LIFE AFTER TOM

Life in the Aftermath of a
Virus Ravaged World

M.J Brierley

Prologue

The rising sun strained his eyes. He sighed; everything was harder these days. He woke early, as always. He sat atop the impressive wooden and metal barricade around the sprawling town and glanced slowly around him. He could see the last embers of the night's fires. Fading ashes yielded to the sun's rising warmth and radiant glow.

He savoured the scalding coffee. His gaze drifted to the wisp of vapor curling off the cup's rim.

The gate was open. The gate was always open, security wasn't a concern these days. It hadn't been for many years, although they'd learned the hard way that there should always be a guard present, just in case. The worst of humanity had died out. Those replacing them had created a stable, albeit fractious society. People would always find something to fight over. This was true even after the events they'd been through. In the early days, people had attacked the town, they had tried to displace Tom and the others, to take what they had. They had to fight to keep what they'd created and had no intention of relinquishing it now, no matter how peaceful the world might seem.

Several years after establishing themselves there, they christened the town Newhaven. The name was party to a lot of debate, with Tom deciding the eventual winner. He liked the way it sounded to say, this was to be their haven, and so it had seemed fitting.

He felt the lines on his face with the tips of his fingers, which had been growing more prominent as the years passed him by. His hair had turned grey. Simple tasks, like moving, now hurt when the weather turned, leaving him sore and frail. He liked it here. He liked to watch the sunrise. If he squinted, he could just make out the sea, far in the distance.

Thirty-five years. They'd been here thirty-five years. Tom was an old man now. His life's horrors had worn him down long before his time. Worn down by the things he'd seem, the things he'd done. His fingers brushed against the unkempt beard on his grey-whiskered face. He wondered where the years had gone, how had they managed to pass him by in the blink of an eye?

His life had been hard. Back before the outbreak, he'd had a usual, standard guy, with a usual, standard life. He'd never admit it, but the virus had probably been one of the best things to ever happen to him, if he was honest with himself. His face dropped as the selfish thought snaked through his mind. So many had died, so many left behind had emerged broken, shells of the people they once were. When the first wave hit, he'd done everything he could to stay alive. After the second wave, humanity was decimated. He found himself in a position of leadership. Firstly, over just a few people, but as the years went by, those prepared to follow him grew.

He'd left the town council years ago. He grew bored of the tedium the role entailed, slowly delegating more and more of it to others, until he managed to make himself almost redundant. Yet, they still asked him for his insights nearly every day. He retired from the daily running of Newhaven to give the next generation the opportunity to pick up the reins. His experience couldn't be replaced though, there would always be a role for him. He wondered sometimes if they did it just to make him feel useful, to make him feel like he was still contributing. He didn't mind. Despite his insistence to remove himself from the official role, he liked to feel useful. It kept him going, he was sure.

For most of the last thirty-five years, he'd been cooped up here. He rarely left the confines of Newhaven. He worked on mundane issues. They were what he expected a town councillor would do before everything fell apart. It was a far cry from the time he spent in the wilderness. The time he spent fighting and killing.

He liked his life, but he did miss those days, they had made him feel alive. He didn't miss the fighting, the killing, but the rest of it, he pined for those. He'd grown to yearn for the old days, the days when he considered himself free. He had a responsibility to these people though, and he vowed to uphold that.

Kate's hand pressed gently on his shoulder, catching him off guard, he froze at her touch. He hadn't heard her arrive. His hearing wasn't great these days. Like the rest of him, it had deteriorated with the passing of time. He smiled at her, as she smiled back. Lines showed at the corner of her eyes. Even after all these years, she was beautiful. Tom smiled to himself; it hadn't been bad, this life.

People were starting to mill around behind him. He could hear the first sounds of the dawn workers. starting their daily routines in the streets below. Pans rattled off in the distance, as kitchen staff began preparing for the breakfast run. The cockerel crowed somewhere on the other side of town, greeting the rising sun.

The first few years building this place had been fraught with risk and danger. They had fought off several raiding parties and passing marauders, attempting to take whatever meagre rations they had. Years of refinement brought significant enhancements. Life had got better. Life had got easier. Tom sometimes worried it was starting to make them soft. He always expected a return to the dark days, and he feared they would no longer be ready for them.

The town had grown. All those years ago, they'd requisitioned just a handful of the secure buildings around the intersected road running through the centre. Eventually, as more people arrived and joined them, they'd been forced to expand, slowly reclaiming every building left standing. Now, temporary structures had been added to the outskirts, evidentially turning into permanent homes, stores, supply rooms and anything else the town may need. More than 2,000 people resided here now. A census was completed every year or so, to try and keep track of the ever-growing and much changing, population.

Trade had been set up with the nearby island community of Boneyard, the government's last stand, all those years ago. The relationship between the two communities had been strong and had endured over the years. The islanders remembered what Tom and Bob had done for them many years prior. They mainly traded fish for crops that were hard to grow on the island, but there was always a growing need for building materials as both communities expanded.

The town now included many skilled workers, or what they considered skilled in these days. There was a pottery studio, which churned out a constant supply of cups, bowls, and plates to replace those forever breaking. A blacksmith, who attempted, usually in vain, to cast new tools for the farmhands, or to replace the rusting screws and bolts holding the structures around them together.

They still had the horses, an entire herd of them now. Riders trained them from yearlings. They were the main form of transport and used for hauling goods on the crudely constructed carts. The fuel had spoiled a long time ago, any vehicles, not rusted from the rain, were useless to them.

All-in-all, Tom thought to himself, the world could have reverted, technologically, two hundred years or more, gone were all the modern conveniences. If it wasn't for the obvious signs of civilisation left scattered around, the crumbling cities, the rusting husks of vehicles, there would be little to show humanity had ever prospered here. The marvels that progress had provided were long gone. Most of it had been nonfunctional for a long time, but the occasional thing had kept running, bravely plugging away as the world fell further apart. They had a small bank of solar panels, attached to the town hall, which was converted from the old hardware store when they first set up camp. These were used to provide limited power to the old fridges and freezers they managed to keep running, to ensure the food they harvested could be kept for longer. They also powered the only form of communication the town had left, a box of radios liberated from one of the nearby army bases. They were useful to keep in touch with scouting or hunting parties. They also allowed them to speak to the inhabitants of Boneyard Island, or the other scattered survivor camps located nearby, without needing to make the demanding journey every time to see them.

The world was slowly coming back together, healing itself from the decades of evil that had rampaged unchecked.

The virus appeared to have died out. Despite the warning the scientists and government officials had spread, no third wave ever gripped the planet. Tom struggled to remember the last time he saw an infected person. No one had an answer as to why. It was known immunity had been a factor in the survival of many. It was accepted that the rate of immunity could now be high enough to ensure spread was no longer possible. They truly believed, after all this time, they had finally beaten the virus that decimated the world. There had been some panicked moments in the early days, when people would become struck down with diseases they were unable to diagnose, but nothing sinister ever seemed to come from it. They had accepted a lot of disease was back, disease that had been almost extinct due to improved sanitary conditions and the marvels of modern medicine. It was difficult to know the difference between them all, without a doctor or any diagnostic equipment or tests. Cholera had ripped through their little town on several occasions, causing massive destruction and death each time. They'd made conceited efforts to improve the sanitation and that now seemed to be back in the past, too, where it belonged.

Most of the modern-day technologies, once widely available, were now rusting piles of scrap. With the exception of the small solar panels attached to the town hall, power had gone out a long time ago and there simply wasn't the expertise available to keep it in repair. The world slowly rotated back an age. The technological age was officially over. The second iron age was well under way.

Tom wondered to himself how many people they could have saved over the years, who had succumbed to simple health issues, if the world had kept turning. He'd lost many friends, and he knew his number would soon be up. It was the inevitable moving of time; it caught up with them all.

Tom felt his face drop as he thought of Bob. The big, jovial man had been a shining light in his life for so long. His resolve had helped this place grow to what it is today. Bob had died a few years ago. He went to his bed one night, an old man, and never woke up in the morning. Complex machinery no longer existed, or at least, if it did, it no longer worked. Bob had soon found himself toiling in the fields, putting his heart and soul into the survival and prosperity of the town. He gave everything for this place, right until the bitter end, when it finally caught up with him. Bob had been in his late 70's and the agreed diagnosis was that age had finally overcome him. He'd had a hard, back-breaking life, even before the world collapsed. He was a leader after it, taking the weight of the town on his large shoulders.

Tom knew he owed all of this to Bob, and more. He owed his life to Bob. The town had been in mourning when the big man passed. They carried his body back to the farm, where the journey first began and buried him in the orchard he used to love watching from his kitchen window. It had been a long, arduous journey, with the vehicles gone. A group of them had made the pilgrimage on horseback. It was only right that he was given the best send-off they could manage.

Tom wiped a tear from the corner of his eye, the big man would have hated to see him shed one for him in the first place.

He smiled and stood.

"Okay," he smiled to Kate. "It's time to go."

CHAPTER ONE

Benny slowly stroked the horse's mane. It brayed softly as he did. He enjoyed the company of the animals, he always had. He'd grown up with them and was more than comfortable around them, even when he was young.

He'd been riding for as long as he could recall. He'd recently turned twenty. He'd been born here and had never seen the desolate and destroyed cities of the old world. This was home. Benny had grown into a respected, useful member of Newhaven. He always pulled his weight and gave his all for the town. Despite his young age, he'd already tried his hand at many tasks to better the town. Finally settling on the one that made him feel most useful, the one he felt he was best suited to.

He removed his hand from the horse, who responded by nuzzling lightly at his shoulder.

"That's enough, boy," he whispered quietly to it. He ran his hand through his shoulder-length brown hair as he watched her walk towards him.

"Hey, Benny. How's it going?" Maria asked as she approached.

He blushed. She was a few years younger than him, but they'd grown up together. There hadn't been many kids in the early days. Not like now, where there seemed to be more of them running around every day.

"Good, thanks," he replied, a hint of shyness in his voice. He silently berated himself. He'd known this girl his whole life, she was his best friend, why was he being bashful around her now?

She laughed; she must have seen it in his face. She then

punched him hard in the arm. Her long blonde hair flailed across her face as she did, obscuring her bright blue eyes momentarily.

"Come on," she said. "We're going to be late." She motioned towards the bay-coloured thoroughbred horse, tied to the thick wooden post at his side. "Are you taking Milton?" she asked.

"Yeah, you know he's the most reliable; never let me down, this lad."

She smiled again. I'll grab one, then we'll head out, okay?"

Benny nodded in agreement.

"By the way," Maria called back as she walked towards the barn. "Your mother is down there. I think she's waiting to see you off." She pointed towards the gate leading out of the paddock.

Benny sighed. She was far too overprotective, that woman. Deciding to get it over with while he had a moment of privacy, he walked towards the gate. At least he might save himself from the humility of Maria witnessing this.

Chloe stood leaning against the post, her back resting against the large oak column.

"Good morning, son," she smiled with fake glee. "Where's Maria? I was looking forward to embarrassing you!"

Benny grimaced. He knew she was joking, but she usually managed it, nonetheless.

"She's just tacking up. She'll be ready soon."

"I wanted to see you off, make sure you knew what you were getting into."

"I know what I'm doing, mum, don't worry about me. Besides, we'll be out with Martin, there's no one who knows what they're doing better than him."

"Martin's an old man, dear. Like the rest of us, take it easy with him."

"He outpaced me last time we went out, easily," Benny replied. "I don't think you need to worry about him."

Chloe laughed. "Yeah, age has been kind to that man. Just be careful, that's all I'm here to say."

"We haven't seen anyone in years," he retorted. "There's been no conflict for as long as I can remember. Seriously, mum, it'll be fine."

Chloe smiled at him, then turned and walked back towards the town without another word.

Benny heard hoofs behind him; he turned to see Maria cantering down the dusty track. She didn't seem to be slowing. He observed her approach intently as she grew closer, her snow-white horse striding freely. His face changed as she charged nearer, concern spreading across it. She was going too fast; she wouldn't be able to stop in time.

He felt the panic rise inside him and quickly turned to the gate, pulling the latch free as he kicked it open. As she approached him, she pulled back on the reins and the horse skidded to a halt as pebbles and tufts of earth showered over him. She's stopped just feet outside of the now open gate. Benny felt his heart race.

"You're going to give me a heart attack," he scolded, panting slightly from sheer shock.

Maria just laughed. "Nah, he'd have stopped alright."

Benny looked to the gate post and then at her sat atop the horse, just the wrong side of it and shook his head.

He let out his breath as he turned to collect Milton. He'd already tacked him up and just had to slip the bridle over his head and mount the saddle. The leather felt surprisingly comfortable. He knew how old it was, leatherwork wasn't one of the skills they'd yet been able to re-master. Like most things here in Newhaven, they were reclaimed from the once great world. Care had been taken to ensure the longevity of everything the town had managed to scavenge. Knowing they were irreplaceable; everyone understood the importance of maintenance.

"Come on!" He shouted as he flew past Maria. Never one to be outdone, he'd immediately put Milton into a canter of his own, galloping past the now stationary Maria, laughing wildly as he did so.

He heard her shout "Whoa!" to her own horse and soon she ran in stride, a length behind him.

The hour was still early and the streets mostly deserted. Mostly. Several shopkeepers or early morning workers had to jump out of their way as they passed. They received a few shouted insults and rebuttals as they shot through town.

They slowed as they reached the main gate, one of only two entrances in and out of Newhaven and the only way that led to the coast and open road before them. The impressive, twelve-foot gates sat open, like they had for the majority of his life. He glanced at the lookout posts as he passed. One man sat lazily in a chair, watching the emptiness that stretched past the barricade. There was no weaponry visible. The bullets had run out years ago. Several rifles remained in town, and if rumour was to be believed, Tom still had a small supply of bullets stashed away. No one had ever seen them, though. They did speculate, if they searched hard enough, they'd be able to locate more. It had been a long time since these things were last produced, but bullets didn't go bad, did they?

Benny often thought they should go looking, see if they could find any. Surely the town would be much better off if they even had a limited supply. Hunting would be easier, if nothing else.

He'd not seen a gun fired for most of his life. By the time he was old enough to join the guard, they'd been more or less obsolete for years. Bows, arrows and axes had replaced them as the main source of weapon, for both hunting and protection.

A sharp whistle from up ahead broke him from his thoughts.

Martin was already out front, patiently waiting on the open road, mounted in the saddle of his own horse. A large, double-edged axe attached to a leather band strapped over his back, a bow over the other shoulder and a machete tucked neatly into his belt. Benny glanced at the quiver of arrows hooked to the saddle. He'd been out on patrols a few times with Martin, the man was a good laugh and very good at what he did. He always took the arrows with him. Benny had only ever seen him fire them at deer, when opportunity allowed. He'd never missed.

He knew Martin had been in the army, back in the bad days, when the old world fell. He'd been the enemy, once. It was well known, by all ages of Newhaven, that the army had turned into the villains, in the pantomime they now thought of as the outbreak. Martin had turned on his own. He'd shown his true colours and his true humanity when he'd joined Tom and the others and set off across the country to find refuge.

The stories of the old days had passed into legend. Only a small contingent of the original townsfolk left had been the founders. Others had joined from the same era, some were even said to have spent the pandemic holed up with Chester, and later Jay, in the debauchery of the city. They didn't speak much about those days. Everyone was equal, now. Anyone who had joined their community and helped it grow in the early days, was revered as peers. Digressions had been forgiven and trust was slowly earned.

Benny had never been anywhere else, but he knew that Newhaven was as close to a peaceful and trusting community as could be possible.

Despite it all, he felt the pull, the desire he supposed most young men must have to leave. There must be more out there, he knew it. There must be. One day, he wanted to go and find it.

He knew about Boneyard. The community there was

thriving. He had thought about requesting to join them, more than once. It didn't feel far enough from home though, it felt like he'd always be under the wing if he stayed, so he kept it to himself. He never told his mother; he knew she'd be heartbroken if he left.

His dad had died when he was much younger. He'd been one of the first arrivals, a younger man, at the time, who happened across the community in its infancy. He'd managed to talk his way in and eventually earned their trust and respect. He'd worked closely with Bob on the farms, becoming the foreman of a small group of dedicated farmhands who kept the rest fed. They'd become good friends, by all accounts, until his dad had his accident.

A horse had spooked, no one really knew what at. It'd galloped down the freshly ploughed fields, trampling his dad in its panic. There was no medical care available, and he'd succumbed to his injuries a few days later. Just bad luck, he was told.

He and Chloe had only been together a few years when this happened. She'd never had another partner. All of Benny's life, he'd never known her to show love for anyone, other than him. Benny's childhood had been just him and Chloe. He felt bad, knowing she was now alone when he left town, or spent wild evenings in the local tavern. Soon, he'd have to leave for good and she'd be all alone.

He frowned at the thought.

"Benny?" Martin asked, watching him thoughtfully.

He shook his head, he'd been daydreaming.

"Yep, sorry, Martin. Good when you are."

Maria chuckled beside him.

"Okay, you two. Let's take care. Today we're patrolling, that's all. Nice, easy and safe."

He pulled two dull-looking machetes from a wicker basket tied to his saddle and handed one to each of them.

"Why bother?" Maria asked. "We've never seen anyone out here."

"Never take that for granted," the older man replied.

Maria and Benny had been out with Martin a handful of times now. They took the machetes and walked a slow perimeter of the town, extending their reach with each lap. It had become part of daily life, the seemingly pointless patrols, despite the lack of others in the area.

Martin clicked his tongue and the large black horse below him walked forward up the crumbling road as the others followed.

It was still early in the morning, the sun only just starting to warm the air. The hoof beats reverberated as they bounced off the asphalt. Benny rubbed his hands. Despite the rising sun, there was still a chill in the air, and he hadn't dressed appropriately. He knew it would warm up soon and he'd find himself sweating in the saddle.

They were following the usual route; a route Benny had walked many times before. He'd been working patrol with Martin and Maria for several months now and was growing slowly confident with each passing shift as they met nothing.

He once again let his mind wander, as the horse he sat atop was doing most of the work, anyway.

He was young, maybe eight or nine. He could barely recall the memory but knew the story well enough to fill in the blanks his young mind hid from him. This was the last time there had been an incident in the town, the last time outsiders had arrived and tried to take everything from them.

It had been late evening, the sun had set, fires illuminated the streets. There was a party. He didn't recall why but had been told it was in celebration of the founding of Newhaven. This still happened every year. It was the biggest celebration the town put together and soon turned to tradition. There was beer, lots of beer. It was brewed in the town, still is. People were merry, dancing around the large fire in the middle of the square, where the two main roads intersected.

It had been a long time since anyone had shown up at the gates. Security had become lax and due to the celebrations, no one had been guarding the entrance.

They just walked in. They pushed open the unsecured gate and simply walked in.

The first Benny knew something was wrong, was the scream. He may have forgotten a lot of that night, but he'd never forget that ear-piercing, blood chilling scream. She must have been the first to see them. Benny did not remember her name, but if he cared to walk to the memorial, now prominent in the town centre, she'd be listed there, at the top of the makeshift cenotaph. More names were added since, of course. More names were added from just that night. It was now a monument to everyone who had passed from the town. His dad's name was engraved there, too.

The gunshot came next. It exploded through the night, the music cut out, as those with the drums and the guitar looked in shock at the scene unfolding before them.

A group of people stood there, a rifle smoking in one man's hands. Benny remembered his face, or he thought he did. Maybe he filled in the details some years later, but in his mind, they were large, dirty, unkempt men. Six of them, wearing matching leather vests, each with a weapon loaded in their hands.

Benny had seen guns before; they were still available in the town when he was young, but he'd never heard one fired, not so close to him.

The sound scared him, it was so loud, like thunder cracking directly over his head. He turned to his mum and cried into her dress. Chloe pushed him behind her, as the rest of the town remained in silence, staring at the new arrivals.

The woman lay dead on the floor, blood mixing with the dirt below her as it crept from the hole in her chest.

Someone walked forward, putting himself between the attackers and the unarmed townsfolk. It was Tom. He was older, Benny remembered him being one of the oldest in the camp, but not like he was today. He was still active and mobile. Benny idolised him for years after this night.

"You in charge?" The man with the smoking rifle asked, his voice gruff and sharp. His greasy black hair was plastered over his forehead, his blue jeans now a dozen colours, stained with dirt and God only knows what else.

"Yes," Tom replied confidently, as he looked at the woman lying dead at his feet. "What do you want?"

The man smiled, a sickening smile, revealing a row of browning teeth and reddened gums.

Funny, after all these years, Benny still remembered the man's poor oral health. The first thought that came to his mind was that the man really should brush his teeth, before he lost them all.

"What you got?" The man said.

"For you?" Tom asked. "Nothing."

The man frowned, fingering his rifle as he aimed it at Tom.

"You might want to watch how you speak to us, or you'll end up face down, like her." He gestured to the woman dead at his feet.

Did Tom snarl? Probably not, but that's how Benny remembered it.

"One chance," Tom said. "One chance, to turn around and leave. After that, you die."

The man laughed, a harsh, booming laugh, from deep within him.

"I don't think you understand the situation here. We got the guns. We gonna' take whatever we want, or you lot, you're all gonna' die."

Tom shook his head sorrowfully. Benny clearly remembered his next action; he'd never forget it. He looked up, just to the side of the man, seemingly looking into the darkness and gave a slight nod of his head.

The next scene was one of pure horror and panic. A bang shot out from the shadows and the man's head exploded into a red mist, before his body slumped to the floor. The others hesitated, only for a moment. A moment too long. The next deafening bang felled another.

Benny had his face pushed into Chloe's dress still, obscuring his view.

He managed to turn it, just enough to see what happened next. As the second man was still falling to the ground, a sickening squelch, one he'd never forget, sounded from the back of one of the others. Benny saw the expression on his face change, from shock to realisation. Then he saw the tip of the blade pierce out from the front of his chest, before it jarred quickly upwards, opening a large gash in the middle of the man. Blood poured down his face from his mouth and he fell without a word. Ava stood behind him, pulling the machete out of his back.

She swung it to her left, where it bit into the next man's neck. He dropped his rifle and as it fell, his already blood-soaked hands grasped at it in a futile attempt to keep it close to him. Ava forced the blade further into his flesh, blood spurting in a wide arc, coating Ava and the ground around them. The man made primeval, guttural sounds, as he desperately scrambled for the blade, his fingers bled as he forced them into the sharp metal. With a final push, she pressed it a few more inches into the man's neck and he collapsed to the ground.

One of the remaining men from the group had come to his

senses and started shooting indiscriminately into the watching crowd; several people fell and more still screamed. Another bang from the shadows quickly cut him down, before the last man standing threw his rifle to the ground and put his hands up. He was shaking and looked terrified; his nose ran as he desperately tried to mumble something incoherent.

Martin walked up behind him, hit him with the butt of the rifle and he fell to the ground. Ava tied his wrists with cable ties, before they both grabbed him by the arms and hauled him away.

Benny didn't know what happened to the man, he didn't really want to. He'd never asked.

He did find out, years later, when he was much older, that the man had spilled everything. He'd told Tom during interrogation the entire story. It was the music, the celebrations, the fire. They had seen and heard them from a long way out and slowly crept to the town. They'd been a small group and they'd survived by taking from others. When they'd noticed the lack of guards, they let themselves in. When their leader had shot the woman, just to make a point, they hadn't seen Martin sidestep into the hardware store. Tom had kept them talking long enough for him to arm himself and Ava had positioned herself behind the group, ready to finish it off when the firing started. Ava always had the blade with her. She'd started wearing it soon after the town was established and had it firmly strapped to his hip to this day.

CHAPTER TWO

Benny was jolted back to reality when his horse came to an abrupt stop. Martin was a short distance in front of him, his own horse halted, holding his fist up in the air, the universal hand action to indicate they needed to stop, quietly. He hadn't noticed the hoofbeats quiet and nearly walked into the back of him.

He craned his neck to peer at what Martin was looking at and he noticed from the corner of his eye that Maria was doing the same.

"Martin?" He whispered urgently. "What's wrong?"

Martin pointed directly in front of him. A campfire lay cold in the clearing off the road, blackened logs in a circle of stone, surrounded by high grasses that waved gently in the slight breeze. There was no other sign of movement. Benny stayed still, waiting for instruction.

After a few moments of thought and reflection, Martin walked the horse to the remnants of the fire, before expertly dismounting.

"Stone cold," he announced, as he touched the back of his hand to the embers. "Whoever was here, it wasn't recent. Maria, when were we last out this way?"

"About a week ago," she replied.

"Okay, so we know someone has been here in the last week. We're not that far from town. It's unlikely they missed us. No one has reported seeing smoke, or we'd have checked this out days ago." He looked behind him, Newhaven sprawling in the distance. "It's not in direct sight of town, it's possible we just missed it."

Benny followed his gaze towards Newhaven. A thick row of conifer trees blocked the view, their branches obscuring any view of the town, other than the high barrier surrounding it.

"Coincidence?" He asked.

"Could be," Martin replied thoughtfully. He clambered back onto the horse. "Eyes open, move carefully. Might be nothing, but we don't know who this was, and we don't know where they are. Last thing we need is to give someone the chance to sneak up on us."

They slowly started to circle the town, the three horses spread out in a wide line, following the faded tracks from the cold fire, keeping each other in sight. Benny searched the floor before him, looking for anything out of place. They found nothing as the hours passed them by. On the fourth lap of the perimeter, when they were only meters from the now impressive barrier surrounding Newhaven, it was Maria who called out.

"Guys," she said slowly. "Check this out." She was pointing to a dense patch of bracken growing from the deteriorating road. It had been partially flattened, the indentation was roughly the right size and shape of a crouched person. It stood out in the wild landscape. Thick tufts of brush and bracken grew in disjointed clumps wherever it had managed to force itself through the cracking pavements and roads. The rest of it stood tall and proud, whereas this patch was flattened, the stalks broken low near the concrete.

This entire area was overgrown; they seldom came out here. Trees blocked the way for anything larger than a man walking and the thick tufts of bracken and brambles kept them to the road further out.

Martin once again dismounted his horse and knelt on the ground next to the bracken. He picked up a discarded plastic bottle and looked at it. It wasn't covered in the layer of grime that rubbish blown in by the wind would be expected to be.

"Can't have been long ago," he said, absently. "It looks like just one person though; I don't see any evidence of anyone else." He glanced around him. "Everywhere else looks fine and there's no trail leading to it. Someone put themselves here and quite carefully too, I'd say."

"Something doesn't feel right," Benny added. "This is weird. Why have we got some guy creeping around? Why wouldn't they knock on the door, say hello?"

"Maybe they didn't know how we'd take it. It's a pretty fucked-up place out there," Maria replied. Martin shot her a sideways glance. He'd never been keen on the younger generation swearing as openly as they did. "Sorry," she whispered.

Benny frowned to himself. Something didn't add up. He walked around the bracken, examining the floor, looking for anything that might hint to who had been watching them. He pushed past tufts of brambles, feeling the thorns catch on his legs. The tracks of their horses were clearly visible where the debris had been brushed aside by the hoofs. The same should be true of whoever caused this. Whoever it was, they must have been on foot and got here very carefully, deliberately.

Martin stood by the barricade, gently running his hand across the mishmash structure. The perimeter had been hastily erected back in the early days and added to year after year. It was now a formidable mosaic of steel and wood, creating a solid barrier that encircled the entire town. There were two entrances through the barrier, one at the front, the large gate they'd walked through and one at the far end of the town, past the stables and paddocks used for the horses. They had guards posted on the front on a shift pattern, so it was always manned. The rear entrance was not. Being so close to the farmland, there was always someone working in the vicinity. It was very unlikely anyone could enter that way and not be seen, no matter the hour. The gate at the other end of town was seldom closed. It led into the thick forest surrounding that side of Newhaven.

After thirty-five years of growth, the trees had finally reclaimed much of the land humanity once took from them. They used the forest for their firewood and to collect timber for the structures being erected more frequently as the years went by. The amount of firewood they used was substantial, people were out there almost every day to collect it. It never made a dent in the forest. The trees eventually settled out behind it to a vast, empty meadow heading inland. There was nothing out that way.

Martin knelt carefully, feeling the soft ground retract slightly under his weight. Foliage grew thickly up the exterior of the barrier, despite their attempts to keep it under control, even their little town wasn't spared the invasion of reclamation.

"You can see in here," he said finally. "There's a small gap, you can see right through to the square."

The square was what they'd come to call the centre of the town, where the main stores and food tents stood. In the early days, they'd erected a cenotaph, where the names of the fallen were etched on. The list was long now and growing each year.

"It's not close, though, I don't think you'd be able to make much out or hear anything. But someone has certainly been watching us," Benny said.

Martin sighed again. "You can also see the track leading out of town. If someone wanted to know our routines, who left and when, this would be the perfect place. We'd have no reason to look over here, much less to physically ride this way. Someone's been watching us, and I'd say for some days, too. But why?"

"The question is," Maria added. "Where are they now?"

"You think they're still around?" Benny asked.

"Wouldn't you be? If you've camped out here, clearly watching for what we assume is a few days, you wouldn't just leave, would you?"

Martin sighed. There was always something. They hadn't seen another person outside the established camps in so long. Newhaven was an open community, if anyone wanted to join them, they would have been allowed, if only they'd asked.

"We'd better try to find them," he said. "They've been watching us; we don't know for how long and we don't know what they want. That cannot be a good thing."

"How?" Benny replied. "We've circled this damn place four or five times now. There's no sign of them."

"This brush is still flat, Benny, they've been here. And recently. Let's spread out, see if we can cover a bit more distance. I'll keep the perimeter. Maria, check out up to the road, maybe a little way up. Benny, head to the coast. It's the most used route for the Boneyard trades, but see if anything sticks out. We'll meet back here at noon." He opened the pack on his back and removed several of the rare and valuable radios. "Take one each, report in if you see anything out of the ordinary." He handed one to each of Benny and Maria.

They accepted them and Benny nodded before pulling Milton around, winking discreetly at Maria and slowly trotting off towards the coast.

"Hey, Benny," Maria called out to him as he trotted off.

"Yeah?" he shouted back.

"Be safe. Don't do anything stupid."

"Would I ever?"

She laughed. "Just, be safe. That's all. I'd miss you if anything happened."

He shook his head, a smile spread across his face.

"See you soon, loser," he called back as he moved out of range.

He walked as silently as the horse below him would allow, which wasn't all that quiet at all. In the years since everything fell apart, nature had reclaimed most of the planet and here was no different. He peered through the gaps in the tall grasses and around the trunks of vine-covered trees, looking for anything out of place. The machete felt comfortably heavy in his hand as he navigated the wilderness, it's dull-looking blade glinting in the sun as he bounced slowly forward.

He stopped several times, just to listen. The birds called feverishly from the trees and crickets chirped from the grass. Glancing around, nothing seemed unusual. Benny had been born into this world; he hadn't known what came before. The cityscapes, empty and reclaimed by nature, were the real world, to him. The thought of these sprawling metropolises filled with anything but weeds and animals seemed strange. Newhaven was a large town, as far as survivor encampments went. There were three other camps they'd discovered through the years within a few days' ride from Newhaven. They'd enjoyed good relationships with them. After the initial compulsory period of distrust, they'd eventually established trade and often made the trek between them. It had taken years before they had any form of real and open communication with them. Most people preferred to keep to themselves in the early days, when marauders were still a constant threat and the introduction of large groups of people inevitably meant the risk of the virus making a comeback.

As time passed and the risk from both had faded, people started coming together. The dark days behind them, they all looked to the future and rebuilding what society they could.

Benny had enjoyed a relatively safe and secure upbringing. He'd heard the stories, of course, but could scarcely bring himself to believe them.

Nearly eight billion people. That's what they had told him the global population was. He didn't know where they all would have gone. It was certainly nowhere near that now. No one really knew, of course, but the elders, how he thought of Tom and the others the generation older than him, often told him they believed up to 99% of the earth's population, pre-pandemic, was now gone. Dead, either from the virus, or each other. There was still debate to which was worse. He'd never seen anyone infected with the virus, but he has seen the worst of humanity. For him, that was by far the scarier possibility.

The population of the planet pre-pandemic still seemed like an unfathomably insane number to him. Air travel and global communication had been a thing of the past. He struggled to imagine a world any bigger than his own little corner of it. The few towns, full of varying numbers of survivors and the island, just off the coast. To think lands sat across the great seas, with potentially millions of people; the thought terrified him, if he was honest. He'd been told so many stories when he was growing up, about all the interesting and different places in the world. He sometimes wished he could see some of it, despite the gnawing fear. That's what fed his desire to leave, he wanted to know what was out there.

He did wish they still had the internet. That sounded cool. The ability to connect with anyone, from anywhere, in a heartbeat. He could only imagine how amazing the world must once have been. He'd heard the other stories, too. The ones that were not so appealing. The lengths people went to, to claim power over others. Chester was an infamous name back in Newhaven, even after all these years. It was common knowledge that the elders had killed him, after an epic and perhaps somewhat exaggerated, fight, back at the city. His own mum had been involved; he knew that much. He'd become a bogeyman, a nightmare story to scare the children who refused to go to bed.

Benny himself had spent long nights in his youth terrified of the man who would come crashing through his door if he didn't do what Chloe told him.

He smiled to himself. They say you can't choose your family, but even if he could, he wouldn't have it any other way.

The hours dragged as he edged closer to the coast. He could see dried hoofprints in the ground, where the softer mud had hardened with the heat from the sun. These would have been from their horses on earlier trips to the cove and not what he was looking for. Nothing seemed out of place.

He'd been out for a long time and knew he'd need to turn around soon to make the noon meet with the others. In the distance, he could just see the lifeguard lookout point. The building had stood on the cliff tops all these years. Despite its wood and glass frame and its open position to the brutality of the elements, it had so far stood the test of time.

He gauged that he could make it if he kept his pace up headed back. It was the only visible structure from all around; it made sense to check it out. Anyone travelling this way may well have used it for shelter. He knew several people from Newhaven had in the past, when their trips to the cove had met poor weather.

It didn't take him long to cross the distance. Despite the slower than normal speed, as he scoured the ground for any form of clues, or evidence that someone else had been here recently, he made the journey in good time.

Milton snorted as he approached the building. The door had been replaced a long time ago with a simple wooden plank, nailed to a few hinges, where the glass had been smashed many years earlier. It was closed. This was not surprising, anyone who used it would have been sure to close and latch the door to prevent it being blown off in the next storm, or it'd soon be useless for everyone.

The glass was smeared with thirty plus years of grime and spray from the sea below, making visibility through the once transparent structure all but impossible.

He dismounted from Milton and tied the horse to the wooden fence running parallel to the sheer drop from the cliff face. He walked to the glass window and peered through. Through the murky window, he saw something lying on the floor. What was it? He rubbed the glass to try and get a better view, but it just smeared the grime into swirls of circular lines. He frowned, then reached for the door.

The interior was musty, an acrid smell floated on the air which he couldn't place. He screwed up his nose as the unfamiliar scent assaulted him. A brightly coloured backpack lay near the entrance, the top open and its contents strewn across the wooden floor. He looked around, clothes, a half-drunk bottle of water and what appeared to be a flashlight lay scattered around him. He doubted the latter still worked; batteries had been a rare commodity longer than he'd been alive. He kicked at it lightly with his foot and it rolled across the floor, coming to a rest against the far wall. The quiet crash echoed dully around the empty building.

Benny frowned. This looked like junk, it could have been here for months. It might even have been left by someone from Newhaven. It was time to leave, he'd need to get a move on to make it back by noon, this had been a waste of time. He shook his head as he stepped back out into the sunlight. He looked out to the sea, listening to the waves gently crashing on the rocks below. It was a mild day, he liked it when it was like this. He let the glowing sunlight warm his face as he closed his eyes, feeling the breeze on his face.

The last thing he heard was the seagull shrieking far out to sea, as Milton brayed softly. Then his world became black as he fell to the ground. He didn't feel the blow to his head, not until after he woke, many hours later.

CHAPTER THREE

"Where the fuck is he?" Maria asked, impatiently. Her horse was growing restless, too, as it shifted its weight between its feet.

"I don't know," Martin replied, scowling at her. His gaze returned watching the horizon headed towards the sea. He pressed the button on the radio once again, nothing but static greeted him.

"He should be back by now." He looked to the watch on his wrist, a relic from the old world that amazingly still worked. "It's coming up to one o'clock. He's an hour late. We'll give him another ten, then we'll have to go looking for him." He tried to keep his voice calm. He'd been in charge of security for Newhaven for over thirty years. It wouldn't do to let his nerves show through, especially in front of a new recruit, such as Maria.

She was visibly distressed; he could tell just by looking at her. Her brow was permanently furrowed, and she never took her eyes off the road leading to the coast. Martin knew they were good friends, of course, they'd grown up together.

He was also concerned. Chloe was one of his dearest friends and he'd always promised her he'd keep her son safe. *I'm overreacting,* he berated himself. *He'll be fine, he's just running late.*

"I'm sure he's just lost track of time. He'll be here any moment now," he said aloud, turning to Maria. "There's nothing out there and he's made that journey hundreds of times. He'll be back." He hoped he sounded confident, but if he was honest with himself, he didn't feel it.

Something was off about this entire situation. Neither he nor Maria had found anything unusual on their search. The coast made sense, though. If someone had been here, that's where they'd go, isn't it? He shouldn't have sent him. He should have left him to patrol the town and he should have checked it out himself.

With every passing second, he felt his heart beat faster. He couldn't take it any longer, he had to know.

"Come on," he said, after an agonising wait. "Let's follow him up, see if he's got himself lost."

Maria nodded, they kicked off their horses and set off towards the coast at a slow trot.

Scanning the floor before her, she followed the fresh tracks, they must have been made by Milton and Benny. They extended past the road and through the meadow. The track was often used by traders heading to the cove. No one had been out that way in days, though, this had to be him.

She increased the speed of her horse as they grew closer to the coast. The small lookout building could be seen in the distance. Next to it, she was sure she could make out the small silhouette of a horse.

She sped to a gallop as the building grew closer. Milton neighed as he saw her and threw his head in the air. She came to a skidded halt next to him and Martin panted as he brought his horse to a more dignified halt next to her.

"What are you playing at?" he asked angrily.

"I saw Milton out here; something's wrong." She said, pointing to the horse tied to the fence.

"That doesn't mean you just gallop off. You have no idea what could have been here. You could have tripped, for God's sake."

Maria scowled, but she knew he was right. She'd let her emotions get the better of her. Benny was reliable and sensible. Something must have gone wrong. She didn't reply but dismounted from her horse and stroked Milton's neck gently. She removed the pack from the horse's saddle.

"His stuffs still here, everything," he held out the radio she'd removed from the untouched pack.

"Here," Martin said from behind her. She turned to see him pointing towards the open door of the lookout. The wooden plank swayed lightly in the breeze, her eyes were drawn to the ground, where a wet patch of blood glistened in the sunlight.

"It's fresh," Martin said. "Can't have happened long ago." He looked around him, as Maria did the same. There was no evidence of people passing through, nothing to indicate a body had been dragged through the scrub at their feet.

Before long, Maria noticed the first droplet of blood leading away from the scene.

"Look," she exclaimed, pointing to the tiny droplet of red staining a nearby nettle. Her gaze followed the track leading away from it. It was the old coastal path. But that path didn't go anywhere. It had fallen into disrepair years ago, most of it claimed by erosion. She pulled the machete from her belt and edged forward, before a hand on her shoulder stopped her.

"No," Martin said firmly. "We don't know who, how many, or why. We can't just go running after them. We need to go back."

"To hell we do," she exclaimed. "It's recent, he could still be around here. There's no way a group dragging an unconscious body got far. If we don't go now, we might never see him again."

Martin sighed. "I know, I really do, please believe me. But I can't risk putting you in danger. I need to get some of my men, then we'll come back out here and figure it out."

She responded by pointing the machete at him, rage etched on her youthful face.

"No!" She screamed. "We're going after him and we're going

after him now!"

Martin nodded. He'd expected this reply. It's exactly what he would have done. He shook his head slowly to clear it. He wasn't going to argue, he agreed with her, he just had to be sure before they traipsed into the unknown.

"Okay. You're right." He conceded, knowing he'd never win this argument. "But stay behind me." He pushed past her to step onto the narrow, crumbling path. He could hear her breathing hard in relief behind him.

The track headed into the overgrown hedgerows, with a sheer drop down the cliff-face below. Martin stepped carefully, small rocks shifting under his weight. He glanced nervously around him. His old muscles were aching. He didn't fully trust his feet on the uneven ground.

Soon, it became clear that there was no way anyone could have taken this path, especially not dragging what they assumed was an unconscious Benny behind them. It didn't make any sense; the blood trail led this way, then soon disappeared. Martin had a terrible thought, and his blood ran cold. He steadied himself and peered over the tall brush into the blue sea below. The drop was substantial; he didn't dare say his thoughts out loud, lest they may be true.

He didn't need to; Maria had the same thought.

"You don't think... "she stuttered, tears forming in her eyes. "You don't think they threw him off, do you?"'

Martin took a deep breath. He didn't want to admit it out loud, but that's exactly what he thought. The track didn't go anywhere, and the blood drops stopped. But no, it couldn't be. The hedge was unbroken, and they wouldn't have been able to get him over it, surely? And why would they have dragged him down here? Why not just throw him off by the lookout, where the cliff had no hedge to block the fall?

"No," he said firmly. "No, there's no way. Not here."

He heard Maria let out her breath; she looked relieved and

must have come to the same conclusion. The hedge row was just too thick. The blood drops stopped, though. What had happened here and where was Benny?

"Back," he barked, the sense of foreboding drawing up on him. That was enough standing on a cliff-edge. As they retreated for firmer ground, Martin took another look around. There was something strange about the blood. There was so little of it dropped to the path, yet a large pool when it appeared Benny, or someone, had been struck. He dropped to his knees, examining the floor closer around the puddle.

His eyes widened in fear. This was a trap. The blood had been planted to lead them down to the edge of the cliff. He looked at Maria, her mouth opening in a scream that never came. She dropped to the floor in front of him, as a dull thud sounded from behind her.

As she slumped to the ground, the figure of a woman emerged in her wake. A large and thick log raised in her hands. Martin tried to unhook the axe strapped to his back. The woman ran forward, screaming. She brandished the log like a bat and swung it wildly.

She was dishevelled, her matted grey hair flailed around her face with every uneven step she took. Her clothes were little more than greying rags and her feet were bare, blackened and hard. A layer of grime coated her skin at every exposed point and her open mouth revealed just a handful of teeth remained in her gums.

She reached Martin before he could pull the blade free. He rolled sideways to avoid the log. It came crashing down where his head had been. The woman did not relent. She instantly changed direction and swung at him again. That awful shriek never stopped. Martin scooted backwards as quickly as he could and the swing from the log missed him once again. The woman was so close to him now, he could see the insanity in her eyes. There would be no talking his way out of this. She snapped her gums together, as droplets of spittle flew from her mouth.

Martin kicked out with his booted foot, connecting to her shin. She shrieked louder as she stumbled back, never releasing the grip on the log in her hands. He took advantage of the momentary pause to regain his footing. Now he stood, he saw her small stature. He must have had a foot on her in height. She'd recovered her balance and ran at him again, the log raised above her head. Martin dodged nimbly, her swing's force propelling her past him, forcing her off balance. As she did, he spun on his heel, so he was facing her from behind and grabbed her arms, hooking them behind her back. She struggled like a rabid dog. The log fell from her hands, but she struggled and squirmed with the force of a person twice her size. Without warning, she reared back her head, connecting to Martins chin. Pain burst from his lip and blood flowed down his face. Her screams overpowered all other noises, as her body thrashed wildly.

Martin positioned his foot next to hers, then with all his might, pushed her sideways. She tripped over his boot and hit the floor hard. She was back on her knees faster than he thought possible. He lunged forward and put his knee into the centre of her back, pinning her to the ground. He used his weight as ballast. He managed to force one of her arms behind her back and pinned it there with his other knee. With his now free hands, he held on to the back of her head. Her odour struck him. She was rancid. His eyes watered in the close proximity, as a fresh assault of stench hit him every time she thrashed her body.

"Stop!" he shouted. To his surprise, she complied. She stopped struggling altogether and lay motionless on the ground.

Rasping, panting breaths replaced the shrieking that had now stopped. Martin spat on the floor next to them, the red blood bright in the afternoon sun.

He felt her go limp beneath him, then removed some of the force he was applying to her, worried he might kill her if he didn't. He was ready for her to take the opportunity to begin her struggle again, to lash out at him, but she stayed still.

Finally freeing the machete from his belt, he stood, leaving her unimpeded on the ground.

"Up," he commanded, to no response.

"Up!" he tried again. She rolled onto her back and faced him.

She was an older woman, older than even Martin, he thought. That meant she'd been around from the days before and from the looks of her, alone for most of them.

There was no recognition in her eyes, they darted around, unfocused. Martin snapped his fingers in front of her face, forcing her focus back onto him. He thought he saw a shift in her eyes, some form of recognition. She seemed to look less like a wild animal and more human, somehow.

"I'm Martin," he said slowly. "Who are you?"

A low growl emanated from her throat in reply. He had the machete stretched in front of him, the tip of the blade pointing at her chest. She seemed to finally understand, as she opened and closed her mouth without forming words.

"I need to check on my friend. Don't move." She showed no response on her face, but her eyes watched him as he slowly backed away.

He crawled to Maria and knelt beside her, never taking his eyes off the unmoving woman in grey. He felt for a pulse. There it was, strong. He nodded to himself; she'd be alright.

"Who are you?" He demanded again, as he moved back to her.

She grunted quietly.

"Where's Benny? The lad who that came from?" he pointed the tip of the machete to the now congealing puddle of blood.

The woman cocked her head ever so slightly and grunted once more.

"Benny." He repeated. "He was here; that came from him. Where is he?"

The woman jumped forwards, in an acrobatic move that belied her apparent years, to rest on her knees, but made no movement towards him, nor to run. She just crouched there on all fours, like an animal evaluating the situation. She raised one of her thin, grime-covered arms slowly and pointed to the blood on the floor.

"Yes, Benny. What did you do to him?"

She took a crouched step forward, moving like a nightmare from a child's dream. She pointed at the blood again. Martin took a step to the side, leaving open space between the woman and the drying puddle. She took another step, never taking her eyes off of him. He nodded and she took one more. She stretched her arm out until her fingers hovered above the red blood, then dipped her fingertips in it. As she lifted her hand, small drops of red blood dripped from her fingers. She hopped to the side and flicked her hand at the bush. Small drops of red blood smeared over them, barely notable. She pointed to the path.

"He's down there?"

She grunted.

"No..." Martin said, realisation dawning over him. "You did that. You put the blood drops on the path. Why? To draw us down there? But why?"

She grunted.

"Because... You wanted us to go down there. You wanted us to try and get through. Then what, were you going to push us off the cliff, sneak up and bash us over the head with that log of yours?"

She grunted, but it sounded different. The pitch was lighter, so he had to assume this meant yes.

"Did you kill him? Did you kill Benny?"

Was that a slight shake of the head? It was hard to tell, she was completely still.

"No... I don't think you did. But I think you saw who did. Is that why you did that, with the blood? Was it for us, or for them?"

She pointed over the meadow, away from the coast.

"They went that way?" he asked. "Who did, who are they?"

A groan from behind them seized his attention for a moment, as Maria rubbed her head.

"What the…" she started but was cut off by shrieking. The woman launched herself towards her, running on her hands and feet like a gorilla, her eyes locked directly on Maria.

Martin had hesitated; he was too far away to stop her; she'd be on top of Maria in seconds.

Coming back to his senses, he launched into a sprint towards them. Maria had raised her hands to protect her face, just as the woman pounced on top of her, clawing at whatever exposed flesh she could see.

He just had time to hear Maria shout "bitch!" before she disappeared under a haze of moving limbs and that greying, dirty cloth. At full speed, he planted his boot into the woman's face, and she fell limp to the side. Blood trickled down her nose and from her mouth as she lay unconscious on the floor, shallow breathing raising her slight frame every few seconds.

"What the hell was that? And what is that smell?" Maria asked in disgust, wiping blood from a deep gash on her forearm. "That'll be fucking infected."

"I don't know. She didn't say a word, just grunts and gesticulating."

"Benny?" asked Maria.

"I don't think so. I don't think she did anything to him. I think she saw who did, though. I also don't think she's all there. I suspect she's been out here, alone, since before."

"How have we never seen her before, if she's been around for that long?"

"Beats me. Maybe she usually hides in the forest. It's a big world. I'm not surprised, really. Not if she didn't want to be found."

"Then why now? Why didn't she just hide now? Why all of this?"

"I honestly don't know," he replied.

Maria looked at the frail body next to her. "What do we do? Kill her?"

"No, I couldn't, I don't think."

"I'll do it. She tried to do the same to us. Crazy bitch."

"No. She might know where Benny is. Or at least, who took him. If we can get her to talk."

"So, what are you saying, you want to wait for her to wake up and then ask again?"

"No, I don't think that'll work. I think we need to get back to Newhaven. Get her cleaned up, see if there's maybe someone with a…" he hesitated. "Er… lighter touch than us."

He studied Maria. Blood had dried over the side of her head where the log had impacted, and her arms and chest were covered in deep scratches.

"Your dad's going to kill me. Or your mum. Probably both," he added glumly.

CHAPTER FOUR

Benny woke with a start. The world was black, and his head pounded. He tried to rub at it, but found his wrists bound behind his back. He started to panic. He was lying in a strange position; he'd been placed face down on... what... a bench? A tree? No, it was moving, he could feel the ground bouncing up and down. He was on the back of a horse. He could feel the binds wrapped around his knees. He tried to groan, but the cloth tied around his mouth prevented any sound coming out. As he came to his senses, he realised he'd been blindfolded, trussed up and gagged. He could feel the fabric against his face.

He tried again to call out, only a faint noise met his ears. He could hear hoofbeats now, they were reverberating off concrete. They must be on the main road; it was the only one around here. Unless he'd been unconscious longer than he thought. He started to panic. If he'd been out for a while, he could be anywhere by now. He didn't know who had taken him, but no one would ever find him, he'd never see his mum again, or Maria. He screamed into the gag. It was louder this time. His throat burned with the effort.

He screamed louder still, putting every ounce of effort he could into it. The gag was coming loose, and he could hear the world clearer now. His muffled yell cut through the air as the horse stopped walking.

It was replaced by his moaning, as a fist swung hard into his midriff, knocking the wind out of him.

"Shut the fuck up." The voice was familiar, but he couldn't

place it. It didn't sound like he expected. It sounded... civilized, somehow. It hadn't sounded angry, or overly commanding, just calm and collected and somehow vaguely familiar.

Still bound and blindfolded, he did as he was told and concentrated only on his own breathing. He felt the horse walk on. Conscious of his precarious position across the horse's rump, he tried to stay as still as possible. Using the rising motion of the horse's footsteps, he slowly managed to raise a corner of the blindfold away from his eyes by pushing his face into the animal and letting the motion move the cloth a tiny amount with each step.

He could just make out a road below him, mostly covered with weeds and moss. He couldn't see which way they were heading, the small corner of the blindfold he'd managed to lift didn't give him enough vision to make out any landmarks.

Hoping he hadn't been unconscious for long; he did the only thing he could think of. He carefully rubbed his feet slowly together, loosening the laces on his boots. Once he felt enough movement inside, he used one foot to carefully lower the boot down his foot, until it hung off his toes precariously. He matched his breathing to the sound of the hoofbeats on the ground and once he had the rhythm matched, he gave the boot a final push.

It fell to the road, landing just as the horse's hoof touched down, obscuring the dull sound of its fall. He waited for some time. He couldn't be sure exactly how long, but he needed to be far enough away from the first boot before he tried again. If he was going to leave a trail, it wouldn't do much good if it was too far away from wherever their destination may end up being.

When he felt comfortable, he repeated the action and his other boot fell softly to the floor. He had to hope it was enough. Enough of a small clue, for when the others came looking for him. They would come looking for him, wouldn't they?

This would all be useless if he was too far from the lookout building and he'd have no boots, which didn't seem great to him, but it was all he could think of doing.

The rest of the journey continued in discomfort, turning to agony by the time the horse finally stopped. Benny writhed on his stomach, trying to keep purchase on the horse, while relieving some of the pressure being placed on his aching body.

He heard the man dismount, his boots crunching into the gravel below. He then felt a hand grab his shoulder and drag him forwards. He fell to the floor, landing hard on his back, grunting.

"Huh," the voice mumbled. "Where are your boots?"

He tried to reply, the gag still muffled him. A moment later, he could feel the knot at the back being loosened and it slid from his mouth.

He gasped and panted; his mouth was dry, and his jaw ached.

"That's what I tried to tell you," he said breathlessly. "They fell off some time back."

The man laughed from somewhere above him.

"Best watch your step then, wouldn't want you stepping on broken glass now, would we?"

He felt the hand grab his shoulder and haul him to his feet. His legs had been bound together at the knees; walking was cumbersome and difficult. He ambled forward, nearly losing his footing in the dark as the man pushed him on. He felt the floor under his foot change; he was walking on wood. He heard creaks as he shuffled ever on. A hinge squeaked in front of him, as a door banged quietly off a wooden wall.

A hand reached for the blindfold, then he felt it being tugged off. He blinked several times. Despite the dim light within the building, it still stung at his eyes after such a long period of darkness.

As the world slowly came back into focus, he studied his surroundings. He was in what appeared to be an old, large, wooden building. Where paper may have once adorned the walls, all that remained was crumbling fragments, forced off by the black and green mould growing in its place.

The floor was made of wooden planks, with no carpet or lush rugs to insulate the rooms. Several of the planks by the walls had rotted through and collapsed in on themselves, leaving gaping holes fading into darkness. He was stood in front of an open door, a figure standing in the doorway, examining him with their head cocked to one side.

He glanced behind him, the man who was presumably his original captor stood there, unmoving. Both figures wore masks obscuring their faces. Neither appeared particularly large, their stature being what Benny would consider about average. He couldn't tell the sex of the person in front of him. They wore a large, thick coat over multiple layers of clothing, the hood pulled up high over their head.

"What is this?" He asked cautiously, keen to avoid another blow to the body.

He received no reply, he hadn't really expected one. The journey here hadn't been full of laughs and conversation, after all.

After a brief pause, the figure in front of him reached for their hood and pulled it back, revealing a face. It was a woman. Still partially obscured by the mask, Benny could only see her eyes and hair. He was sure he could see anger in those brown eyes, cold hatred staring back at him. She stepped aside and the man behind him pushed him hard in the back. He stumbled forward, the bonds at his knees buckled him and he fell to the floor. With his hands still tied behind his back, he had nothing to break his fall and felt his nose crunch under the impact.

He groaned and rolled onto his back. Blood was already seeping into his eyes. He blinked rapidly to clear it and sat as upright as he could, watching the rest of the blood drip off his face, settling in his lap.

The door was still open, and the woman stood stationary, watching him. He spat blood, pooling from his mouth, onto the floor between them, never breaking eye contact with her. Her eyes narrowed and she silently closed the door between them. He heard a lock turn as darkness flooded the room.

As he once again waited for his vision to adjust to the dim light, he started trying to free his hands. The bonds were tight, but the constant movement from the long trip had given him a small amount of leeway between his wrists. It wasn't enough to free his hands, but he was able to stretch a small gap to give him marginally more movement.

He awkwardly stood, the rope around his knees biting into him and shuffled to the edge of the dark room, looking for anything sharp that he could use to his advantage. It didn't take long before he came across a broken floorboard, one edge protruded from the ground and ended in a jagged break. He positioned himself in front of it and started rubbing the binding up and down the edge.

Although he knew the noise from the fraying fabric must be quiet, it sounded deafening in the silent room. He kept going, until his arms ached and his muscles burned, begging him to stop. Eventually, he heard the sounds of the rope fraying. Using as much strength as he could muster, he pulled his arms to his side and the rope finally broke. He rubbed his wrists, red welts already appearing on them. He untied the rope around his knees and stretched his extremities.

A scrape from the other side of the locked door made him freeze. He heard the key turning in the lock, then the door sprung open.

The woman stood in the doorway, a rifle in her hands. It wasn't pointed at him, but the threat in her demeanour was evident.

She smiled. At least, he thought she did, little lines appeared in the corners of her eyes, the mask still obscuring the rest of her face.

Benny hadn't moved and stood in the corner of the room, slightly hunched, with his arms stretched out in surrender.

"Took you long enough," the mystery woman said, the mask muffling her calm, soft voice.

Benny didn't know how to respond, so he stayed silent.

"Here is how this is going to work," she continued. "We want you, alive. If you want that, too, then you do what we say, when we say it. Understand?"

He nodded. She patted the gun.

"These things still work. Sure, ammo is rare as shit, but if I need to, I'll waste one on you, just make sure you've got that."

She didn't sound aggressive, or even angry. She was calm, collected and speaking very reasonably.

"Okay," Benny said, nodding his head. "I understand."

"Good. Now, you don't need to stay tied up, but we will do it again if you misbehave. There's someone in this hallway, at all times and another outside that window." She pointed to the window on the wall behind him. It was so covered in grime; he hadn't even registered it led outside.

"You stay here, and you'll be okay. Try anything and you won't be. It's simple, really."

"Who are you?" Benny asked, his voice catching in his throat.

"Don't you worry about that," she replied curtly. "You'll find out soon enough."

She leaned her hand around the open door and grabbed the back of a wooden chair. It scraped across the bare floor as she dragged it into the room and sat down.

"We don't want to hurt you. Not at all, it's just circumstance and opportunity, is all," she said.

Benny felt the lump forming on the back of his head, which was still throbbing in pain.

"Doesn't feel that way," he said.

"I am sorry about that, but how else would we have got you here? I'm sure you'd have fought back, if you'd had the chance to do so."

He shrugged; she was probably right.

"You know my people will come after me, right?"

"We're counting on it."

He froze at this comment, as the blood drained from his face.

"This was all a trap?" he asked. "For who?"

"For those in charge at Newhaven. This should get their attention. The original plan was to hide out by the gate and snatch whoever came along, but I'm told our man was spotted, or traces of him were. He had to make a quick break. And you just came wandering along, all alone. It was too good an opportunity to pass. We'd intended to be a few more days, give us time to get things ready. But no matter, this works just as well."

"For what?"

She didn't respond.

The silence descended between them, both staring at each other.

Finally, she broke the void. "Hungry?"

"I... erm... what?" That caught him off guard.

"Food. Would you like some? This could take some time; we don't want you starving on us. You'll see, we're not all bad. We just had no choice."

The entire building was as dilapidated as the room he'd been in. He wondered absently what it may once have been, before it fell into disrepair. Completely wooden, the floors, walls and rafters stood bare, whatever decoration was once applied had long since rotted away.

Most of the windows were blown out, some with just jagged edges of glass remaining set in the frames. The room he had been placed into seemed to be one of the few that had the glass intact. The kitchen was no better. The room was long and narrow, with a large table pushed up against the far wall. Dirty looking plates sat on the table, a bowl of... something had been placed in the middle. Two men sat either side of it.

"Stew." The woman announced. She had seen him staring. "Rabbit. It's good."

His mouth salivated at the thought. He hadn't eaten since that morning and the day had taken it out of him.

He approached the table and the two men moved out of his way. They also wore masks. One of them might have been the man who brought him here; he wasn't sure. He helped himself to a bowl and put a full ladle of the brown liquid and meat pieces inside.

He hadn't realised how hungry he was until every last drop was gone. He drank down the thin liquid left in the bottom. He could feel the grease from the rabbit coating the inside of his mouth.

The three people with him in the barren room hadn't moved, nor had they removed their masks. He still didn't know who they were, or what they wanted with him. He looked at them in turn. All three were watching him, not moving, not talking. Just watching. What did they want?

"What's with the masks?" He asked, trying his luck in light of the hospitality.

The woman answered him. "We don't know where you've been, and we need to protect ourselves the best we can."

Benny laughed. "What from?"

She frowned, her forehead wrinkling. "From the virus, of course."

He stopped dead. "The one that ended the world? That hasn't been seen for what, thirty years."

"Is that what they tell you?" She asked. "It's around. It will always be around. Some are immune to it, sure, but not all. Eventually, it's going to get you."

He laughed. This was preposterous. He knew all about the virus, of course he did, but he also knew it was long gone. Faded into obscurity, consigned to history, along with most of the human race. Something nagged at him, though. Something in the back of his mind told him she was right, and that he'd known it all along. He'd never seen an infected person. He struggled to remember what he'd heard back in Newhaven. There was something, some small speculation. It was something one of the founders had heard, a long time ago. What was it?

He clicked his fingers as it suddenly came back to him.

"You're talking about it being engineered, designed to keep killing?"

"That's right. It's not rumour. It's true. The virus was the final solution. The final solution to humanity. It was designed to kill us all."

"That can't be true," he retorted in disbelief. "You can't believe that. It may have been engineered. Sure, it's possible, but who would create a virus that would kill everyone, including themselves and their loved ones?"

"We believe," she said slowly. "That it went wrong. We believe that there was a cure, or a vaccine. Whoever created it had intended for it to be a weapon. Something they could utilise against their enemies. But they misjudged nature. They misjudged what evolution had a funny way of doing, in a very short amount of time. Personally, I believe at least half the people in this room are probably infected. Perhaps immune, but carriers. We know many people are. But not everyone. I believe it's only a matter of time. Then we truly will all be gone."

Benny scoffed. "That's crazy. It can't sit dormant for over

thirty years, that's just not possible."

"Why not?"

"It's just not," he stammered, the doubt creeping into his voice.

"We all know what was said that day in Boneyard. It's stuff of legends, what Tom and Bob did over there. We know what the workers told them. Why would they lie?"

Benny didn't answer. He'd been thrown off guard. They knew all about the founders of Newhaven, it appeared. That much didn't surprise him. When they'd referenced the town on his arrival, he assumed they knew of it and were looking for something to trade to get in, him. But they mentioned Tom and Bob, by name. They knew more than they were letting on.

He shook his head. "No. You're wrong. It's done."

She smiled that sick, terrifying smile, back at him.

CHAPTER FIVE

The barricade around Newhaven came into view as the sun was setting on the horizon behind them.

Several people stood at the open gate, gazing over the open expanse they traversed. Martin watched as a figure came running to greet them. He knew who it was long before he could make them out.

"Hey, Kate," he sighed. He knew what was coming.

She ran past him, stopping at Maria.

"What the hell happened to you?"

"Long story," said Maria wearily, absently rubbing at the dried blood on her face. "How about we get inside, and I'll tell you about it."

"I don't think so," Kate roared. "You will tell me now!" She turned on Martin. "You had one job. One job, Martin, to keep the kids safe. Look at the state of her. Honestly, I've a right mind to..." She trailed off. "Where's Benny? And who is on the back of your horse?" She'd only just noticed the lifeless figure Martin had slung across the horse's rump, tied lightly on with rope.

"Mum," Maria said from behind. "We need to talk, all of us. It's bad."

"I'll get your dad. Meet me in the stables."

Kate, Tom, Maria, Martin and Ava stood in the stable. As Maria finished removing the tack from her horse, Martin retold the story of the last few hours.

"Oh god," Tom said. "Chloe will be devastated."

"Dad," Maria said, addressing him. "I don't know about that, but she'll go bat-shit crazy."

"I'll get her," Martin said. "She needs to know. I want to check in on our 'guest' again, anyway."

The woman had been taken directly to the medical centre, which in reality was little more than a repurposed front room in one of the old homes that fronted the centre of Newhaven, staffed by an older lady who had once worked in a hospital. No one was quite sure what she'd done, but she was the closest to a doctor they had and so she'd been adopted into the role. They even referred to her as the Doctor, being the closest to medical staff they had. She had to work with remedial tools, of course, old, herbal remedies and whatever they could rustle up from the forest. The stores of modern drugs, antibiotics, surgical gear and the other things they once took for granted were long depleted. It would be a very long time, if ever, before they came back.

She had promised to call for them when the woman woke up. In the meantime, she was to clean her up and tend to her wounds. Maria had rejected the chance to be checked over, insisting she was fine. She had rubbed disinfectant from the dwindling stores over the deep cuts, caused by the woman's fingernails.

Martin left, leaving the four of them alone in the barn.

"So, tell me again," Tom said. "What happened?"

Maria sighed, then told the story from her perspective for the third time.

Tom and Kate had Maria several years after the establishment of Newhaven. She was not planned, but they weren't upset by the news. The pregnancy and subsequent childbirth had been fraught with danger. With the lack of modern medicine and care, stillbirths and labour complications had risen. The town had been fortunate, with most mothers and their newborns, surviving the traumatic experiences relatively unscathed.

Chloe had her first child several years before they did and the two grew up together, best friends throughout their childhood. They played in the nearby forest and fields together, completely inseparable.

There were a few other children their age, but throughout their teenage years, they remained as close as ever. When Benny had first approached Martin to join the security force, Maria had instantly signed up too. They were known as the security force, but the reality was that they spent most of their days trotting around the town perimeter, or lazily watching the road from the vantage of the main gates.

Tom and Kate had been so proud when Maria joined up, showing willingness to work for the community, to better what they had. So had Chloe. Benny had been showing signs of wanting to leave, deep down, she thought he still did. He was a growing man and she worried he'd want to explore the world, as dangerous as that may be. When he'd approached Martin, she'd been overjoyed. It had just been the two of them since Jason, Benny's dad, had died years earlier. Bob had been the one to break the news. She remembered the day like it was yesterday. She'd cried, she'd cried all night. It was only when Benny had entered her room, sucking at his thumb, with tears in his eyes, that she'd vowed to stay strong, for him. All of them have survived a brutal world, none more so than Chloe in the dark days. She'd grown comfortable here in Newhaven. It was safe and secure. It was home. All of that was going to change.

"Damn," said Tom, after Maria finished the story once more. "And we don't know anything else? That woman, she said nothing?"

"Not a word, she just tried to scratch my eyes out."

Kate laughed. "I can see why," she said lovingly. Maria shot her a sideways glare.

"She wasn't right, that woman. There was something off with her."

"Martin thinks she's been out there since the beginning. Possibly alone. Can you imagine that, alone for over thirty-five years. Living through the horror that was the outbreak, then complete isolation? I'm not surprised she might seem a bit crazy."

"She saw, though," Maria said quietly. "She saw what happened to Benny. I don't know what she was trying to do, with the blood spots. I don't get it."

Kate thought to herself. "I guess it makes sense," she said eventually. "If you guys hadn't turned around, you'd have been stuck on a crumbling cliff path, with a sheer drop a few inches away. she could have quite easily pushed you both off. I don't think she's that crazy. She had the forethought to think of that. That's something."

Maria frowned again. She'd been pushing to get back out there, to go searching for Benny from the moment she arrived back to Newhaven. She didn't understand why they weren't putting together a small force and going after him. With every passing hour, he could be getting further and further away. Or he could be dead. She didn't know either way.

Kate had rationally argued that without knowing which way he had been taken, their only option was to try and get the woman to talk. She hadn't woken since Martin knocked her out and none of them really knew if she was even still capable of forming words.

Martin appeared at the door with a frantic-looking Chloe next to him.

"When are we going?" she asked, her voice high and shaky. There was a fire in her eyes, a fire that hadn't been seen for many years.

"We need to figure out where, first," Martin added. He nodded to Tom. "The woman's awake, but she's not making any sense. She's not happy about the entire thing, by all accounts, either."

"Okay," Tom said, leaning on the walking stick he'd started taking most places with him. "Let's go see if we can calm her down."

The woman was shrieking and thrashing violently on the bed. She'd been strapped to the metal frame using old leather belts. Her wrists bled where they dug into her as she squirmed in an attempt to get free.

Kate walked over to her and started whispering quietly in her ear, being careful to avoid getting her face close enough to be unintentionally hit.

The woman was cleaner, the layers of grime on her skin had been washed away, presumably by the doctor as her wounds were dressed. She had a large, purple bruise forming on her face, the imprint of Martin's boot could clearly be seen. He blushed to himself. He'd had no other real option, though.

They watched in fascination as the woman slowly calmed, her eyes locking onto Kate; a sense of calm descended over her and she stopped shrieking. Kate kept whispering to her and ran her hand through her matted hair.

A few minutes passed, before Kate turned towards them and gestured them over with her hand.

The woman's eyes scanned over each of them, darting from one face to another, but she made no attempt to move. Her ripped and stained clothes had been removed. She'd been dressed in a simple pair of light trousers and a plain white t-shirt. Maria thought she already looked more human and much frailer. She looked old. Her skin was sunken, resting over her bony face, almost too big for the skeleton underneath. The dirt had hidden much of the evidence of age when they'd first met. It was hard to believe the woman in front of her was the same one that was able to attack her with such ferocity and speed hours earlier. She looked so fragile.

"I'm Kate, do you know your name?" The woman's eyes flew back to lock onto Kate, but she made no attempt to reply.

"It's okay. You're safe here. No one is going to hurt you. We just need to speak to you. Can you speak?"

The woman's mouth opened slightly, but no sound came out.

"Take your time. You're in Newhaven. This is where we live. There's lots of people here and it's safe. There's no virus. No one is going to hurt you here."

The woman let out a low groan at the mention of the virus, but she kept still.

"it's okay. It's gone. You're safe," Kate repeated. "We need your help though. The man you saw taken, he's very special to us, and we need to get him back. But we don't know where he is. I'm hoping you might. I'm hoping you might help us?"

A low gurgle emanated from the woman's throat.

"I'm sorry, I can't understand you. Would you try again?"

The woman rasped louder, just as intelligibly.

"One more time. We really need you to try."

A nonsensical word came from the woman. It didn't mean anything, but it was progress. She looked annoyed with herself, like she knew what she wanted to say, but couldn't physically get the words out. She tried again, before breaking into a violent coughing fit.

"It's okay, it's okay," Kate cooed, as she brought a glass of water to the woman's lips. She took a sip and nodded her head up and down.

"I think we're getting somewhere," Kate said to the others. "This could take some time. I'll stay with her. You guys see what we can put together to go after Benny. As soon as we have some information, we'll be taking off, so make sure you're ready."

"We already know which way they went," Maria protested.

"Why don't we just go?"

"You know which direction they left the lookout; you don't know where they went after that."

"What makes you think she will. She only saw what we did, I don't think she followed them. She was too busy trying to kill us."

"You might be right. But we need to try. We need to know what we're headed in to. I promise, if we don't get anything in a few hours, we'll go out anyway. We will get Benny back," she turned to face Chloe. "I promise."

Martin had been to the rest of his security crew, looking for volunteers. They'd all put their hands up when he asked if anyone would ride out with them. He was proud of these men and women. They'd come from nothing, no military background, no training, but they'd been fantastic in their duties here in Newhaven. He pointed to two of them, Vincent and Steve, both middle-aged men, who had been in the role for a long time. The rest of his crew were younger, most of them born here and had never seen real combat. He was sure they'd be able to handle themselves, but for this, he only wanted the best. They understood, someone had to stay and make sure Newhaven remained safe. Especially now.

Tom stood watching them, leaning against the corner of a building. When Martin noticed him, he nodded his head, indicating he should join him.

"It's time," he said, removing a key from his pocket. Martin looked at it and nodded back in agreement.

The storage room hadn't been opened in years. There had been no need to. The door creaked and dust flew through the air as they stepped inside.

"You think they'll still be good?" Martin asked.

"I hope so. They've been dry, I don't see why not." He pulled back a thick blanket, which had been hiding a large metal filing cabinet, stood upright against the wall. Pulling open the door, he revealed the row of gleaming rifles inside.

"Five rifles and forty-one cartridges. Let's hope it's enough."

"It will be," Martin added, as he picked up one of the rifles. "It's been some years since I've handled one of these. I forgot how good they feel in the hand."

Tom chuckled. "I'm not so sure about that. I don't mind not having them. Brings back some bad memories. Some I could do with forgetting."

Martin nodded slowly. He understood what Tom was insinuating. The last time they'd had a large cache of weapons and ammo was back in the old days, when they found themselves fighting the remaining government and the soldiers left on the mainland. Once Boneyard had fallen, the soldiers mostly deserted from their posts and camps in the forests. He knew a few who had joined other camps. Most went their own way. They likely died in the ensuing chaos, taking their weapons with them to the grave.

Boneyard still had access to a large selection of them. They'd offered them in trade, more than once. Tom had always rejected the proposal. He knew he might need to take them up on the offer soon, if they needed to replenish their stocks. He didn't like the weaponry, he saw it as an omen leading to worse times, but it was good to have in an emergency. An emergency like this.

As the world recovered, divisions would start to show once more. People always needed something to fight over. Survival had been a good distraction, but it was fast coming to an end.

The world sat on a knife edge. Tom worried about which way it was going to fall. Thirty-five years of peace had made people weak; it had made people trusting. That was the same thing, to him.

"Give them out as you see fit."

"One for you?"

"No. I don't want one. I'll be coming, of course, but I'll do it with what I've got."

"Are you sure, Tom? You're not a young man, anymore. You're needed here."

"I'm needed by every one of the folks who live here, Martin. Including Benny. Lead by example and all that," he laughed.

"Ava said she'll come, but I've asked her to stay here and oversee things. She's probably best placed to keep it in order."

"That's for sure. She'll have them whipped up before you know it."

They shared a chuckle.

"Here we go again," Tom said quietly.

"Here we go again," Martin agreed.

Chloe stood bolt upright as Kate walked across the paddock towards them. They'd been ready and waiting in the stables for an hour now. Chloe was as eager as Maria to set off. Her child had been kidnapped by no one knew who, and she wanted him back. Now.

"She spoke," Kate exclaimed. "It took some time; I don't think she's said a word in years. Her name is Caroline. She fled to the forest at the first outbreak and has been living out there ever since. She's more or less feral at this point. I don't know how we've never come by her before, it looks like she's been around this area for years. She knew all about us, all about this place. I did wonder if she was responsible for the fire, but I don't think so. She also knows about the other settlements nearby. Not all of them, but she's been around a lot of them. One man took Benny. He tricked him. He put a bag where it could be seen inside the lookout point, then hid around the corner. When

Benny came out, he hit him around the head and that was it. Tied him up, slung him over a horse and took off. Caroline didn't follow them; she saw you two coming soon after and thought you were with him. That's why she tried to get you off the cliff, but to be honest, I don't think she thought that through properly. I don't know if she could."

"So, we've learned nothing?" Chloe asked, desperation in her voice.

"No, not exactly. The man was wearing a mask; she couldn't say who he was, but she did recognise the horse, she thinks. She seems to remember animals much easier than people. She says they've been up and down this way for a few weeks, scouting out different places. They always come from the same way. Onto the main road and head south. She's seen four different people. Always masked, but she's sure they're the same. Three men and a woman."

"It's a start," Maria added, slinging her backpack over her shoulder. "We'll do the same and see what we see." She reached for one of the rifles leaning against the stable door. Martin moved to stop her.

"I'm taking one," she said firmly. "I know how to use it, I'll be fine."

"We don't have enough and when would you have fired one in your life?"

She smiled. "I'll be fine. I've been taught by the best."

Martin looked to Tom, who nodded in reply, then he moved his body to allow her access to the weapon. With only five rifles, and an average of eight shots each, he wanted to make sure they were in the right hands.

He'd take one, of course and both Vincent and Steve would have one. Maria had the fourth and Kate had already helped herself. Everyone else would need to make do with the machete, the axes and the bows.

He looked around at the people with him. All of them, he

knew and trusted with his life. He knew they could look after themselves, but he felt like he had to say something regardless. Sensing he was gearing up to make a speech, the others fell silent and watched him. His confidence fell flat, and no words came.

He shrugged. "Let's go," he said, slightly deflated.

CHAPTER SIX

It was a typical, dreamy sunny day. The sun was still making its ascent over the sky, he squinted as he looked towards it, deep from the corn field. He giggled; he was having a lovely time. If only he could find her. She'd be around here somewhere, she always was.

"Benny!" he heard the high-pitched voice call him, hidden within the corn, followed by a laugh. "You're never going to find me!" The voice wasn't that far away. He'd find her.

He couldn't keep the smile off his face as he pushed his hands through the stalks, expecting her to be hidden behind each one of them. The crops were not yet full hight, but he and Maria were still young, and the tall stalks towered above them.

"I'm going to find you, Maria," he giggled, pushing his way through the corn. He heard a laugh to his left and veered off in that direction. The field was thick with crops. It was going to be a good harvest this year.

Benny and Maria had been playing for most of the morning, while the adults toiled. He thought he glanced her long blonde hair and giggled harder, moving towards her. She wasn't there, he frowned, she always won hide-and-seek. She was lighter than him and could move through the corn like it wasn't there, while he crashed through it like a bull.

"Maria?" he called.

"Ben-ja-min," she replied in a singsong voice. It floated in on the breeze. He turned again and ran in the opposite direction. The crops were taller than he was; he could only see the area immediately in front of him. He could run right past her and never see her. She knew it too.

"Too slow," she called, her voice moving further away from him.

He groaned in frustration and turned back the way he'd come. He always lost. He wanted to win, just once.

"Maria!"

That giggle again. She was further away now.

"Come on!" he whinged. "This isn't fair. I don't want to play anymore."

He was young and prone to a sulk. He knew he was doing it; he was going to lose, and he didn't like it. Maria was always kind to him. He knew if he told her he'd had enough, she'd come to him. He was right again. Out of the thick stalks, she suddenly appeared, lunging towards him and poking his nose with her finger.

"Bop," she said with a giggle.

He leapt forward and his fingertips brushed over her arm. "Got ya!" he giggled.

"That's not fair. You cheated," she whined.

He laughed. "Well, I won, didn't I?"

"Cheater."

"You're it!" With that, he turned and ran into the crop, disappearing out of sight.

He ran, pushing past stalks, breathing heavily. He could hear her crashing through the field behind him. Despite being several years younger than him, she was much more nimble and faster than he was, and he knew it. He didn't mind when she caught him, he liked the chase. He kept running, he didn't know which direction he was facing now, he just kept running.

He wasn't paying attention. He glanced behind him; he couldn't see her, he was trying to stop himself from laughing, he didn't want to give his location away that easily.

He grunted as he ran into the wooden fence. He fell to the ground and felt tears welling up in his eyes. A cut had opened up on his forehead. The fence was level with him. He'd run into it headfirst. He sat in the dirt and pulled his knees up to his chest. The tears came and he raised his head, wailing to the clear sky.

"Come on, lad. You'll be just fine, it's only a cut."

Benny looked up. Bob stood over him, the big man's frame blocking the sunlight from his eyes. He was a kind man. Benny liked him; he was always happy, and he made him laugh.

He sniffed and wiped his nose.

"I'm sorry, sir," he mumbled.

"Don't be sorry, lad. Kids play. Nothings broke. Well, probably," he laughed as he noticed the blood dripping from his head. "Maybe your noggin. But I don't think it'll cause much trouble. Full of sawdust, that head of yours." He playfully wrapped his knuckles lightly on the side of Benny's head.

Benny laughed and Bob lowered his hand. Benny took it and felt himself being pulled to his feet, just as Maria came crashing through the corn.

"Benny?" she asked, her eyes wide with worry. "Are you okay?"

Bob laughed, that full, deep, booming laugh of his.

"He'll be fine, especially now you're here lassie. He wouldn't want to cry in front of you," he winked at Benny. "Come on, the pair of ya. I've got some lemonade here and we'll get that head of yours cleaned up." Maria took his other hand as he led them through the fence and into the nearby barn.

"You really do need to be more careful in there. I know, you're only playin', but it's easy to get hurt out here," he glanced at Benny. His dad had died out here a few years earlier. Benny didn't remember it, but he knew Bob had been there.

Bob had done everything he could to try and save his life, but it'd all been in vain; he died before they could get him any treatment. Not that anything they could provide would have helped.

Benny was too young to really understand what had happened. He knew the basics but didn't really understand how it had all unfolded. He'd been around horses all his life. He used to make Chloe nervous when he'd run between their legs. He'd always been fine; he wasn't sure why his dad hadn't been.

Bob poured them both a glass of lemonade. It was sweet and sour at the same time and Benny sucked his cheeks in as he sipped at it. Bob had wiped the trickle of blood away from his head and he sat on a bale of hay, his legs swinging over the edge.

"How's ya mam?" Bob asked him.

"She's good," Benny replied. "She's back working with Tom and Kate. I don't know what they're doing. She's out a lot, now."

"She's just makin' sure you're safe. She's good at that. We are all in good hands while she's around." He smiled kindly. "Tell her I want to see her down here more often. I know she don't like comin' out this way anymore, but it'd be nice to see her."

"I will, sir," he promised. He didn't see Chloe as much as he'd like to. He was only eight or nine and wanted to be around her. She'd always been there after his dad died. He'd grown used to her company. Recently, that had all changed. He found himself alone at home or running through the fields with Maria. He didn't mind the latter, but he didn't like to be alone.

He looked up to see Bob staring at him, smiling though his large, bushy, grey beard.

"You know, lad, you're always welcome to come hang out here with me. If you're lonely, you know? I'll find something to keep you busy. If you want, of course."

Benny smiled, a grin spreading across his face.

"Can I come and play tomorrow? Mum's going to be out all day."

"Of course you can. Just come down and find me. You're always welcome, lad."

"I want to come, too!" Maria said, pouting.

Bob laughed. "You too, of course. Just don't tell your mam I let you climb over the bales. She'll have me for that, if she finds out." He roared with laughter. It was infectious, and Benny and Maria started laughing, too.

The following morning, Benny woke as the sun shone through his window. Their house was located near the centre of town, as all the founders' homes seemed to be. He thought of it as a house, but it wasn't, not really. It had once been, now it was segregated into several homes. No one needed an entire house to themselves, anymore. They had two rooms. One was used as bedroom. Chloe slept on the bed pushed against one side and he slept on the floor over the other. She'd put a curtain up, to give him some privacy as he grew.

The other room was adjacent to their bedroom. A single, small and sparsely decorated room, with an aged sofa and a small coffee table. There wasn't much need for anything further. The cooking was a community affair, the large tent off the intersection was used to feed them all. Cooks started early, preparing food for the population. It wasn't as many back then, but it was still a mammoth task. The food was cooked on an open fire, fed by branches from the nearby forest. A metal grate was elevated above it, resting on thick, metal legs. As the town grew, the cooking facilities were upgraded. Eventually, a brick oven was built. The process was still more or less the same, but it felt much more efficient, somehow. The lavatories were on the edge of town. They'd been dug when the town was first established, but like the cooking facility, they'd been upgraded over the years. There was limited privacy, but in reality, they were nothing more than wooden shacks, with what could best be described as a long drop below.

Showers were now available. Again, they were outdoors and provided cold water only. The water was collected from the gutters running along the roofs of the buildings. A system had been fabricated where they all ran into several central collection tanks, large black plastic, with a mishmash of pipes and tubes transporting the water via gravity to where it was needed.

Bob had designed most of the water and irrigation system. He was good at it; he'd done similar all his life back on the farm.

There had been discussions over changing the piping for something of a metallic construction, which could be routed through an open fire in an attempt to bring warm water to the town. It hadn't had much traction so far, but the thought was that as winter approached, it would become a popular topic of conversation.

Benny pulled the curtain back, revealing the empty half of the room on the other side. He sighed to himself. She must have quietly crept out before he woke. Even at his young age, he knew she was busy and would be there with him if she could, but he still felt the pangs of loneliness when he woke alone. He dressed, then headed to the kitchen tent to get himself breakfast. Everyone knew everyone in Newhaven and there were no safety concerns, so Benny and the other children were really left to do whatever they wished. Schooling was a thing, but it wasn't the same as the eight-hour long days that children were subjected to before everything changed. They learnt the basics, but most of their school days were spent learning skills that would help them in later life. They learned how to farm, how to build and how to fight, although less emphasis had been placed on the latter recently. The school was held three times a week, and today wasn't one of them.

The tent was nearly empty; he wondered how late he'd slept. There was a small amount of the thin stew left in the large pot, but none of the servers remained. He helped himself to a bowl and used the large ladle to scoop some out for himself.

Once he'd finished his breakfast and licked the drips from the bowl, he returned it to the dirty pile, which was overflowing with used bowls and utensils and headed down towards the farmland. He skipped happily as he did. He was looking forward to his day with Bob. He hoped Maria would be there too. It didn't take him long to find Bob, the big man visible from some distance. Bob didn't do much of the manual labour anymore, his age had caught up with him. He was still the most competent of anyone in Newhaven, so he acted instead as the farm foreman, handing tasks to others and overseeing the work as he hobbled across the uneven ground.

Benny waived as he ran the rest of the distance until he arrived at Bob's side.

"Benny, boy!" responded Bob, scooping him off the ground with one arm and spinning him around. "Glad to see ya' kid. Ready to get to work, pay your way?"

Benny giggled as Bob dropped him back to the ground and nodded enthusiastically.

"Okay then," Bob boomed. "So, this morning, you and me are gonna' feed all the horses. They're in the barns, because we can't stop them eating the leaves off the corn, so they've been put in jail for a few days." He cast a quick, toothy grin at Benny. "Ready?"

"Yeah!"

They headed to the barns, Benny jogging every few steps to keep up with Bob, even with the limp. How long had Bob had a limp? He frowned as he thought back to the last few times he'd seen him. He didn't remember him limping before.

Bob must have caught him looking. "Don't worry about me, lad. Just a bit of age getting into my old bones. I'll still outpace you!" he smiled as he walked even faster.

Benny smiled as he deliberately increased his pace to a jog to keep up with the man's stride.

They spent the morning completing simple and easy tasks. They fed hay to the horses, mucked them out, and emptied the used straw onto the pile behind the barns. Bob cracked jokes at every opportunity, Benny laughed along to them all.

With the sun high in the sky, Bob called him off his current task, checking the chicken coops for eggs and put a plate next to him. There was a sandwich on the plate. Bread was a treat, he didn't have it often, due to the difficulty in making it for such a large group of people. Thick slices of cheese were inside, another treat, and infinitely rarer. The town had a small herd of cows. He had no idea how they'd got there, or how they kept them, but he knew they didn't produce enough milk to provide for them all, there simply wasn't enough of them.

"Shh," Bob said with a wry smile, as he shovelled his own cheese sandwich into his mouth. "They'll be a riot if they find out," he finished through chews of the bread.

Benny smiled and ate his lunch happily. The crusts had been cut from the bread and the cheese had a fantastic salty flavour. He enjoyed every last bite, licking the crumbs from the plate when he was done. He smacked his lips comically and Bob rewarded him with a warm smile.

"Benny!" the voice echoed through the barn. He couldn't hide the smile spreading over his face.

"Maria," he replied joyfully, then frowned at her. "You're late."

"Sorry," she replied sheepishly. "Dad wanted me to go outside with him. He showed me how to track deer."

"Lovely," said Bob. "Venison on the menu tonight?"

"No. We didn't find anything. But I got to fire Dad's gun, that was awesome."

Benny thought for a moment he saw Bob frown, but when he turned to look at him, his face was as jolly as always.

"Why don't you two go play?" Bob asked them with a smile. "We're about done here, you've been too efficient, young man.

Sun's out, may as well go and enjoy it!"

Benny smiled at Maria, who nodded excitedly. "Hide-and-seek?"

They ran through the crops, like so many times before, giggling and laughing as they ran. Maria pushed into him with both of her hands.

"You're it," she screamed, already running in the opposite direction. He took off after her. She was already blended into the crops and out of sight.

"Maria!" He shouted, as he'd done many times before, then stilled to wait for her call back or to hear the sound of a close-by laugh if she'd hidden somewhere nearby. He heard neither and so pushed forward through the towering stalks.

"Maria," he shouted again. A scream replied.

He felt the colour drain from his face. It had come from in front of him, but where? He couldn't see anything and quickly descended into panic. He ran, shouting her name as he did.

He heard a quiet cry; it was her; she was close.

"Maria, are you okay?" He called.

"Benny?" she replied through sobs. "I'm here."

He dropped to his knees, hoping to see better where the leaves didn't obscure his view. There she was, just a few meters from him now. He crawled on his hands and knees until he sat next to her. She clutched her ankle. Already it was swollen and red.

"What happened?" He asked.

"I think it's twisted. I hit the ground wrong. It hurts, Benny," she sobbed.

"I'll get Bob."

"No. Please, don't leave me."

"Okay. I won't. Promise. Can you walk?"

She shook her head.

He bent down next to her. "Jump on my back," he said. She

looked at him for a moment, then slowly pushed herself to her feet, grimacing as she did. She wrapped her arms around his neck, as he stood while she clung to him.

"Benny, Maria? What's goin' on. Are you two okay?" Concern showed on Bob's face as he watched the pair of them approach the barn.

He'd sent them away and taken the opportunity to rest. Spending just the morning with Benny had taken it out of him, he'd been dozing in the sun when he first heard them coming.

"It's Maria, she's hurt her ankle."

Bob's eyebrows raised as he started to understand the situation.

"Good lad," he said quietly. "I'll take her from here. We'll go see the doctor." He picked her up in his giant hands and turned towards the town. He walked with her in his arms as Benny watched him go. The limp was worse.

Maria had a splint wrapped tightly across her ankle, bandaged up to her calf. Bob had left to find Tom or Kate and told them both to stay put, so the two of them sat in the middle of town, idly fiddling with the leaves littering the ground. The doctor had announced that Maria would be fine; she'd just need to keep weight off her leg for a little while. She'd then kicked them out and returned to her work.

"Thank you, Benny," Maria said quietly after a prolonged period of silence, blushing as she cast him a sideways glance.

He smiled. "Of course, anything for you."

CHAPTER SEVEN

The sound of hooves beating off the road filled the air around them as they rode away from Newhaven. They were as prepared as they would ever be and headed off to the south, trying to pick up any trail that might help lead them to Benny.

Seven horses, loaded with seven riders, five rifles and forty-one shots. That's all they had, and that would have to do.

Martin was sure they could have easily got more people to go with them, out of a town of nearly 2000, he'd have no problem finding more volunteers, but what was the point? None of them were trained, he'd rather keep the search party small, people he could trust and people he knew could look after themselves.

He rode at the front. Maria and Chloe kept pace by his side. Vincent and Steve walked the flanks, with Kate and Tom holding back. Tom never admitted it, but he was getting old, and life had been hard for him. He wasn't the man he once was. It was difficult to believe he'd been only a few years older than Martin. He turned to glance back at him and saw the old man clutching the reins, his pace slower than the rest. He sighed. Maybe it'd happen to him. One day he'd wake up and before he knew it, he'd be as old and frail as Tom looked. These things do have a habit of creeping up on a person.

They rode for most of the afternoon, keeping slow along the road so as not to miss anything that might provide a clue to Benny's location. They spread out as best they could, trying to cover every inch of road. Scouring the ground before them.

He nearly missed it. It was so inconspicuous that he nearly walked right by it. The road, even after all these years, was still strewn with debris and detritus; it could just have been another item of junk, discarded by the wayside.

It caught his eye, but only in a passing glance. He had to take a second look before drawing the horse to a halt.

"What is it?" Maria asked.

He pointed to the boot on the road beside him.

"Is that Benny's?" he asked.

She frowned at it.

"Maybe..." she replied, her face deep in thought as he examined the boot on the ground.

Chloe hopped off her horse and picked it up. She studied the side.

"Yes," she announced. "It's his."

"You sure?"

"Yes," she replied. "I'm sure. I've spent long enough tripping over the damned things. This is his. I'm sure of it."

"Then we're on the right track. That's good."

"You think it fell, or he left it for us?" Maria asked.

"I think he left it, kicked it off, maybe. I don't see a boot just falling off. That's good news. It means he's alive and he's thinking about how to escape. He's left this for us to find, so he knows we're coming after him. He knows he's not alone."

Tom and Kate finally joined the halted party as Chloe held the boot in the air for them to see.

"That's from ours, alright," Tom added, confirming the thought the group already had. Martin could hear him panting from where he stood. He looked exhausted from the few hours ride. Any strength he'd shown back at Newhaven had been sapped out of him. He'd aged years in just an afternoon. His grey hair looked thinner, the deep lines in his face more pronounced.

"Tom, look, if you want to turn back, it's no problem. We've got this," Martin said, hesitantly.

Tom shot him a glance; he knew the answer before it had left his lips.

"I am not turning back. I'm fine, and I'm good to help."

Martin looked to Kate, who smiled sadly. Tom was stubborn. Always had been and in his older age, that'd just gotten worse. There would be no persuading him. Kate shook her head slowly, so only Martin had seen. He knew then she felt the same thing. This would need to be discussed, but now was not the right time. They had to find Benny, and a power grab midway through a rescue mission would not be a good thing.

"Okay," he conceded. Changing the subject, he added, "we're on the right track, that's good. We'll be losing light soon, so let's keep going while we still can."

They continued on, passing the flowing meadows on each side of them as the sun slowly descended over the treeline in the distance. Rusted cars, long since abandoned, littered the landscape. Some remained on the road, where they'd run out of fuel, or had been forcibly stopped. Others had been pushed away, rolling down the gentle inclines into the meadows below. None were discernible of what brand they once might have been; it was all the same now. Rusted, twisted metals, a relic of a bygone age, one that would not be seen for a long, long time again.

Most of the buildings still stood, although neglected for so long, their shells remained sturdy. Small cottages, the occasional petrol station and other roadside shops lay abandoned as they rode further south. In the days shortly after the outbreak, these buildings had been a haven for people fleeing the towns and cities. As things became more desperate, they became a menace to anyone passing. People could, and often would, jump out of them or shoot from within them.

Martin had experienced both, back when he was on patrol. He remembered the fear when they walked near one of these abandoned buildings, in the middle of nowhere. They'd have to search it, usually finding them clear. Not always, though...

Martin hadn't felt that dread since he was back in the army, but he felt it today. He studied their broken windows as he passed, looking for any sign of movement. The situation had him on edge and he was determined to be ready for anything. He cast frequent sideways looks to Tom. The man had led them for all these years. He'd been a close friend, and Martin loved him as such, but something wasn't right with him. Despite the close age between them, Tom had aged so much faster. His body was letting him down at times and Martin feared now his mind was, too. He was slowing them down. He was a burden to this party, yet he refused to leave. Should he just tell him outright?

No, he couldn't do that. Tom was still in charge, and he'd just have to accept his judgment, no matter how skewed he thought it might be right now. He frowned to himself. This could become a problem before much longer.

Chloe arrived next to him, pacing her horse to keep in step with his. She cast him a sideways glance and he turned his attention to her.

"Something's going on with Tom," she said. As if she had read his mind.

Martin nodded. "He's getting on; it happens to the best of us."

"Not if it affects my chances of getting my son back. I won't let it, Martin. If Tom isn't up for this, we need him to go back. He'll be more use back at Newhaven, we can't be worrying about him here."

"I understand. I'll keep an eye on him, but it'll be fine, Chloe. You know Tom. He wouldn't be here if he didn't think he could do it." He kept his own worries to himself. He had to be shown supporting a united front, even when it was to Chloe. This concerned him, though. Chloe had been with them since the beginning. Longer than Martin, even. He would have expected her to side with Tom till the end. It must have been more obvious than he'd originally thought.

"There!" Maria shouted, pointing to the road. The sun was well on its way down and the light had faded. Martin had to focus his eyes on the part of the road Maria was pointing. Partially hidden behind the tall grass, sat Benny's other boot.

"Good," he said. "We know we're on the right track. It's getting dark, though, we'll have to set up camp soon. We can't go much longer."

The others agreed, as they veered off the road into the woods blanketing the roadside until they came across a small clearing. They dismounted their horses and tied them to the nearby trees, allowing enough slack so they could graze the floor around them.

Martin watched as Tom slowly jumped from his horse, his face distorted in discomfort as he hit the floor. He grimaced as he regained his balance, before Kate rushed to reach for his shoulder and help him stand straight.

He shook his head and turned away. Removing the canvas from his bag, he began to hook it to the nearby trees to set up shelter for the night.

The low fire burned away in the centre of the clearing. They'd kept it small, just enough to give them warmth, whilst hiding the light and the smoke from the roadside. The row of trees between them would help keep away prying eyes. They didn't know how far they had left to travel, and it wasn't worth the risk of being spotted here.

Maria volunteered to take first watch. She was eager for the night to be over so they could continue the search for Benny. This would be the first night Benny had been away from them, she missed him already.

The trees were full of the sounds of animals as she sat quietly on the edge of the camp, staring into the darkness at shadows dancing in the moonlight. She listened to what she thought might be an owl, hooting somewhere in the distance and tried to imagine what the world would have been like, before the end. She'd never known that world, only what people had told her. Billions of people. People everywhere. The thought made her feel ill. The town was large by her standards. 2000 people was a lot of people. To imagine cities of millions was unfathomable.

She knew, of course, about the technological marvels that had gone extinct along with the bulk of humanity. The internet, computers, cars. She knew the theory of all of these things but didn't see their benefit. She struggled to imagine or understand a life that seemed to have no purpose. A life spent idly wasting time. Counting down the days until one day, there would be none left to count.

She was lost in her thoughts and hadn't heard him approach. She jumped as he carefully touched her back.

"God," she said in shock. "Steve, you scared me."

Steve laughed. He was younger than Martin, but not quite in the same generation as Maria. Steve had been born shortly before everything ended. He didn't remember much about the old world and had now spent all of his adult life at Newhaven. He'd been a small boy when he arrived. One of the first. He'd watched the town grow along with him.

His parents had died in the first outbreak, he didn't remember anything about them. He'd been taken in by his uncle. When things got too bad, they tried to make it to the government camps, all those years ago. They hadn't made it, they'd got nowhere near. He later discovered that their failure had likely saved his life. They squatted in abandoned buildings for the first year or so, surviving on what they could scavenge or steal. It was heading into winter when they came across Newhaven, quite by accident. His uncle knew the town that preceded Newhaven, they were headed to see if there was anything left in the small general store that could be pilfered. Instead, they'd come face to face with the crude, unfinished barrier.

It was Martin who had first greeted them, although it was with a rifle pointed their way. He remembered that day clearly. This strange man, dressed in green fatigues - it had been before Martin gave up his traditional army gear - no sign of fear on his face, protecting his people. It was that first meeting that made Steve want to follow in his footsteps, it's why he joined the guards, once the roles were formalised. He could only have been five or six, when he first met him, but the memory had stayed with him throughout his life.

Steve's uncle had died many years ago. Tuberculosis, or something, so the doctor had thought. There was no way to accurately diagnose these things anymore. The virus had been clear and decisive, the other diseases were still as cruel as ever. He remembered his uncle's last few days, spent in agony, writhing on the makeshift bed. He'd watched him grow thin and gaunt over a few short weeks. It was a relief, in many ways, once he died. He still felt guilty about that. Deep down, he knew his uncle would have wanted it to be over.

He was a teenager then, perhaps sixteen, and more than capable of looking after himself. He'd started an apprenticeship with Bob, tending to the small herd of cows. He wasn't old enough to start work with Martin. He'd have to wait another two years before they would let him do that.

The farm work had been fine, and he'd been glad to be contributing, but he counted the days until he turned eighteen. On his birthday, or as close to it as he could accurately predict, he'd walked into the guardhouse, disturbed Martin as he ate his lunch and demanded to be allowed to join him. Martin had accepted with a big smile and a firm handshake. That had been the start of his nearly twenty-year career to now. It might not have been quite as exciting as he'd hoped, aside from a few isolated incidents in the early days, but he felt fulfilled in doing it. He was good at what he did.

Bob had been sad to see him leave the farm but understood his decision. He'd grown close to Bob in the two years he spent there and was one of the few who accompanied his body back to the farmhouse by the orchard when he died.

He brushed his blonde, curtained hair out of his face, tucking it neatly behind his ear.

"Couldn't sleep?" Maria asked.

"Nah," he replied. "I'm used to it; I usually do night watch. I like the quiet. I like the sounds you can hear out here when it's dark."

"Is it like this at night in Newhaven?" she asked. She'd been in Newhaven at this time, plenty of times, but never really paid attention.

"Yeah. It's lovely, really. It's peaceful." The quiet sat between them for several long moments.

Maria broke the silence with tears that ran down her face. "I'm worried about him," she sniffed.

"Me too," he replied. "Me too."

"We are going to find him?" she asked, needing the validation.

"We are," he replied. "Never leave a man behind. You and Benny are new to our little crew, but you'll see, we never leave a man or woman behind. I was sick with worry when it got back to town he'd been taken; of course I was always going to come out to help."

She smiled hopefully. Steve wasn't what she might call a friend, not yet. He was good with a machete and proficient with a bow. He was loyal, caring and understanding. Maria smiled as she watched him stare into space. There were worse people to be stuck out here with.

"Now, why don't you go and get some sleep. I'll take over from here. Not much to do, other than watch the stars."

The smell of roasting meat woke Maria the following morning. The sun heated the inside of her canvas tent as she wiped the sleep from her eyes.

Emerging, she saw that she was the first awake. Steve had set a small fire at the edge of the camp, and something was roasting on a spit atop it. It sizzled as fat dripped down the wood onto the hot embers below.

"Now that smells good," she said sleepily.

"Rabbit," he replied with a smile. "The trick is to wait till twilight, then shoot them in the face with an arrow. Works every time." He chuckled at his own joke as Maria rolled her eyes.

"Managed to bag a couple overnight," he added. "Plenty enough for all of us."

It didn't take long before the aroma drew the others from their slumber. One by one, they joined them by the small fire. As all seven of them warmed themselves in the rising sun and burning branches, Steve removed the blackened rabbit loin from the fire and handed it to Tom.

"Might be a bit dry, but it should keep you going."

Tom accepted the meat eagerly as Steve turned the legs, still roasting above the embers.

"How did you manage this?" Chloe asked, eyeing the loins jealously.

"Easy," he smiled, tapping the bow at his side.

Once they had all eaten and packed away their camp, Steve and Maria led the horses to a stream a short walk away within the trees to drink, filling their own canteens as they did so.

"Have you slept?" Maria asked as she topped up the metal flask in her hands, noticing the black bags under his eyes.

"I got a few hours last night, that'll be okay. I'm used to it," he replied.

"You should have woken me. We could have swapped."

"Nah, that's fine. Honestly, I'm alright. I don't mind it. I'm as fresh as I need to be."

"Thank you, Steve. I do appreciate it. I hope you know that. I'm sure Benny will too. He always liked you. He'll be pleased to know you're out here looking for him."

"Of course," he smiled back, before he turned away from her.

"Let's go find our Benny, eh?" he said quietly.

The others had packed the camp down by the time they returned. Several folded packs scattered on the floor as they milled around.

Steve walked Tom's horse over to him and helped him onto it.

The others mounted their horses and they all headed back onto the road.

CHAPTER EIGHT

Benny stared at the empty wooden wall, alone with his thoughts in this quiet room. His neck hurt from the awkward position he'd slept in. There was a rusted metal bed frame here, but no mattress. He'd ended up curling into a ball on the floor, hugging at his knees and trying to sleep. He hadn't managed it particularly well, but he was sure he'd at least managed to get some.

He'd need it. He knew what he was going to do, and he needed to be rested and ready to do it.

He'd been here for less than a day. He didn't have a watch or anything to tell the time from without being able to see the sun, but the breaking twilight barely coming through the grime-covered window told him it was still early. He'd probably been here for just twelve hours, although it felt like a lot longer. His head still throbbed; whatever damage had been done when he was knocked out was still hurting him. He ran his hand over the wound and felt the scab forming on the back of his head.

He stretched his arms out and heard his shoulder pop in its sockets as he did. One way or another, he didn't want to spend another night here. He stood by the closed wooden door, his ear rested against it as he listened for any sign of movement.

He heard nothing. He did the same at the window. He'd been told someone was keeping guard out there and that they were armed, although he hadn't seen them yet. It made sense and he wasn't prepared to risk that they were lying about their numbers. He'd been knocked out already in the past day, he didn't want to add being shot to that count.

When he was satisfied there was no movement in, or outside, the run-down building, he put his plan into action. He'd spend a long time thinking about this, locked inside that dark room after they'd fed him the previous night. His plan was simple. The floorboards were lifting in various places, where time and the damp had pulled them from their nails. He was going to lift them and lower himself into the crawl space below. From there, he hoped he could make his way to the other end of the house, out to freedom. It sounded so simple in his head, he idly wondered why they hadn't perhaps expected him to do it. Or maybe they had. He would have to be slow, quiet and careful. He needed to go now. He needed to be long gone before they came to check on him.

He didn't know their schedule. He had no idea when they might rise, nor if anyone was left on guard overnight. It was a risk he had to take.

The boards came loose with little effort., the rotting wood separating easily from the rusted nails that had once held them firmly in place. As quietly as he could manage, he pulled three of them slowly away from the floor and laid them softly against the door, jamming them under the handle. He hoped that might give him a few more seconds when they did try to enter. They came up with ease, leaving the large, rusted nails sticking out from the joists below. He supposed they were fairly rotten and wouldn't do great as a barricade, but it would hopefully buy him a bit of time, if he needed it.

He dropped down to the space below the building. It was only just wider than he was, writhing in the dirt. Thick planks blocked his path and more than once he had to turn around as he tried to navigate his way through the labyrinth in near pitch darkness.

His arms burned, his eyes watered and the dust choked him. He tried not to cough. Every movement was agony in the small space, but he could see the faint signs of the morning glow through a grate lying tantalisingly close in front of him. He was nearly there. He steadied his resolve and pushed on.

Almost dragging himself now, he inched closer until eventually, he could reach out his hand and touch the plastic grate. It was secured to the building somehow. He didn't see anything to release it from his position, so he had to assume it was screwed onto the outside. He pushed at it and felt it give under his hand. The brittle plastic let out a low crack.

He smiled to himself, probably the first time he'd smiled since before he entered the lookout point. This was going to work. Soon, he'd be heading home. Soon he'd see his family again.

He pushed against it. Slowly at first, then he added a little pressure. The plastic bent outwards, then one of the plastic strips on the vent cracked completely, revealing the light outside. Time had weakened it to the point of failure. He kept pushing, another one gave to the pressure, then a third. He gave it one final shove and the remaining plastic gave way before him. The hole they left was large enough for him to clamber out of. He saw his arm for the first time since he'd crawled under here. It was black with dust, cobwebs clung to every available space, he could only assume the rest of him was in a similar state.

He heaved himself slowly, and as quietly as he could, through the narrow gap. He felt the breeze on his face as he pushed himself into the open. His lungs were burning; he desperately wanted to cough, he could only imagine what he'd breathed in under there. He knew he mustn't; he had to get away, then he could clean himself and find something to drink.

He was completely outside now. He could see the trees around him. A road led off from the front of the building, a narrow single-track one; it must lead back to the main road. He glanced around, wondering which way he had come from? He hesitated, trying to decide which way to run. He made up his mind to run for the trees. He could figure out where he was once, he was safely far enough away from this place.

He glanced around him one final time, everything seemed quiet still. There was no sign of anyone else in the vicinity. He'd need to pass open ground to get to the tree line, the gap between the building and the nearby trees was substantial. He'd just have to run for it and hope for the best. The building now behind him was massive, much larger than he'd first assumed. It was three stories high, and judging from the length of the side he stood against, the kitchen and the room he'd seen, we're only a small portion of the ground floor. He wanted to know more about it, where was he? He didn't have the time to worry about that now, he needed to get away.

He took off at a sprint, not stopping to look around. He felt the branch of the first tree whip off him as he plunged himself into their cover. The foliage was thick and he had to slow his speed to avoid tripping or becoming tangled in the thick weeds bracketing the ground around him. He pushed through, looking for a clear route. He hadn't made it far before he crashed into the tall, steel fence.

"No..." he moaned to himself, running his hands along it. It was solid slats of what appeared to be steel, buried deep into the ground, with small gaps between them he could barely fit his hand into. The slats were connected together by metallic wire, almost an inch thick and placed at the bottom and top of the fence, running horizontally along the structure. Looking up, he saw the row of razor wire circling the top; it was far too high to jump, and he'd never be able to climb over the rows and rows of jagged, sharp teeth. He worked his way down, looking for anywhere he might be able to push through. He started to panic as he realised the fence likely surrounded the entire building. It must have been here since the world fell, there's no way they could have put it up. It had been designed to secure the entire property. He didn't even want to think what from.

He reached a corner; it angled 90 degrees and he saw that it ran all the way back behind the building. He stood frozen in indecision. The trees were higher here, he might be able to climb them and drop over the sharp wire. He looked at the height of the fence, he had more chance of breaking his leg in the fall.

He had only one option, he'd have to walk out the main gate. He turned and started to make his way back through the dense trees, headed to the point he first entered. He just had to hope they hadn't noticed he'd gone yet and that no one was watching the main entrance.

As quietly as he could, he pushed through the branches until he could see the vent on the side of the building he'd pulled his way out of. He glanced around and still saw no movement. The single-track road sat agonisingly close; he could make it if he sprinted. Was there a gate on the front? He'd have to find out, there was nothing else for it. He held his breath, then let it out slowly, trying to calm his nerves. He felt the sweat drip down his neck. Then he heard the click.

He froze, not daring to turn his head. It was close, just behind him. If he ran now, that would be the last thing he ever did. It had all been for nothing.

He put his hands in the air, spreading his fingers to show that he had nothing concealed within them. He felt the barrel of the rifle push into his back.

"Back you go," a growling voice said. He walked slowly towards the front door of the building and the man kept the rifle pressed up against him every step.

He felt ashamed of being caught. He'd been so careful and hadn't seen this coming. He knew things would get worse for him, now. They wouldn't risk him escaping again.

As he arrived at the large oak front door, the man reached around him and knocked three times; the sound echoed through the nearby trees.

He heard a bolt slide from the other side. The woman from the previous night stood there, looking dazed and confused. She wasn't wearing her mask. She was older than Benny had thought. Lines etched around her mouth and eyes told of a hard life out here. Wherever out here actually was.

She blinked her eyes several times, registering the scene in front of her. Then she let out an audible sigh.

"Why couldn't you just stay put?" she asked, almost sorrowfully.

"Found him over by the trees," the man said, nodding with his head at the area they'd come from. "Looks like he busted out from the crawlspace. Didn't know this place was surrounded though. If he'd gone straight for the road, we'd never have known."

The woman looked at him. "Come on. Might as well have some breakfast and get yourself cleaned up." She said as she moved aside to let him into the hall beyond the door.

"I really don't want to hurt you," she said, as Benny tried to chew the corner of something indescribable, he'd been handed.

The other two men had obviously woken, and they stood either side of the door, rifles on their shoulders, watching him.

"If you'd just stayed put, this would all have been fine. You know we're going to have to tie you up now, right?"

He didn't reply; he just looked at the food in his hands. It had an earthy, raw taste, but he couldn't place it. It wasn't exactly unpleasant, but he wouldn't go out of his way to eat it again.

"Hopefully, this won't take much longer," she continued. "A few days, maybe. We're ahead of schedule, but we're not yet ready to move out. We need the others to arrive, first."

He was listening, but he didn't want to give her the satisfaction of knowing that, so he continued to pull at the food.

"It's not our fault, you know," she said quietly. "They left us no choice. They let us starve, while they live in luxury. They have it all and we have nothing. We didn't want to do this, but we had to. We have people we care about, too. We'll do anything to make sure they're safe."

He looked up; his curiosity got the better of him. "Who did?" he asked.

She smiled sadly. "Newhaven," she said.

Benny stopped chewing. How did they know about Newhaven and what was she talking about? Newhaven was an inclusive settlement; all they had to do was ask and they would have been let in, given a share of the spoils, in exchange for taking a share of the workload. They always needed more people. There was never enough to keep everything running as it should.

He'd never seen this woman before. But there was something about the man, which one... he couldn't tell, but he'd thought he recognised something familiar in his voice, on the journey here. Were these people from Newhaven? Had they been there? No, he'd have known, no group had joined Newhaven for years.

"What do you mean?" he asked her.

"You'll find out soon enough. There's plenty of time for that later," she replied.

His mind raced. He'd never explored the possibility that these people might actually know him, or at least know the town. He thought it had been opportunistic. They heard stories, roaming gangs, kidnapping people, forcing them to do unthinkable things. He always thought this was just stories told to frighten the children, but yesterday he'd believed it to be true. Now, he didn't know what to think.

"Have you..." he hesitated. "Have you been to Newhaven?"

She smiled. "Oh yes. Many years ago, now. It almost feels like another life. I've certainly lived another one out here. It was good to hear that Tom is still with us, although I was sad to learn about Bob. He was always such a lovely man."

"How do you know that?"

"We've been watching you for some time now. It wasn't just by chance you ended up on that coast. Not you, specifically, of course, anyone would have done, I suppose."

"For what?" He asked.

"Bait. Trade," she shrugged. "It hardly matters. I know Tom and while we have one of his, he won't come in shooting. Always far too precious about life."

"Tom is a good man, if you ask, he'll help you. You don't need to do this."

"No," she snapped at him. "He's a dead man. We did ask, once. And look at us now. If Tom wants you back, he'll pay with his life. When the rest of us get here, that's exactly what he'll do."

Benny felt his blood run cold. They couldn't be serious. All this, to kill Tom? An old, kind man? What had happened between them? What past could this woman not forgive, or forget?

The moments passed as he stared in disbelief. The woman didn't say anything, she just watched him thoughtfully.

"Who are you?" he finally asked. "Why do you want Tom dead?"

"A memory," she replied. "A part of your past, which they want to disappear. We all are. But we won't, not quietly. Tom is the reason for all of this. That's why he has to pay. He must pay for what he did to us, for what he put us through. We've lost so many. So many..." her voice quietened as her thoughts drifted away.

His brow furrowed in confusion, what she was saying made no sense. He'd have known. If Tom and the others from

Newhaven, had been the cause of so much death and hardship, surely, he'd have known.

"What happened?" he asked.

She glanced at him, torn from her memories.

"You don't remember? Of course you don't, you were so young. I remember you, Benny. When you were a small child. We came to Newhaven, looking for hope, for shelter. It was okay, but then some of ours did some... unpleasant things. Tom took it out on all of us. They forced us all out. We tried, a few times, to make amends, but he'd never have it. He slammed that door in our face every time. He left us here, to starve, to live like rats. He let us die." She glared at him now, hatred in her eyes.

He had been young, but he had a fleeting memory of these people, now she'd retold the story. What she said, it wasn't how he remembered it. He remembered the anguish the older lot, his mum, Tom and the rest had gone through when they decided to banish these people. It hadn't been easy. They'd felt the pain of what they did, too. But what choice did they have? These people had attacked them, put all of their lives in danger. What did they expect.

He looked up; her eyes still glared at him, boring into his soul.

"Do you want to know what happened next?"

He didn't reply, nor did he break his gaze.

"The man, our leader, Kingsley. His wife, she killed herself after it happened. She had kids. Young ones. They didn't last long. After she died, they were on their own. They died that winter. I don't know what of, but that was what started it all. Watching those children waste away to nothing. That hurt. It hurt us all. More died, of course. Many more. We lived in squalor; it was inevitable, really. It all could have been prevented. If he'd just let us stay."

Her eyes wandered off again. Benny was done with this conversation. This woman wasn't right, she wasn't rational, and there was no reasoning with her.

CHAPTER NINE

The seven horses trotted noisily up the deserted road, the dull thuds of their hooves bounced off as the concrete as they sprang off the weeds and moss slowly claiming it back.

The morning was overcast. Dark, angry-looking clouds hung in the sky. The sun of daybreak had been replaced and the wind picked up, whirling around their faces as they rode.

Martin shivered despite himself and wrapped his coat further around his chin. The first drops of rain fell gently on his face.

They'd been riding for an hour. They'd found nothing further to indicate where Benny might be, but kept to the road, heading south. They were spread evenly across the road, so they could keep an eye on every part of it. Tom's progress was still slow, and the others had to adjust their pace to prevent him being left behind.

"Anything?" Chloe shouted, her voice competing with the wind.

"Nothing," Maria replied, from the far side of the road, riding next to the hedgerow. "I don't even see hoofprints, there's nothing to suggest anyone has been here in a long, long time."

She frowned; they should have seen something by now. How far could these people have got? Benny should have been back at Newhaven at midday. Assuming they rode all day, he could still be miles away. Still, she'd have expected to see something.

The road was long, winding and utterly deserted. The deteriorating buildings had become less frequent, as thick tufts of thorns and brambles bracketed them in. The trees could still be seen in the distance, towering high into the sky.

The rain grew harder and faster, Chloe raised her hand to protect her face from the downpour as they pushed on. She could hardly see; the thick drops of water were falling furiously. Her clothes were soaked, water ran down the back of her neck. The floor under her feet was quickly becoming a tarnished mess of weeds and mud, despite its concrete base.

She barely heard Martin when he shouted. He was pointing off the road, to a clearing in the thorns under the thick trees.

"In there!" he shouted again; the sound barely reached her ears. She didn't want to stop. Every hour they spent stationary was an hour longer her son could be getting further away from her. She begrudgingly followed him in, and the rain immediately eased as the canopy far above offered some protection from the elements.

"We're going to have to wait for this to pass. We can't see a thing as it is. If we keep going, we'll miss something," he panted.

Chloe nodded. She didn't want to, but knew it was the right decision. She shook her hands and drops of rain flew from them. The horse snorted as it blinked water out of its eyes. They dismounted and stood on the soft floor. The horses immediately started to graze as they left them to it, collecting in a tight circle, as much for each other's body heat, than to hear what they were saying.

"As soon as it passes," Martin assured Chloe with a nod. "The moment it stops, we'll be back out. Don't worry, Chloe, we'll find him. We just can't risk riding right past him and I couldn't see a thing out there. If anyone was watching, we'd never see them, either.'"

"I know, I know. I'm just eager to find him."

"We all are, and we will. I promise you that."

The lightning interrupted the rest of his speech. They looked to the sky, which was pointless, as the trees towered above them.

The thunder followed instantly.

"That was close," Maria said.

"Too close," Steve replied. "Should we be here?"

"Would you rather be somewhere else?"

He shrugged.

"Here's safer than anywhere else," Tom added. "The lightning will pass. The trees will keep us safe."

Martin grimaced; he wasn't sure that statement was entirely accurate. Tom should know that.

The next flash of light blinded them. It had been even closer. The horses reared up on their hind legs. The following thunder was deafening as it hid the first sounds of the cracking wood around them. As their ears stopped ringing, Steve heard it first. His head shot up, looking in every direction, seemingly at once.

Maria looked at him curiously, before she heard it too.

"One of them is coming down!" she shouted. "We need to get out of here."

It was too late; one of the large trees a few rows back began to sway in the wind, more violently than the rest. It creaked and groaned, before the massive trunk split with an ear-piercing noise. It was falling away from them, into the forest.

Thank goodness, thought Tom, watching it fall. He was too busy concentrating on the tree; he never saw the horses coming. The noise had them spooked. As a collective pack, they'd broken free of the branch they were tied on, ripping it from the tree it grew out of and ran towards the open road, the thick branch bouncing perilously behind them. Right through the group stood in the clearing.

Steve pushed Maria as hard as he could; he watched her fly through the air and crumple onto the floor, just outside of the path of the horses. The branch still attached to their reins; they dragged it along with them. It bounced off the floor, high into the air, before crashing back to make contact with the sodden earth. He jumped to the other side, hitting the ground hard and tucking into a roll. As he came to a stop, he saw the others scatter, Chloe had got clear, but Kate had been running back, right into the path of the rapidly approaching stampede. What was she doing? He followed her path. Tom stood there, not moving. It was too late; she'd never make it. None of them would. He watched in abject horror as the two horses at the front ran past Tom, one either side. The next three avoided him too. The final two bumped him with their shoulders. At the speed they were traveling, it sent him sprawling to the ground, Steve watched as he disappeared under a blur of legs.

Tom lay on his back, his arms stretched out, just as the branch trailing the horses bounced back to the ground and crashed around his head.

Kate was there first, sliding to the ground on her knees as she approached him. She grabbed for his hand, screaming. Steve stood and ran towards them, arriving just behind Martin. The others remained where they sat or stood, watching with grim expressions.

Tom's face was a mess. It was bloodied and his features were disfigured. Steve realised with a sick feeling in his stomach that the trunk had crashed directly into his face. His nose was misshapen, and his jaw hung open at an odd angle, the left side seemed to be missing entirely. Blood seeped into the mossy ground around him.

"He's alive," Kate screamed at them. "He's breathing. Just."

Steve pushed forward and held his ear to Tom's chest. He could feel it slowly rise and fall. He was alive, she was right, but the rasping gurgle coming from the disfigured remainder of his mouth wasn't a confident sign he'd be okay.

Steve rustled through the backpack strapped to his back and pulled out a handful of white bandages. He handed them to Kate, who began dabbing at the blood pooling around Tom.

"We need to get him back to Newhaven," she said shakily.

"See if you can get the horses," Martin shouted over to Maria and Vincent. "They won't have gone far. Get them back here. Now!"

Maria ran towards the road without replying, with Vincent hot on her heals, trying to put the nightmare version of her dad out of her mind. Martin had been right; the horses were huddled together a short distance away. They'd stopped running and the rain fell around them.

She approached the horses carefully, her arm stretched in front of her as she made comforting noises. They were nervous and took a step back but made no attempt to bolt from her. She reached for the reins and held firmly onto the leather. Vincent approached behind her, as she handed three of the reins over to him, taking the four herself. She released them from the branch, which lay in the road, just away from them and walked them back to the clearing.

Kate still knelt above Tom, the white bandage had turned completely red. Martin looked up as they approached.

Maria hid her face in her sleeve as she watched from the perimeter, the horses reins still clutched in her other hand.

"Good," he said. "Bring two of them here. Keep the others out of the way."

Maria handed over two of the four horses she held to Chloe, who accepted the reins and walked the animals away from the clearing.

Martin gestured to Steve and took Tom by one of his arms. Steve grabbed the other. They slowly and carefully lifted him to his feet. His head lolled around with every movement, as he remained completely unresponsive. Chloe positioned one of the horses next to them and they carefully hoisted Tom onto its neck. He was sprawled over the animal's mane, his arms hanging limply on each side.

"What have you got to tie him on with?" Martin asked Steve, who responded by searching his pack.

"Nothing," he said finally. I've nothing that'll do it, I'm sorry."

Martin glanced around. "Maria, take the bridle off that one," he pointed to the other horse she held. "Set it free, we'll use that."

She did as she was told; the horse trotted a few steps before it came to a stop by the others held by Vincent. She passed the leather straps to Martin, who immediately tied them around Tom's limp form and the neck and body of the horse.

He turned to Kate and asked, "will you be okay riding this back to Newhaven?"

Kate nodded in reply. He cupped his hand, and she used it to mount the horse. Picking up the reins, she nodded to them, before turned to trot out of the clearing, heading home with a dying Tom strapped in front of her.

"Steve, go with her. Makes sure she gets Tom home safely."

"What about you guys?" Steve asked.

"We'll keep going. We still need to find Benny. Tom wouldn't want his accident to stop that. Get some speed on, if you can. You need to get Tom to the doctor, quickly, or he won't make it. We've got one of the radios here," he patted his pack. "Call when you're back at Newhaven. I'll let them know you're coming. Be quick, Steve, he doesn't look good." He turned to Maria. "What you do is up to you. I'll understand if you need to go back with your parents. We can do this."

She wiped tears from her eyes. "There's nothing I can do for dad. I'll stay, let's get Benny back, make sure this was worth it."

Steve nodded, then ran to the closest horse, expertly jumped onto the saddle and took off after Kate. The group watched as they rejoined the road. Then they took off at a canter back towards the safety of Newhaven. Water splashed from the horses' legs as they galloped into the distance.

Martin took a moment and breathed deeply. He closed his eyes and let it out. The rain was easing, and the wind had calmed.

"Okay," he said, finally. "Let's go. We've got a job to do."

The journey continued at a much slower and subdued pace. The rainfall had turned the ground to slush and removed any hope of tracking earlier movements. The events that led to Tom being injured played on their minds, as they walked in silence.

"Do you think he'll be okay?" Maria asked as she walked beside him.

"I honestly don't know. It didn't look good. He's been acting funny for a while now. We can only hope so."

"Is there enough of us left to do this?"

"Again, I don't know. That depends on what we come against. We'll have to hope so. Help is hours away, at best."

She nodded. "There's no way Chloe will turn around, anyway. Nor me. We've got this far; we have to keep going."

"Of course." He smiled.

The clouds were breaking, and the sun finally started to shine through. They felt their clothes slowly drying as they rode.

"What's that?" Chloe asked, pointing to a glint of metal shining through the trees.

Martin hadn't noticed it, but now she'd pointed it out, he could see that there was something there. He walked over to get a closer look.

"It's a fence," he said, perplexed. "A really big one, at that." He strained his neck to look through the treeline. "It looks like it goes quite far down. I think it's a perimeter of something. Come on, let's see if we can figure a way in. It certainly seems like something we should check out. Leave the horses here, just in case."

They jumped from their saddles and tied the remaining horses to the trees.

They kept low and to the shadows the canopy provided. Creeping slowly parallel to the metal fence. At points, the trees thinned, allowing them to see the massive metal pylons that thrust into the air. They were evenly spread a few inches apart, towering high into the sky. Razor wire coiled over the top. There would be no climbing over that.

Before long, the road branched off, a single-track road headed through an open gate. The ground around the entrance was pitted with hoofprints.

"This looks promising," Martin whispered.

"What is it?" Maria asked. "Or rather, what was it?"

He glanced around. "No idea. No signs or anything. Something well protected. The perfect place to hide out, I'd suspect. Maybe some army thing, or just someone's home. They might just have been sick of folk trespassing. I don't think it matters. Come on, let's see if we can get closer."

They silently crept down the track, keeping as close to the overgrown hedge as they could. A huge building soon came into view. It looked like a wooden cabin, but on much larger proportions. They crouched nearby, looking for any movement.

"It doesn't look like anyone's here," Maria said. "Should we go in, just to check it...." she was interrupted by the low creak of the front door opening. They watched as a man walked out. A mask concealed the lower part of his face. He had a rifle slung over his shoulder but didn't appear to be out here for any reason. He stretched, before walking to a nearby hedge and relieving himself.

"They don't expect anyone," Martin said. "That's weird. They must know we'd be coming?"

"Maybe they didn't think we'd find them, or that we'd be this quick. Or maybe there's more of them. We can't take it for granted. We don't even know they have Benny. They might just be hiding out here, completely unrelated."

"Let's hope not," he replied. "We've got nothing else to go on here."

They watched for a time longer. The man made two further appearances from the front door and once someone walked from the side of the house to greet him, before retreating back to whatever he was guarding around the back.

"You think that's all of them?" Chloe asked.

"I doubt it, but I don't think there's many more. We can probably just storm the place, if we want to."

At that moment, a noise behind them made them stop in their tracks. It was laughter, floating on the wind.

"Quick," Martin hissed. "Over there."

He sprinted to the nearby trees and was soon enveloped in their shadows; the rest followed. They could see both the house and the track that led up to the front door from where they were. Down the track, a group of people walked. He counted as they came closer, nearly fifteen people. All of them looked armed. Where had all these weapons come from and how did they still have working ammo?

He already knew the answer but didn't want to admit it. They'd been so busy playing house; they'd never really considered what else could be going on out in the world. There were plenty of caches of weapons around. The ammo would be fine for many years, in the dry, airtight containers. The rifles were simple, not prone to jamming. As long as they were cared for, they would last as long as they needed, as was proved by the one he had in his hands.

The group approached the building and the large front door opened before they got there. They were greeted by a woman; she wasn't wearing a mask. Martin thought she looked familiar, but he couldn't place her. The memory was at the forefront of his mind, he just couldn't quite access it.

The group and the woman greeted each other. They were too far away to hear what they were saying, but it was clear they knew each other.

The radio buzzed in his pack, he swore under his breath as he fumbled for it, hoping the sound wouldn't traverse the distance to the building.

"Go," he whispered into the mouthpiece.

"Martin," came the cracking voice from the other end. "Tom. Tom didn't make it. I'm sorry Martin. Tom's dead."

He closed his eyes. The others heard the words too.

"Okay," he replied, trying to hold back tears as he reached his hand to his eyes.

The group crouched in stunned silence. They'd expected this, the state of Tom when he left was worrying. They would have to mourn later. They had a job to do now, and they couldn't lose two members of their group in one day.

Maria's face fell into her hands, as she silently sobbed.

Martin shook his head to clear it, then whispered into the radio, "contact Boneyard. We might need their help."

"Already on it," came the stoic reply.

He hesitated. "Kate, I'm sorry."

"So am I."

Martin quietly stowed the radio back into his pack. The group stood around the building, where they were still locked in conversation. Someone was gesticulating, pointing wildly in random directions. The woman stood aside. Martin gasped. Benny was standing limply in the illuminated doorframe.

He had rope tightly bound around his wrists and ankles, but he was alive. He limped as he was pushed into the open so that everyone could see him. The woman was talking, but they couldn't hear what she said from their position hid in the grounds. One of the group laughed, then all pushed forward into the building. The door closed behind them, and they were out of sight.

CHAPTER TEN

The explosion rocked through the flotilla. Michael looked to the sky, the billowing black smoke from above the hangar was already spilling into the air. He didn't know what could have happened and frankly, he didn't much care. The fuel was stored over that way, maybe there had been an accident?

Something strange was happening today. He'd been queuing on the food barge for his meagre breakfast when he saw the soldiers lead those men away. He'd asked around, no one seemed to know what was going on. To be honest, no one else really seemed to care, either.

It wasn't that unusual, he supposed. The army and those government types often took issue with a person and extracted them from the flotilla, never to be seen again. It was safer to stay out of it.

He'd never seen these two before, though. One was a big man, memorable. He was sure he'd remember if he'd run into him before. What if they weren't from the flotilla? He thought to himself as the queue slowly moved.

No one new had arrived in months. Michael wasn't sure how many were left alive in the world out there, anymore. The government, or the soldiers at least, sometimes gave them updates on the state of the world. It sounded bad. Every story was worse than the last. He'd watched the helicopter take off the day before. It hadn't arrived back yet. He pondered the men he'd seen taken away as he slowly shuffled forwards. A surprising amount of people had ignored the explosion altogether, him included. He wanted his breakfast and if he left now, he'd go hungry till lunch. It wasn't worth it.

The more he thought about it, the more he was positive he'd never seen those men before. No. He'd remember if he had. The smoke didn't stop. It kept billowing, high into the sky. He frowned; this was probably not a good thing. He'd likely end up having to clean this up.

Like most of the people living on the flotilla, his days were spent sitting around, not doing a great deal, just hoping for the chance of work from the government. If you worked, they gave you extras. It might be food, or fuel, but they paid. It was better than nothing. There was a lot of competition for any roles they could provide, though. Very few people living here had any form of steady or permanent employment.

Those who farmed and provided the food were the lucky few. They were 'paid' with the best food, fuel for their heaters, or occasionally, forbidden treats, like cigarettes or alcohol, depending on what the soldiers had managed to pilfer from the mainland at the time.

He dreamed of that life. He'd give anything to get fucked up, just one more time. A few people on the flotilla had tried to create their own distillery and it hadn't gone well. He'd tried a shot of one of the spirits they'd created once; he still wasn't sure if it was a poor attempt at alcohol, or just fuel from the barge tanks. The reality was that they simply didn't have the resources, or expertise, to create a floating community. Not one that any of them would appreciate, at least.

Michael lived in one of the pleasure boats, roped up towards the edge of the flotilla. He'd not arrived on this boat, he arrived a few months earlier, when the authorities on Boneyard were still accepting refugees. He'd rowed from the mainland in a small, requisitioned rowboat he'd found moored at the coast, after hearing rumours of the settlement there. When he arrived, he had been greeted by soldiers brandishing guns at him. They were fully kitted out in hazmat gear, thick suits, the masks, everything. He'd been forced into a tent set up on the airfield, subjected to various tests, where his blood was drawn, samples taken, and various implements inserted in places he'd rather not recall.

He'd been declared virus-free and given a permit, which was really just a piece of green card with an official-looking stamp on it, to set up home on the island.

The pleasure boat was not empty, but one of the crew rooms had recently been vacated. Michael later discovered the owner had killed himself, not able to accept their new reality, he'd used a broken piece of flexible piping to draw the fumes from the boat's heater unit into the cabin. He'd closed the windows, forced towels in the door gaps and let the noxious gases take him. His body had been removed before Michael arrived, so he'd taken whatever shelter he could get. That man's weakness, or bravery, depending on how you looked at it, had provided an opportunity for him. It was better than trying to sleep in the grass.

He'd made some friends here, or companions, at least. He'd arrived alone, everyone he knew on the mainland was long dead by now. He'd watched most of them die. He never understood why he hadn't joined them. Sometimes, he wished he had. He tried to be part of the community, but when everyone seemed to live in squalor and perma-poverty, it was hard to keep the sense of belonging going.

He arrived at the server and gratefully accepted the bowl of something, he wasn't sure what, but the bowl of something edible. He sipped at the grey liquid as he watched the scene unfold in the distance. People were now heading in numbers to the open wasteland before the hangars, something had clearly taken their attention. Voices were raised. He finished his food before moved closer to get a better view. It was them. The two men the soldiers had taken, they were walking towards the flotilla. One of them had a gun. He heard it shoot into the air, making him jump, even from this distance. He put the empty bowl on the closest table, not bothering to return it for cleaning and hopped back onto dry land.

He was close enough to hear them now, the big man, the one with the large, bushy grey beard said to no one in particular, "it's now yours."

He added something else, but Michael couldn't hear what he said over the noise of the crowd. He watched as people changed direction and started marching towards the bunker. With a sudden realisation, he understood what they meant. These men had caused the explosion. They'd opened the bunker. They had liberated Boneyard.

He ran to join the throng of rushing people, packed tightly together on the narrow track. Pushing his way past the slower walkers, he soon found himself towards the front of the crowd. Movement was slow and cumbersome, either due to the amount of people trying to use a small path, or hesitation by those at the front at the prospect of facing soldiers with rifles, he wasn't sure. He saw the entrance to the underground bunker, the door sat open on its hinges. He'd never seen it open and felt the excitement building inside him. People halted as they reached it, no one seemingly willing to take that first step over the threshold. Michael had very little to live for. He took a deep breath, then walked into the concrete structure. Others followed closely behind.

He walked with an undeserved confidence, not knowing where it came from, or what he hoped to find. He had no idea where he was going. Deeper and deeper into the dark tunnels they travelled, the noise of the crowd behind him bounced this way and that. He came across a large room, which branched off in two directions. He looked to his right; a small group of soldiers stood there. They looked unsure, watching the mass of people approach them. They were armed, rifles in their hands. They exchanged a look for what felt like hours, before the soldier at the front raised his hands, unstrapped the rifle strap from his shoulder and placed it on the floor between them. The rest soon followed suit without a word.

Michael picked it up. It felt heavy in his hands. He nodded once to the soldiers, then continued his march down the corridor to the left. The doors were all open. Someone had been here. He saw the bodies, strewn across the ground. Trying not to look too closely at them, he reached for the handle to the last door, a big oak door that looked very out of place in this deep tunnel. It swung open and he heard a gasp and a whimper from inside.

Three people were inside. They looked pathetic. They were older, wearing crisp suits, but all three of them tried to hide behind the backs of their chairs. It was pointless, of course. There was nowhere to go. This bunker had only one entrance and it was now crammed full of the other refugees.

"Please," an old man closest to him pleaded. "Please, don't hurt us."

This was them. The people in power. The last remnants of the government. The reason for his, for their, suffering.

The others rallied behind Michael. Some shouted threats at the three cowed people in the room. More than one suggestion was shouted to just shoot them and be done with it. There wasn't much sympathy for them in this crowd.

Michael had silenced the baying mob behind him with a simple gesture from his hand. He had no clue why, but people seemed to have accepted that as he was the first one through the threshold; he was in charge. No wonder people managed to get in these situations, if that's how they were happy to elect leadership.

"No," he called back to the crowd. "We're not as bad as them. We know what they did to us, but we won't do the same to them.

They'll be given a fair trial, and a fair sentence." He had no idea where these words had come from. He'd have happily strangled all three himself, but with the weight of potential power draped over him, he felt the need to be merciful. At least that's what he later told himself.

To jeers and shouts, the three people had been frog-marched out of the bunker. A sham trial had been held the same day, on the barge that usually housed the kitchen tent. The result has been known long before the decision was announced. Michael had been insistent, though. They would be democratic and everyone would have the opportunity for a fair trial, starting now.

There were plenty of calls for them to be executed, but it was agreed in the end they would be set to sea, for the world to claim its revenge on them. Their rickety rowing boat as pushed to the mercy of the tides the same night, no one wanted this hanging over them.

In total, seven soldiers had been left in the bunker. Just seven. The two men had killed a few, but the low number of soldiers surprised the inhabitants of Boneyard. They'd been subdued by so few, so young. All of them had handed over their weapons and denounced the previous administration. Michael saw the benefit to keeping them around and offered them to chance to join the community they were going to create. All accepted and over the years became valued and important members of the Boneyard society.

There wasn't enough room within the bunker for all the refugees. Some had managed to claim the sleeping bunks and moved in, but most returned back to their homes on the flotilla that night, Michael included.

The preceding days were hectic, he didn't remember them

very clearly anymore, everything had flown by in a blur.

His position as leader seemed to have been cemented, purely by the fact that he walked into the bunker first. He took to the role gratefully.

The first few years had been difficult. Despite his unofficial election, there had been many attempts at power grabs by various refugees. All had been peaceful. The remaining soldiers, and their weapons, appeared loyal to him. He'd never had to ask them to prove it, but the threat kept most dissidents diplomatic. Things soon settled down. People were organised into groups, based on their skills. Building work started. Simple homes were installed on the airfield, houses made of concrete and wood. Boneyard had plenty of supplies, the government had made sure it was well stocked before they evacuated there. This included building materials, amongst tonnes of dried foods, stored water and a large cache of weaponry and ammunition.

The extra food helped keep people happy and fed. The weaponry had been locked away safely, deep within the bunker.

The story of Tom and Bob and what they had done, spread through the community like wildfire. Only one soldier had actually spoken to him, and he told the story of what they'd done at every opportunity. They soon passed into legend. Michael vowed to try and make contact one day, once their own commune was thriving.

The days passed to months, and just as quickly into years. Boneyard island was thriving. Everyone had a home. The bunker and associated power production capability provided by the solar panels, offshore wind turbines and ocean wave energy, captured by the oscillating water columns located close to the rocky beach, provided the entire community with modern commodities. Lights worked, heating was commonplace, and food was cooked in electric ovens. Some people still resided on the tied together boats. Michael supposed they liked the feeling, perhaps they'd grown used to it. They had been offered permanent homes on the airfield, but they'd rejected the offer with a smile.

They still had the helicopter. It had arrived back hours after the bunker fell. The pilot surrendered on his landing, seeing from the air what was happening. The tank was nearly empty and there was no replacement fuel to be had, not after the explosion. They knew some remained on the mainland but hadn't made the trip to collect any of it yet. They hadn't needed to. Boneyard provided everything they needed. The fishing boats had been untied from the flotilla and put back to their original use, the sea provided a bounty the land simply could not match.

The virus has stopped commercial fishing overnight. In the short time since the first outbreak, the sea stocks had recovered exponentially, and they expected it would only grow brighter as time moved on.

The island had everything they could ever want, but Michael yearned for more. He wanted to know what the situation was on the mainland, he wanted to know if the virus still ravaged the population, if there was anyone left alive.

He arranged for a small group of them to make the journey. He'd lead it, of course, he'd never ask anyone to do something he wasn't prepared to.

In the short months since the insurrection, he'd become a leader, both in his attitude and in the eyes of others. He'd offered to hold some form of election, but was shot down, most told him he was a sure thing anyway, so why bother.

They set off with the high tide the following morning. The boat they took was one of the few motor-powered boats that still retained a small amount of fuel in its tanks. It didn't take long before they reached the shoreline. They had debated sending the helicopter out to scout before they departed, but that was deemed to be an unnecessary risk, with no guarantee fuel would be located for its return journey. A boat was less likely to be spotted.

They arrived at a cove on the coast and anchored the boat in the shallows. He wanted to meet the two men who had set them free, the men who had liberated them. That was why he really came out here. Why did he think they'd be close to the coast? He didn't, but he hoped so. They made the journey to Boneyard from somewhere and if he had to bet, he'd say it was close.

They spent a few days scouting the coastline as they made small incursions inland. They came across nothing of real consequence and were almost ready to give up when they noticed a figure in the distance. It appeared to be riding a bicycle. It was a comical sight, as they crouched in the long grass, watching what appeared to be a large man cycling up the road.

They watched as he disappeared down a smaller side road, headed towards something hidden by the trees. They slowly crept to the same road and made their way down, carefully staying far behind. Soon, they could see a makeshift barricade, constructed out of old cars and various pieces of wood and twisted metal. A man stood above it, a rifle over his shoulder.

The buildings protruded from behind it, their red brick facades dominating the landscape. It didn't appear to be a large town. It looked like any old place before everything ended. Glancing up the barrier, Michael saw that it extended across the road, using the building on each side to keep it secure. He wondered how many people could be inside. There couldn't be many, they didn't have the space.

They cautiously approached, being careful not to show no aggression. Although they had their own weapons, they kept them securely strapped over their shoulders; to show they meant no harm, they hoped.

"Stop there!" the man shouted. They did as they were told.

"Who are you?" He asked.

"My names Michael. I've come from Boneyard Island. I'm hoping to find the two men who were out our way a few weeks ago. Did they come from here?"

The man paused as he studied them. He wore green army fatigues, Michael hoped they hadn't made an error of judgment by coming here. What if this was another of the mainland bases, full of scared recruits. Would they simply shoot them? It was always the risk. The man shouted something over his shoulder, to someone inside the barricade. The door swung open noisily.

The two men he's seen at Boneyard stood before him, flanked by a woman fingering a rifle in her hands.

"Hi," the one closest said with a wide smile. "I'm Tom, this is Bob," he pointed to the large man next to him. "It's nice to meet you."

CHAPTER ELEVEN

The boat silently pushed up onto the soft sand. Four men and two women quietly slipped out onto the beach. Each of them carried with them a pack and multiple rifles strapped across their shoulders. They knew where they were headed. The moved to the coastal path and started the walk towards Newhaven. They would be there before nightfall. The man at the front led them through the meadows, silently instructing their movement with military precision.

They traversed the overgrown landscape, heading ever closer to their destination. They were armed, trained and ready for what was coming. They'd been called upon and would not let them down. They moved silently through the long grass, keeping low to avoid detection.

The gates to Newhaven stood before them, closed. They'd never been closed before, not since the early days. Times were changing. The call from Kate had been decisive and to the point. Newhaven was in trouble, with no weaponry to speak of to defend themselves. They knew Tom had died. She'd told them how, and they would pay their respects in due course. Tom had been a huge part of Boneyard, as had Bob. They formalised trade and helped the island grow. They liberated it in the first instance, the man knew they owed everything they had to those two men. As soon as they asked for help, the people of Boneyard were always ready and willing to assist.

He walked to the gate and rapped his knuckles on it. The

sound was carried by the metal structure and soon, he heard the creak of the lock being undone. The gate swung open, and Kate stood before him. She smiled and wrapped her arms around his neck. They'd been friends for many years now.

"Michael," she said tearfully. "Thank you for coming."

"Of course. We're always here for you, you know that. Kate, I'm sorry to hear about Tom. Truly. It's a sad, sad day."

She smiled sadly. "He'd have wished to see you again, one last time."

"I'm sure he would. But we don't get to choose when we go, and we can't plan for it. Not in this world."

He looked older than she remembered. She supposed that happened to them all, her included. Like the rest of them, Michael was an old man now. He must have been a few years older than Tom, although he looked in much better shape than Tom had, even before his accident. His short grey hair was thinning around his temples and his sun-kissed olive skin was wrinkled around his eyes. He was still a muscular man. He'd always been in good shape, but the diet and hard work after they took over Boneyard had given him a physique people would have paid for before the virus.

She smiled sadly. "It was coming, Michael, and he knew it. Part of me wonders if he only went out on this rescue mission because there was a chance he could end it all."

He looked quizzically at her. "What do you mean?" he asked.

"Tom had a few issues. He kept it to himself, but he was coming to the end. He knew it, I knew it. I only went with him to keep an eye on him. The doctor thinks early onset dementia. Of course, without the diagnostic equipment, we can't be sure, and he was very young for that. It rocked him. He found out a few months ago. He'd been a bit spacey and reckless ever since." Tears flowed down her face. "I shouldn't have let him go. I should have fought to keep him safe here. I just wanted him to be happy and I thought one more adventure would do him good."

"He'd have liked that, I'm sure. There's no way he'd have wanted to go quietly. Maybe it's for the best." He stopped to look at her, hoping he hadn't gone too far with his flippant comment. She didn't look upset, so he guessed he'd been on the right track and continued. "He had a good life. He was a strong leader. Just look at what he did here in Newhaven. Dying of something silly, that would have haunted him."

She raised one eyebrow. "Getting crushed by a branch being dragged by horses isn't silly?" she asked.

He laughed half-heartedly. "You know what I mean. I'm sorry to bring this back to earth, Kate, but we've got a situation, so I believe. We should solve that first, then we can give Tom the proper send-off he deserves."

"Of course," she said, trying to stay strong and keep the quiver out of her voice.

They sat around the oak table in the town hall. Six people had made the journey from Boneyard, along with eighteen rifles and boxes of ammunition.

"Two days ago, a group of unknown people kidnapped Benny. That's Chloe's boy, if you haven't met him," she addressed this to the others from Boneyard. "They had been around here, scouting out Newhaven. We don't know why. Last night, Martin and the others stumbled across their camp. There's between fifteen and twenty of them and they all appear armed. We don't know what they want, or really where they've come from, but it's looking likely they are headed here. Even if they're not, we need to get Benny back and we simply don't have the weapons to deal with them. We're low on people too, for that matter."

"You really should put more into training your folks, Kate."

"We've had near on thirty years of peace, Michael. We haven't seen the need."

"How many have you got, trained, I mean?"

"Maybe a dozen, if we're lucky. Most people here who can use a rifle are from the old world. The average age of Newhaven has gone down considerably since it was first established. We've been concentrating on producing food, supplies, that kind of thing. We've always been able to count on the other camps for anything else."

"They won't be much help," Michael said. "They're just too small, and I doubt any of them have working weapons, either. Luckily, I believe in keeping each and every one of my people ready for whatever comes next. That includes keeping them up to date on weapons training. I've brought these guys, five of my best. Although I wish you'd told me how many there were beforehand, I might have brought more."

"I'm sorry, Michael. We weren't fully aware of the numbers they had until it was too late. Martin and the rest are still out that way, just watching them. They haven't moved yet."

"Where are they?"

"About fifteen miles or so off to the south. They have a few horses, but most of them are on foot, so we figure if they do come this way, we've got some time to prepare."

"That's the plan?" he asked, his eyebrows raised.

"No," she replied. "Ideally, we don't want them anywhere near here. We'd rather go out to them, if we can."

"Do you have the horses?"

"Four are still out, one possibly lost, so we've got just around twenty left. Plenty to get us all there by nightfall."

"And then?"

"Then, we find out what they want and get Benny back. It doesn't really matter in which order."

"You said you have people watching them?"

"Yeah, Martin's over there. He's got Chloe, Maria and Vincent with him. They have a radio, so we're hearing if anything happens. It's been quiet for a while. They're holed up somewhere, so I don't want to keep calling them, just in case."

"Understood," Michael replied. "At least we'll have some backup when we arrive."

The exchange had been brief, but that's all they had time for. They knew they had to leave soon, there would be time for catching up later, once this was over. Michael had made the journey to Newhaven several times over the years. At Tom's invitation, he'd come sometimes just to spend the night, to catch up with old friends. He really did care about these people. He thought of them as an extension of his own home, of the people back on Boneyard. There was no way he would have rejected their plea when she called a few hours earlier. They communicated with the radios, both sides had them. They were set to an open channel that they could all use, although they also had another channel they could use if they wished not to be overheard. They tried not to use that, as they wanted their communities to be as open and honest as possible. That was the channel Kate had used to contact him earlier that day. That's how he first understood the severity of the situation.

Within the hour, they saddled up, placed their packs around their backs and loaded their rifles in their hands.

Ten of them stood outside the open gate, the six from Boneyard, Kate, Steve and two of the younger guards. They had debated taking two more, the most the horses would be able to carry, but there hadn't been anyone they could trust on this task. That had been a sobering indictment of the town and training they'd put into it. Tom had adopted a policy some time ago of focusing on the economic improvement of the town, rather than training the younger people to become soldiers. Kate had often thought he was trying to make up for his violent past. Trying to prevent any of the inhabitants from having to go through some of the things he and the others when through, when he was a younger man.

They set off, loaded with minimal provisions. If this went the way it was expected to, they wouldn't need them. They'd be back by morning, or they'd be dead.

They kept a steady pace as they travelled. It was mid-afternoon, they'd have a few hours of light before they'd be forced to slow as they travelled by just moonlight. Michael made several attempts at idle conversation as he trotted next to Kate. She wasn't in the mood. She'd recently lost her partner, her best friend for most of her life and hadn't yet been able to properly grieve.

The sun was setting in the distance, as long shadows descended from the trees. They'd slowed to a walk to give the horses a chance to rest before the final push. They wanted to arrive after nightfall to conceal their entrance. It had seemed like the best plan, although Kate now wished they'd left sooner, she dreaded the thought of travelling in the dark. Steve rode next to her.

"How are you holding up?" he asked.

"I'm okay. I promise. I won't be, when the time is right. But right now, we have things to do."

"I understand that, but it's okay to show your pain. You don't need to be brave for us, you know that, right?"

She smiled back at him; the low light barely illuminated her features.

"Thanks, Steve. But I'll deal with this my own way. What I need is for people to let me do just that."

"Got you," he smiled back. She was worried he might be offended, but he hadn't shown any sign of that.

As they rode into the descending darkness, her mind swam with images of Tom. Tom in his younger days, the days they'd first met. Tom when peace finally fell on Newhaven, that contented look he'd get in his eyes. Then Tom as he grew older, the look of confusion on his face some mornings. Then Tom after the branch destroyed his face. The blood that pooled on the ground...

She shook her head to clear the image. That was something else that could haunt her after all of this. Another image to add to the collage in her nightmares.

"How far off? Michael asked her. She hadn't heard him approach.

"Not far now, I don't think. According to Martin, the entrance is another mile, maybe two up this road."

He nodded. Then soon we'll need to leave the horses. We'll be seen from a mile away if we show up on them."

"Martin did the same. We should try to find his and leave them all together."

"Sounds good. You know where?"

"We need to get to the fence, first. It's quite close to the building, so we'll need to be quiet about it."

He frowned, "that's a bit closer than I would have liked. Maybe we just find somewhere out here, instead. Martin didn't know what they were coming up to, we do. A dozen or more horses are likely much more noticeable than the four they've got tied up out there."

"Okay," she agreed. "Let's get another half mile or so, then we'll look for somewhere to jump off these things and go in on foot."

They continued in silence. The nocturnal sounds, reverberating from the forest, rumbled through the darkness. With no light to guide them, the horses were tentative with every step.

"This'll do," Michael called out. "Can't see shit, may as well leave the animals here and walk the rest."

No one argued with him. Soon, the horses were tied up to the nearby trees and the ten of them walked as silently as they could muster up the road.

"There," Steve announced, pointing into the dim. "I think we're here." The others strained to see what he pointed at. The moonlight reflected off a steel column, another gleamed close by.

Michael nodded in the dark, not that anyone could see him.

"Okay, silence from here on out. We follow the track, meet up with the others, then we storm the place. From what I've heard, we have up to twenty well-armed folks in there. We'll try the non-fatal approach, but I fear we'll end up guns blazing, so be ready for it."

The others nodded in agreement.

"Guys," Kate whispered. "Where's the horses?"

"What?"

"The horses, Martin's horse, the rest. Where are they?"

"Maybe they tied them up further in the forest, to keep them out of sight," Michael suggested.

"Maybe," Kate replied uneasily. Something felt off.

They met no resistance as they approached the building via the small, single-track road. Kate had spoken to Martin a few times, although not recently, and he'd described clearly where they hid. She saw the area he had described and pointed the others towards it. They crept as low and quiet as they could to the clearing. There was no one there. The woods appeared deserted. Panic threatened to overtake Kate. She tried to keep her composure, checking the trees nearby, but they should be here. This is where they had said they would be. What was going on?

There was no evidence that anyone had ever been here. The building was dark and quiet; it looked as dilapidated and abandoned as any of the others they'd passed on the journey.

"What the...," she muttered quietly.

"Do you think they've been found? Maybe they're inside." He pointed towards the building.

"I don't know," she said slowly. "I think they would have tried to tell us."

"Maybe they couldn't? What worries me is that there were twenty people and we're met by this," he raised his arms out, extending into the din around him. "I know it's late, but I would have expected to see something, to hear something. Light, guards... where are they all? Are you sure we're in the right place?"

"Unless there happens to be two identical places here, both surrounded by a massive fence, then yeah. I'm sure."

"Then we need to assume that something's happened and not something good." He turned to address the rest of the group. "Take care, guys. Something is off here. Let's not be taken by surprise."

He heard the familiar sound of rifles being readied as the group comprehended the danger, they were potentially in.

"Can't stay here," he said quietly to Kate. "To the building?"

"Yeah," she said. "That's as good a plan as any. What do you think this place is?"

Michael raised an eyebrow at her. "This is the old rifle range. It was around for years, before. It was like a club for the rich and tasteless. They'd have drinks in the lobby, then shoot in the forest out back. The fence was to keep the guns secured, or something like that."

"Sounds like you've been here," she said to him.

"Not personally, but I knew of it. I just figured everyone did. It's been around for years. We used to drive past. You could hear them shooting clays out back in the meadow."

"We weren't from this area, originally," she replied. "Never seen this place before. It's not like the signs are still around.

Why's it so big?"

"To show off, I suppose," he shrugged. "Maybe it was something else, before then. I don't really know much more."

She rolled her eyes, visible even in the darkness.

"You asked," he said simply.

Static buzzed from her radio, making them both jump. They looked to her pack, the tinny voice, barely audible, muffled through the fabric. Static distorted the message, the panicked voice at the other end was shouting, begging.

The only sentence Kate could make out was *"help, they're here'*. Her blood ran cold as she fumbled for the radio.

"Repeat," she almost screamed back into it. She could hear Michael shushing her but didn't register his protests in her panicked state. She'd lost the love of her life, her daughter was now missing as well, she couldn't lose her home, too.

"Newhaven?" She asked, urgency cutting through her words. "Please, come in. What's happening, what's going on?"

Only static replied to her.

She looked to Martin with fear in her eyes.

"No..." she whispered.

CHAPTER TWELVE

Martin shifted his weight from one foot to the other. They'd been keeping watch for several hours and he was starting to cramp up. No one had emerged from the house since the group had entered. Light flooded out of the window and the occasional shadow was seen passing from the glow inside.

He tapped Vincent on the shoulder. "I'm going to try and get around the back, see if there's any better vantage over there. Stay here, keep your eye on the front."

Vincent nodded as Martin crept into the undergrowth.

The trees around the building were thick and weeds spilled out of every crack in the ground, traversing the uneven ground was slow going and difficult. He kept the building to his left, staying just inside the treeline to avoid being seen.

Voices floated on the breeze from inside. They were raised, an argument, perhaps. He hoped so, the more discontent inside, the more he could use that to their advantage. They couldn't risk an assault, not with the amount of people inside. They'd be sure to lose, and probably get Benny killed in the attempt, too. The image of Tom kept flashing to his mind, no matter how badly he tried to repress it. The blood dripping from his misshapen mouth... He shook his head. He had enough images in there to keep him awake for the rest of his life. Now he'd have several more.

He crept further around the building. It was big, really big. It wasn't in good condition, like most of the older buildings around here, neglected and close to collapse. The structure was wooden, it had a large footprint, and extended far through the grounds, with a slate roof. The windows were mostly intact. He saw a broken vent leading to the crawl space under the building and momentarily wondered if he'd be able to make it under. He thought better of it, imagining his ageing bones trying to crawl under that thing. He didn't want to get stuck under there. He'd surely be caught, or die alone in the dark, if he did.

Movement caused him to freeze. There was a man in a mask walking from around the back of the building. Like the rest, he had a rifle in his hands, but didn't seem to be showing too much concern. Martin guessed he was on guard, and likely getting a bit bored of it. He waited for him to pass, then followed the trees to the end of the building. He could see down the back of it, now. It was dark and hard to make out anything of substance. The trees continued around, so he kept his current line and started his way down. He was hoping for somewhere he could see in. Somewhere he could creep up to the window and see what was going on inside.

He knew this could be risky, but sitting in the dark like rats was getting them nowhere. Even when Kate and the rest arrived, they'd still be outnumbered. If he could figure out where these people were sleeping and how many of them were likely to be up at any time, it'd give them a fighting chance. Right now, he only wanted to find where Benny was. They'd need to avoid getting into any sort of firefight around his location, in case he was taken down in the crossfire, or out of revenge.

He could see light spilling to the ground a short distance in front of him. A window was open and the light inside was on. He looked around; the guard hadn't returned. He wondered what his route was likely to be. Would he come back the way he'd gone, or would he do a full check of the perimeter and arrive on the opposite side of the building?

He frowned. This would be risky, whatever way he approached it. He'd just have to be as careful as he could and try.

He inched forward towards the window, keeping his head low and out of sight of anyone who might be lurking inside. As he approached the window, he listened from outside to the silence within. Slowly, he peered his head over the rotting sill, and he glanced around the room. It took a moment for his eyes to adjust to the bright light within, supplied from an old, burning oil lamp. He briefly wondered where they got the fuel from, considering what the age of the lamp must be.

The room was large and empty. A door opposite the window firmly closed. It was bare, aside from a wooden table in the middle. A bottle of water sat alone on the table, the colour slightly brackish. Martin crept back to the treeline, having conceded defeat with seeing anything of use. His hearing pricked up; had he heard a noise? He looked worriedly around him, but the grounds were still eerily silent. Then he heard it again, muffled voices, coming from within the building. He stilled his breathing; it was coming from the next room over. The window to this room remained dark. He adjusted his position trying to get a better view. He again approached the building, as quietly as he could manage. The window was covered in a thick layer of grime. He used the sleeve of his jacket to slowly rub at it, removing just enough to press his eye up against the glass.

He could just make out Benny inside. He was curled on the floor, his legs bound together with thick knots of rope. The door was open to the hallway beyond, a thin beam of light spilled over him. Other than the bonds securing him, he seemed uninjured, aside from a streak of dried blood that ran down his neck.

Someone stood in the doorway, talking to him. He was replying, but Martin couldn't hear the exchange. He strained to hear better. The glass between them was making that impossible. At least Benny was safe and alive. He'd seen him in the door, but now he knew for sure. He retreated back to the safety of the trees and headed back to the others.

He barely saw them as he approached, their silhouettes were

scarcely visible under the glow of the stars.

"He's alive," he whispered, as he approached. He heard Chloe sigh in relief. "He's in a room around the back. I don't know if we can get him out without being heard, but once Kate arrives, I think we should try."

"Can't we break him out now?" Maria asked. "If he's out the back, we'll break the window, grab him and run."

Martin shook his head. "There's a whole group of armed people in there. All we'll do is get ourselves and probably Benny, killed. We'll need to wait. It won't be much longer now, I'm sure."

"Wait for what?" Maria asked.

"I don't know," he replied. "Hopefully some of them will leave. Or at least, head to another part of this building. Or for reinforcements to arrive, the guys from Boneyard. We need to even the odds."

"How would we know? We can't see from here."

He shrugged.

Vincent furrowed his brow at the door. "I think there's movement out there," he said quietly.

The other turned to follow his gaze. The door hadn't opened, they would have heard that, but he was right; they could see the bushes at the front of the building rustling.

"An animal, maybe?" Chloe asked, a hint of fear penetrating her voice.

Vincent frowned as he looked at the source of the noise.

"No, I don't think so. I think it's..." he was cut off at the sound of a shot, then he fell to a heap on the floor without another word. A single wound in his heart.

Martin stared at his lifeless body, frozen in shock.

They had no time to react, they hadn't comprehended the situation before they were surrounded. A dozen masked men, all armed, formed a circle around them, weapons raised, shouting at them in muffled voices through their masks.

Martin glanced at his fallen friend and threw his own weapon to the ground. The others did the same. Maria pursed her lips, the anger clear in her eyes.

Someone walked into the circle, slightly smaller than the rest. They laughed. It was shrill and high-pitched. They removed the mask obscuring their face.

"Hello, Martin," Bev said, flashing him a bright smile. Her rotting teeth flashed in the dull starlight and her eyes burned with joy.

As they were marched into the building, Martin turned his head to look at her, walking next to him. She looked triumphant.

"Why are you doing this?" he asked.

"Because of what you did to us."

"What? I don't understand. I haven't seen you for nearly fifteen years. What did we do to you?"

"When you kicked us out."

"When you attacked us!"

"When you kicked us out," she said again, firmly. "We had nothing. We came back here, empty handed. We lost men, good men. And you banished us. We lost more, that winter. We couldn't feed them all. People got sick. Not that kind of sick. The old-fashioned type. But they died, anyway. We lost it all. Men, women and children. We lost them all."

"You attacked us," Martin repeated softly. "You killed people. You must have known there would be no going back."

"I vowed that winter, that I'd get my revenge. It didn't matter how long it took. I'd get it."

"So, you took Benny?" Martin asked.

"I'd rather have gotten the girl. But she wasn't around. At the time," she glanced at Maria. "Now though, I should think this will work rather well."

"What?" Martin asked. "What are you talking about?"

"Tom!" she screamed. "I'll kill him when he comes for her."

"Tom?" Martin repeated, with confusion on his face. "You blame Tom for all of this?"

"Of course. He banished us. He took away everything. Everyone I cared about died."

"Tom had nothing to do with this. You attacked us. Tom let you live; that was his only mistake."

She smiled sweetly. "That might be true. At least he'll get to fully realise that mistake, before he dies."

"Tom isn't coming."

She stopped walking and the man following behind nearly stumbled into her.

"What?" she asked, her eyes narrowing.

"Tom had an accident. He's not coming. I don't think he'll be coming ever again."

He stared at him for a long moment, then shrugged her head. "No matter."

After a brief pause, Martin asked, "was that you, skulking around outside Newhaven?"

"Not personally," she said. "But it was us, yes. We've been planning this for a long, long time. We've been to Newhaven countless times, and you've never seen us. You've grown soft, the lot of you. That's why we finally decided to act. I don't think you can beat us. You're a spent force. And now I'm going to prove that."

Martin shook his head and let the conversation rest; he had nothing left to say to her. Bev smirked and jerked her head to the armed men surrounding them. They were pushed forward by the handles of rifles, stumbling into the open room within.

They were pushed into a small, dark room. There was no light coming through the grime-covered window as they bumped into the sparse furniture. Martin looked around as his eyes slowly adjusted. The room was decrepit, like the rest of the building. The walls were bare wood, the floorboards uneven, cracked and rotting.

"Fuck!" Maria shrieked in frustration, her voice cutting through the darkness.

"Maria?" A voice from the other side of the room asked. "Guys… is that you?"

"Benny?"

His face appeared from the shadows.

They stood, looking at each other in disbelief for a moment, before they embraced, clutched tightly in each other's arms.

Martin clapped him on the back. "It's great to see you safe, Benny. I'm relieved."

Benny smiled back and absently rubbed at his shoulder, where Martin's hand had connected, possibly harder than he had intended.

The door had been slammed shut and the group were left alone in the dark room. Martin walked to the window and pressed gently against it.

"Don't," Benny said. "They're out there. I've tried."

Chloe walked up to him and wrapped her arms around him. He let his head fall onto her shoulder and felt the tears leave his eyes. Sometime later, they had no way of knowing exactly how long, the door to the room creaked slowly open. Light flooded in from the hallway beyond.

"Out," the masked man stood in the doorway commanded. He had a handgun pointed into the gloom. Martin glanced behind him and saw the others. At least three other men, they held rifles close to their chests. It wasn't a fight they would win. He resigned himself to whatever they had planned and walked past him into the hallway. The others followed. Benny, at the back, approached the threshold when the man raised the pistol to stop him.

"Not you," he said.

Benny's face creased up in confusion, but it was Chloe who spoke.

"He's not staying with you. He's coming with us." The men around her raised their rifles, pointed at her chest. She scowled at them. "I've not come this far to find my son, for you bastards to keep him," she spat.

One of the men forced the stock of his rifle into her stomach as she doubled over, hitting the ground hard. He grabbed her arms and dragged her out of sight.

"Mum!" Benny screamed, as the man stood to block him. He tried to push his way through, and the man hit him hard in the face with his pistol. Benny hit the ground with a grunt, feeling the blood streak down his face. He tried to get back up, but the man's boot connected with his ribs, sending him sprawling several feet across the cold, wooden floor.

Maria made to move towards him, before Martin grabbed her arm and shook his head silently. She paused, then hung her head, looking to the floor and allowed herself to be led away from the room, tears flowed from her eyes as she heard the screams from Benny every time the dull kick connected with his body. His screams and grunts grew distant as they were led to the far end of the building, through a door and out into the dark.

Chloe sobbed as she was led away from the sound of Benny's screams. The men had a tight grip on her and there was nothing she could do.

"Why?" she sobbed, at no one in particular.

The men stopped, one walked to face her. He pulled his mask down and her eyes widened.

"David?" she asked in disbelief.

He held his finger in front of his mouth.

"The boy doesn't need to die. This is all I could do to save him. She agreed to let him live, but not unscathed. It'll hurt now, but he'll live," he whispered to her. "It was never meant to come to this. None of us wanted this, just her. Only Bev. I am sorry, Chloe. I really am. For everything. We're too far in now. I hope you believe this is for the best."

Chloe stifled her sobs, with the backdrop of Benny's moaning fading away. David replaced the mask on his face and dragged her out of the building.

"I don't understand," she mumbled as the tears fell from her eyes.

CHAPTER THIRTEEN

The young woman approached the makeshift camp. It had been five years since the outbreak. Five years since she last had any real sense of normality. She'd been only a teenager when the first wave happened. The second wave had killed all of her family. Her parents became sick early on; they died within days in their bed. Her little brother lasted longer. It took him in the end, though. She fled the city when the gangs took over. It wasn't safe, especially not for a young girl like her. She headed for the forest. She didn't know what she hoped to find, anything would be better than what she'd left.

She'd come across a small group of survivors, with the same plan. They were living in make-shift tents, hunting for sustenance in the forest and cooking their spoils over a central fire pit dug into the hard earth. Winter was beginning to bite. She was under prepared. She'd grabbed some clothes when she left, but after a life in the warmth of a heated home, she didn't have what she'd need to survive the harsh winters in the wilderness. When she stumbled into the camp, the people had been concerned at first, keeping her at a distance, in case she was infected.

After a few days, when it became apparent, she wasn't, they began to welcome her in. They were friendly enough, made up of two families and a few other wayward travellers who had also stumbled across them. They gave her warm clothes and helped her set up a tent in a corner of the camp. She joined in with the meals and before long, she felt like she had a family again. For the first time in longer than she could remember, she was happy.

They discovered Newhaven several weeks before they first made contact. It was purely by accident. Two of the group were scouting for game, heading further and further out. They had a supply of bicycles used for longer trips; they'd managed to take them from a nearby town when the camp was first set up. Their chains were dry and their frames rusting now, from years of being stored outside with little maintenance. Soon, even they would be gone. The local wildlife was learning to avoid their camp. Newhaven shone in the distance, the barriers tall and imposing. Fires lit inside illuminated the skyline. They held a meeting, all of them sat around the fire as they discussed their next move.

They were struggling now, there was no denying that. Hunting was harder, the ground was solid and the food running dangerously low. There had been some illnesses sweep through the camp, they thought due to the poor sanitation they employed, mixed with their dwindling diets.

Their small camp had grown, but the resources were not enough to sustain them. They knew they needed to do something. They'd need to move out, or find a way to bring provisions in. This town, it looked like it was thriving. They'd seen horses, crops being grown, even in the winter months. They could only imagine the stores they might have, the supplies they would have locked away in their stores.

The conversation was going around in circles. Half of the group wanted to approach them and try to join their community. The other half wanted to mount an attack and take what they needed to survive on their own. The split was more or less down the middle, those who wanted to approach this peacefully were generally the newer settlers. The original founders, they wanted to attack.

She was in the middle. She hadn't started this camp, but she'd been here for a long time. It felt like home. She didn't want to leave it and put her safety in the hands of strangers.

In the end, the lack of a suitable plan answered the question for them. They'd have to make contact and hope these people wouldn't shoot them on sight.

They agreed that she would go. She was a young woman, now in her early twenties, although even she wasn't sure exactly how old she was now. She was capable, but unassuming. They hoped that no one would see her as a threat and that they would hear her out.

It was early morning. The sun was making its way up into the sky, but the cold still bit into her. She wrapped her coat tightly around her neck. The others had stopped a short way back. They were hidden in the long grass. They'd brought what they could, but they doubted it would be enough if this went wrong. They just had to hope the people on the other side of these gates would show humility and help them.

She made no attempt to conceal herself, as she approved the large metal gate. A man watched her with interest from his wooden seat, high up above her. He had a rifle, but he made no move towards it as she ambled closer.

"Hello?" She shouted up. The man stood.

"Hi," he replied with a smile. "Everything okay?"

His voice was calm and kind, but with an edge of concern. She wondered how many times this man had been approached and how many of those times had been peaceful.

"I'm Beverley, er, Bev," she said, waving her hand. "I'm not armed. It's just me."

"Just you?" the man asked.

"Yes, just me. The others are back there," she waved her hand behind her. There was no sense in lying, in case their approach had been watched.

"Why?" the man asked.

"We felt it might seem a bit aggressive if we all showed up with guns. This felt safer."

The man raised his eyebrows at her but didn't reply.

"We're looking for help. That's all," she hoped her voice sounded as calm as she has intended it to.

"This is Newhaven," the man called down. "And we've never turned anyone away yet. Hold on, I'll come down."

The man who opened the gate was a younger man, dressed like a soldier. He had a kind smile and there was no malice in his eyes as he offered his hand.

"I'm Martin," he said. "Pleasure to meet you." She smiled back, eyeing the three men behind him, each holding rifles, glowing at her, not entirely looking like his sentiment rang true for them all.

He saw her watching them and smiled. "Don't worry about them, they're just grumpy, didn't get enough sleep last night."

She didn't feel reassured by his jokes.

"The rest of your group," he asked. "Are they far?"

"No. Just over the ridge, in the long grass."

He nodded. "If they leave their weapons, they're welcome to come. If we go to them, will they shoot?"

She hesitated for a moment. "No. No, I don't think they will."

Martin turned to the man behind him and nodded. The man set off in a brisk walk towards the ridge.

"Let's hope you're right. I like Vincent and I'd quite like him to come back in one piece." He smiled again and Bev returned a small smile of her own.

The town was incredible. She walked through the clean streets, her neck craning to view everything, trying to take it all in. It was as close to the old world as she'd seen in a very long time. Buildings lined the weed free road that ran through the middle of the town. People pushed carts and the aroma of meat cooking floated through the air.

"How long have you been here?" she asked in awe.

"A little over four years now," he replied. "There was about twenty of us, originally. Now there's nearly 700. Most of them arrived, just like you did."

"Where are we going?" she asked.

"To see the boss," Martin smiled. "Don't worry, he's an alright type, really."

She smiled, watching in awe as the people walked past to start their daily duties.

They entered a brick building, nearly in the centre of town. It was bright and warm. Chairs furnished the room. It had none of the mildew and mould smell she'd come to associate with anything remaining from the old world.

A table sat against the far wall and a man sat behind it, writing something on a piece of paper in front of him.

"Tom?" the soldier said, as the man looked up.

"This is Bev. She's just arrived at the gate. There's more, Vincent's gone to invite them in."

The man, Tom, smiled.

"Welcome," he said kindly. "Please, take a seat. Are you hungry?"

She tried to reply, but no words left her throat. She'd expected an interrogation, not breakfast.

The man, Tom, just smiled at her. "Martin, grab a bowl of food for her, would you?"

"Sure thing," Martin replied as he left the room.

"So," Tom studied her. "I assume you've come here for a reason." Here it was, the interrogation, it just wouldn't be aggressive as the ones she was used to.

"Yes," she replied confidently. "We are from a small camp, about fifteen miles south. We've been there since the beginning. It has been going okay, but recently things have been getting harder. We came across your town here a few days ago and wanted to ask for your help."

"Help?" Tom asked.

"That's right. We're low on food, we're out of fuel. We're on the edge right now. Without help, we won't survive."

"You are welcome to stay here. All of you. We've never turned anyone away and don't plan to start now. We have food and accommodation. We can house you all."

"I..." she started. "I don't think that's what the leaders were hoping for. I don't think they want to give up our camp."

Tom looked at her. "Then, what do they want?" Caution had snuck into his voice.

"Food, supplies. That's all."

"I hope you understand, while we are true to our word and do want to help, we're not in the habit of just giving away our provisions. I do hope that's not why you've come today."

Her gaze fell. She had expected this, if she was being honest. The town looked perfect, and she knew a lot of their camp would want to move here at this man's invitation. The families that started their camp, though, they'd never let them. They had adopted power over these people, and they wouldn't let it go easily.

Tom still watched her, although he hadn't said anything more. The expression on his face was unreadable.

"We can, however," he said. "Come to some arrangement, I am sure." She felt her hopes rise.

"We trade with many local settlements. There's always something to include in a barter. What do you guys have?"

She thought. She thought hard, they had nothing. Nothing at

all. They hunted for food and barely got enough of that. They got their water from a stream, there was nothing special or rare about that. They lived under tarpaulins, strapped to trees. They had nothing that these people would possibly want. Nothing at all.

At that moment, the door opened, and Martin walked in, a steaming bowl in his hands. He passed it to Bev. It smelled delicious. Steam wafted from the top; some kind of meat was braised in water within. She cautiously took the spoon and tried the smallest mouthful. She soon finished the lot. The stew had been flavoured; the meat was tender; she hadn't eaten anything like for a very long time.

"Thank you," she said gratefully to Martin. Turning back to Tom, she added. "With this as an option, maybe they will take you up on your offer!"

He smiled kindly. "Let's hope so."

The door opened again, and the other man dressed in the army uniform stood there, Vincent, she thought that's what Martin had called him. Behind him, stood the rest of her group. They no longer had their weapons, she supposed Vincent must have been able to persuade them to leave them outside. The smell of the stew still lingered on the air, and she saw several of them start to salivate, swallowing quickly.

Tom stood and addressed them. "Bev has told me what you're after and I've made our position clear. We offer refuge here, to any that need it. We'll feed you and offer you a warm bed for the night. You're welcome to stay, for as long as you like. We are also always open for trade. But we cannot, and will not, give our stores away for nothing. I won't do anything that threatens the future of my people here."

He looked at them one by one, waiting for a reaction.

This had happened before, of course. People would show up and demand that they were given provisions, offering nothing in return. It did not usually end well. These types of people were often difficult to deal with, conceited and self-serving. He'd learned from experience to be strong from the offset and put quick boundaries in place.

A man walked forward from the small crowd. He was a larger man, with black, curly hair around his round face.

"Sir, with all respect, we've got nothing to give. We are desolate out there, and you sit here with so much."

Tom smiled. "I know what it looks like, but I'm sorry, that's our stance. Will you think about joining us?"

"I can't do that," the man replied. "I have my own people, we have our own home, we can't just leave it. We won't."

"I'm not saying we won't help you. Of course we'll do what we can. But I can't just let you walk away with half of our stores. It's not the way the world can work."

The man grunted, showing his displeasure.

"Why did you come here?" Tom asked. "What did you hope to achieve? We've not been in this room for five minutes and it's obvious there was no plan here."

"We hoped you'd see sense. We hoped you'd pick another path," he snarled back.

Tom sighed. "Look, go and have some food, talk it over, as a group, and we'll discuss this further in a few hours. But know this, you won't just be walking out of here with whatever you like."

They stared at each other silently over the table. Bev felt the discomfort wash over the room. Most of the people here would have happily joined this camp, it was far superior to their own.

Their leader, the man who had spoken was Kingsley Fox, a landowner from the local area before everything changed. He'd left with his family and set the camp up first in the forest. He was a kind man when Bev had first joined the camp, but the years of hardship and difficult decisions had hardened him. He'd grown used to people doing what he said, and he didn't like to be told no.

He had genuinely believed he could walk up to this town, and they'd give him what he wanted. Perhaps to avoid confrontation, Bev wasn't sure what really went through his mind.

His wife and two children were back at the camp. She was a meek woman, who spent most of her days inside the large tent he'd set up for them. Bev had lived in the camp for five years and she'd barely spoken to her in all that time.

Kingsley broke eye contact first, and turned his back on Tom.

"Fine," he spat. "We will discuss your proposals and come back to you." He stormed out of the room without another word. The others slowly filed out behind him. Bev glanced at Tom, giving him a sad smile and followed the rest.

They sat on one of the long outdoor benches under the kitchen tent, pitched almost in the centre of the town. The guards had escorted them out of the building and walked them over. They stood a short distance away, giving them their privacy.

"We could take it all," Kingsley hissed. "Look at them. Half a dozen guards, at best. We could take this entire place right now."

"How?" Bev asked. "Your weapons are out in the grass, as we've got no idea that this is all, just the guards you can see. Look at this place, all of this, you really think you could just walk in, and they'd roll over?"

He sneered at her. She'd never really warmed to him. He'd always been polite and sometimes friendly, especially early on, but recently he was becoming more and more unhinged.

"We should think about it," another man added from across the bench. "This place looks nice; I wouldn't mind moving here."

Kingsley slammed his fist on the table, causing those around him to jump. "No!" he screamed. We will not abandon our home. That's all we've got."

They sat around the cold bench for a while longer, finishing their food. No one spoke, as they all sat with their own thoughts. Kingsley stood.

"It's time to go." He said and without a backwards glance, strode off towards the gate.

Tom watched them leave from the window in the town hall. He rubbed his temples. This wasn't going to go well.

"Martin," he called to the young soldier, who stood by the door. "Get a few more folk out here with you. I don't think this is done."

Martin nodded and left the room, leaving Tom alone in the quiet.

"Fuck sake…" he whispered to himself.

The group headed back to where they'd left their packs and weapons. They were all still there. No one from Newhaven appeared to have followed them. Bev scanned the landscape before them and saw no movement.

Kingsley picked up his rifle and checked the stock. He gestured to the others.

"Let's go."

They arrived back at the gate less than an hour after they'd left. Martin watched them approach. They were trying to be subtle, but there just wasn't the cover out front. He let his breath out, he hadn't realised he'd been holding it, and loaded his gun.

Seven of them stood at predetermined intervals on the barricade. It had been built to allow shooting positions, with the hope being they'd never have to use them.

The group approached. He peered through the sight and

settled the crosshatch on Kingsley.

"Please don't do this," Tom shouted from the barricade. The group looked up; they had hoped to arrive undetected. Bev had expected this; these people weren't as naive as Kingsley seemed to think they were.

"I will not let my people die, because you're to selfish to share," Kingsley roared back at him.

He never managed to bring the rifle to face Tom. The bullet pierced through his heart before he could.

Martin's rifle smoked and his face wore an expression of regret. The group froze in horror as their leader collapsed to the ground before them, blood soaking the frozen floor.

Bev dived sideways, hoping to use the long grass for cover, as she readied her aim. She fired, without a target and heard the ping from the metal barrier. The others followed suit. Several shots returned from Newhaven. They no longer seemed to be aiming to kill. The shots peppered the ground around them, forcing them backwards. Before long, they were out of range of the weapons being brandished by the people of Newhaven. She turned to the others, no one else had fallen.

Glancing towards Kingsley's body, which was laying alone in the grass, she said. "Let's go home. We've got nothing here now."

Tom watched as the survivors crept towards the trees and off towards the south.

"You think that's it?" Martin asked.

"No, he replied. I really don't."

CHAPTER FOURTEEN

Back at the camp, Bev and the others licked their wounds. Kingsley was dead. They'd told his wife, she hadn't visibly reacted, which Bev thought was a bit odd, but left her to grieve in her own way.

They sat around the fire in the centre of the camp. After their trip to Newhaven, it seemed even more basic now. Just a scattering of tents around a large fire pit. It was cold and drafty. Food was hard to come by and survival was by no means guaranteed.

Bev felt guilty. She hoped, with Kingsley dead, they could try again, and perhaps join into the community in Newhaven. She suspected many of the others thought so, too.

"That went well," she said, after a long period of silence.

"Kingsley was a fool," one of the men commented. "We should have taken them up on their offer. They'll never let us now; they'll never trust us."

Bev's stomach rumbled at that moment; she wondered if the others could hear. They'd had to cycle, and it had taken it out of them. They didn't have horses like Newhaven did, they didn't have anything, aside from the few rusting bicycles they'd manage to pilfer from the old world.

She glanced at the emancipated faces around her and finally understood. The trip couldn't fail. If it failed, they would all die.

She stood and spoke to the group.

"We have to go back. Unarmed and we'll beg those people to forgive us. We'll die out here, otherwise."

"You think they'll listen to us?" someone replied.

"We've got to hope; what else can we do?"

They stared glumly around. The day had not gone to plan. Bev didn't think anyone here had expected Kingsley to be as heavy-handed as he had been. What had he hoped to achieve? Was he trying to show power over people he'd never met, and expect they'd just give up their own stores? They had more men, more supplies, possibly more weapons, although she didn't see many on display during their visit.

She stood in quiet reflection for several long moments.

"We'll work." She said finally. "That's what we'll offer them, labour for food."

With resolve in her heart, she set off back towards Newhaven. No one offered to follow along with her.

The journey left her sore and aching. This was the third time she'd completed it in a little over a day. The ground was becoming unstable, the concrete breaking and being pushed apart by the weeds intent on reclaiming the world. She felt every bump in the road as she cycled quickly over them.

She approached Newhaven much quicker this time, with no others to slow her down and she had a good sense of where she was heading.

She saw the man, Martin, standing on the barricade. He watched her approach. She stopped the bicycle and let it fall sideways to the floor with a thud. Holding her hands out in front of her, she cautiously approached the gate.

"That'll do," Martin said, as she drew near. "Where's the rest?"

She glanced to her side; Kingsley's body had been removed. Could she still see the red stain on the floor where he had lain?

"I want to make amends," she said. "What happened here, that wasn't our doing. It was his."

"Wait there," Martin replied, his voice echoing around the open expanse as he disappeared from view.

Moments later, the doors creaked slowly open, coming to a rest with just enough room between them for a person to walk through. Tom stood in the narrow gap; he was smiling.

"I'm glad to see you back," he said.

"Really?" She asked, incredulously. She'd expected anger, maybe to be shot at.

"Yes," he replied. "There's people like that all over, it doesn't make everyone bad."

She knew he meant Kingsley.

"I wanted to apologise. What happened here," she indicated at the ground around her. "Wasn't what the majority wanted. We came looking for help, not for war."

Tom nodded at her knowingly. This wasn't the first time something like this had happened. Of course, in this world, it was more common than not. But just like Chester, the man who still made appearances in his dreams, many years before, it only takes one.

"My stance remains the same," he said, after brief hesitation.

"I understand," she replied. "So, I come with an offer. Most of us don't want to leave our home. It may not be this, but it's ours, and its home. I hope you understand that."

"Of course."

"So, I offer you this. We'll work for you. In exchange for what we need, we'll work your farms, or your kitchens. Hell, we'll clean your toilets, if that's what you need."

Tom considered her. It wasn't a bad exchange. Newhaven was still lacking in people, there was never enough to get everything done. The town was still being built up. Truth be told, they might have struggled to house all the people from this camp, no matter how few of them there were. This could work for both parties.

He nodded. "Okay, that works. Come in."

They walked through Newhaven, Bev carefully in step behind Tom. A few people cast her glances as she passed, a few sneers were visible. Not everyone was happy with what had happened with Kingsley. She expected some resentment, even if they hadn't killed anyone from this place.

Tom walked her to the farm on the edge of the far end of Newhaven. A barn stood solitary at the edge of the field, its door ajar. Tom knocked on it and waited patiently. When no one arrived, he knocked again.

"Bob," he called.

"I'm a comin'," a voice replied from inside. "Give us a moment."

Tom looked at her and shook his head. "Likes his midday naps, this one," he said, smiling.

A big man arrived at the door, his hair unkempt and his bushy grey beard had small pieces of straw stuck in it. She saw Tom gesture to him, and he quickly brushed them out.

"Yeah... sorry about that, fell in the straw," Bob said.

"Sure..." Tom replied. "Bob, this is Bev. She's come back from the camp down south."

"She was with that group from earlier?" Bob asked.

"That's right. But it's okay. They want to work. They want to offer their labour, in return for some food."

"I reckon we can work that," he said, a large smile beaming over his face.

They talked for a while longer, Bob showed her around the farm and the tasks that needed to be completed. She watched with enthusiasm, feeling hopeful that this could work, that this could provide them with a future.

After a filling lunch of bread, real bread and broth, she left to return back to her camp. They hadn't given their home a name, it had never been fitting of one. As she cycled back, she wondered if they should.

She arrived home with an optimistic outlook. She was sure the others would be as excited as she was at this opportunity. The camp was quiet. People milled around, but without really doing anything. An air of desperation cast around them, floating over their heads like thick, black clouds. Several people looked at her, their eyes wide and hollow.

She smiled. "They'll have us."

Smiles returned to her. People rushed towards her, all talking at once.

"Six people. They need six people to help on the farms. In return, they'll give us enough food to feed the entire camp for every day we're there."

"So, we're doing the jobs they don't want?" asked David.

David was around the same age as her. He'd arrived after her, on its own after making his way out of the towns when the outbreak got bad. He had a bit of a temper, but had been a useful member of the group, always willing to put his shift in. Even after months of near starvation, he retained his bulky mass, an intimidating man with a square jawline and thick black hair.

"No," she replied firmly. "These are jobs they don't have the people to do. Ploughing the fields, sowing, that sort of thing. I said we'd clean the toilets if they asked us to. They'll feed us; I don't really care what they want me to do."

He turned away without a reply.

"We start tomorrow. I need five volunteers to come with me. It's a long ride, we'll need to leave at first light." People murmured around her, without talking directly to her. She felt her hopes dashed, what if no one agreed to go?

David stepped forwards. "I'm in," he said, before turning and walking to his tent.

Several others volunteered soon after and Bev went to sleep that night believing this would be the last night of her dire life; tomorrow would bring a new dawn, a new day and a new future.

The morning arrived and she stood patiently waiting for the others. She hadn't slept much the previous night, she wanted to make sure she was up and ready to go in time. She wasn't going to risk ruining this chance. Soon, the six of them pushed their bicycles onto the rutted road and set off on the long journey to Newhaven.

She was grateful for the bicycles, without them, she didn't know how they would have got there. It was still early when they arrived, tired and sore, but ready. Martin met them at the gate, as he had done before. There were extra guards with him this time, she wondered if that was due to the additional people she had brought with her. Their demeanour calmed once they saw the group was unarmed.

They were taken to the kitchen tent and given breakfast. Bob met them there, jolly as she had ever seen him. He sat with them as they ate, detailing the work he needed help with and letting them pick what they wanted to do. She had not expected that. Most of them took the easier-sounding tasks, but she wanted to throw herself into it and prove her worth, so she agreed to try to plough the field with one of the cob horses he had in the barns.

David kept quiet throughout until Bob finally turned to him.

"You've been quiet, lad. Where would you like to be today?"

David glared at him but did not reply.

"Right," he said, uncertainly. "We'll find you somethin', no worries there. You any good with fencing?"

After a brief pause, David nodded, the slightest movement of his head. Bob smiled.

"Right on. I got some fencin' needs fixin'. Aye, you'll be great at that. Okay, come on, you lot, I'll get you started."

He walked them around the farmland, depositing people with their tasks as he did so. Eventually, it was just him, Bev and David. They walked over the bumpy field, as Bob explained how to use the makeshift plough he'd made from old wood and rope. She listened eagerly, before accepting the reins and moving off to attempt to follow his jumbled instructions.

Bob walked in silence with David. They were out of earshot of the others, before David abruptly stopped and turned to him.

"We'll do your work, but only because we need your food. We're not friends, and I don't need you acting like we are." He spat fiercely.

Bob just smiled at him. "Maybe not yet, lad, but we could be. You'll see."

David hammered the nail into the fence post, a pointless exercise, the post was rotten. It wouldn't last long, no matter what he did. He hadn't felt the need to voice this, it wasn't his problem. He'll do this work and get food for his fellows. Bob had left him alone, he was pleased about that, he wanted to be alone. He'd watched as they entered. Taken in the security of this place, the guards and their weapons. He wanted to be sure he was ready, if anything were to happen.

A rustle in the grass behind him made him pause. He didn't turn, but he listened intently. There it was again. Footsteps. Small ones. He turned and saw a young boy stood behind him with a curious expression on his face.

"Who are you?" the boy asked.

He smiled. This child was innocent from all of this. "I'm David," he said, extending a hand. The boy grabbed two of his fingers and shook them.

"I'm Benny. I play here."

"Is that so? Well, don't let me stop you, go ahead and play."

Benny watched him a while longer, before skipping off to pick flowers from the hedgerow. He stayed close for the rest of the day. David felt himself lightening up; the kid was alright. Better company than the rest of them.

They returned home that night laden down with supplies. The people of Newhaven had been true to their word, and before they left, they provided them with baskets of crops, wrapped meat and small bags of herbs and spices. They returned the next day and the next. Each time they returned home late into the evenings, with enough provisions to keep their camp fed for days.

The arrangement worked for the next few weeks. Spirits in the camp were improving and more people volunteered to go to Newhaven, giving the initial workers some much needed respite.

Bev rose early, ready to start her shift. The sun was barely above the horizon as she walked from her tent to the small shack they used to store the bicycles. She stopped suddenly. Most of the bikes were gone. By her count, there were nearly a dozen missing. She glanced worriedly around. The camp was deserted, aside from a solitary figure sitting by the fire. It was Kingsley's wife. Kingsley's widow. Bev ran to her, as she stared vacantly into the glowing embers of the fire pit.

"Where are they?" she demanded.

The woman returned her stare, her eyes were blank.

"Gone," she said softly.

"Gone where?"

"Gone. Gone to take it."

"To take what?"

She giggled. "Newhaven, of course."

Bev felt the colour drain from her face. What had they done? She ran back to the shack, grabbed the closest bicycle and pedalled like her life depended on it.

She could hear the gunshots, long before she arrived at the open gate of Newhaven. People screamed inside, interspersed with the sound of rifles firing. She dropped the bicycle to the ground and ran through the open gate.

The scene that greeted her was complete chaos. Several bodies lay in the road by the gate. She didn't recognise any of them. The street was eerily deserted, the kitchen tent, usually bustling, lay empty, a large pot tipped over, its contents still dripping over the side of the table, pooling on the floor below.

Another shot rang out in the distance, over towards the farms. She took off in a sprint towards the sounds of the commotion. She jumped over several more bodies, one or two of which she thought she recognised from her camp, but the injuries and blood made it impossible to tell at the speed she travelled.

She rounded the last building, just before the open expanse of farmland greeted her. There was a running battle underway. She saw David, a rifle in his hands, crouched in the grass, shooting at something or someone, just out of sight. Others crouched near him, all from her camp. It dawned on her what they had done. They must have arrived early, the guards let them in, probably with smiles and greetings, and they had slaughtered them in the street. That must have been the bodies she first encountered. Someone must have gotten wind of them, as there were shots being returned.

She watched in horror as a figure in the distance stood and ran, soon to be dragged down by the bullet that entered their chest. She couldn't see from here who it was, but she heard the screams. It hadn't been a clean shot; the person was still alive. The scream cut out abruptly as death overtook them.

David pushed forward, keeping his rifle aimed in front of him, pushing through the long grass. She was nearly behind him now. She dropped to her knees, trying to avoid being caught in the crossfire. He was just feet in front of her.

"David!" she shouted. "What are you doing?" Tears rolled down her face.

He looked at her, a wild look in his eyes and his mouth set in a permanent sneer.

"This is ours now," he roared. "We're taking it. I'm not working for these *people* anymore. They've got so much, but they're just conceited enough to believe they are untouchable. They just let us in." A sick smile spread across his face as he turned to face his victims in the distance.

"No," she said quietly, more to herself than to him.

He let off another shot, the sound was deafening this close to the rifle. Her teeth rattled and she realised she was shaking. With fear, or anger. At who? She wasn't sure. She saw movement to her side and spun to face it. It was Chloe, she could see her trying to flank them, using the hedgerow for cover.

She'd grown fond of the young woman, who ate with her at lunch sometimes. She was always kind and had been one of the first to introduce herself to the group when they first entered Newhaven. She moved to tell David but thought better of it. Resigning herself to her fate, she stayed quiet.

David was so focused on the figure in front of him, he didn't even register the movement. He was aiming towards Bob. She could make the big man out, even across the field. He had a rifle in his hands. It was stupid to think these people didn't have a store of them. A man near them fell; he didn't make a sound, just slumped over where he stood. The sound of the shot followed moments after, when the blood was already staining his shirt red. It came from the building behind them. David had been so engrossed in Bob that neither he nor the others had noticed they had been completely surrounded. Someone was shooting from the windows and another from the camp fell in a crumpled heap.

Bev collapsed to the ground as her legs gave out. She tried to stop the tears, but they kept coming. She covered her face with her hands and waited for the end.

It never came. All she heard was the familiar click of a rifle and the voice behind her.

"Don't move, not a muscle."

Chloe had the barrel of the gun pointed directly at her. Her husband, Bev didn't know his name, had his rifle pushed into David's back. David hesitated, then threw his gun to the ground, a look of pure indignation on his face.

Whatever he was trying to do had failed, and with it, their future fell apart.

She, like the other survivors of this failed attacked, was bound and marched to the town hall. Including her and David, only five remained. The rest were dead in the fields. She wondered if they might execute them. She wouldn't have blamed them, looking at the dead littering the ground, it's what she would have done.

Tom looked crestfallen. His face showed only sorrow. Bob looked angry. She'd never seen that look on his face before, and it worried her. The child, the one David had struck up an almost friendship with, hid behind Chloe's legs, watching the scene in front of him.

"Why?" Tom asked.

No one answered, as David spat on the ground by his feet.

He shook his head. "Pointless..." he murmured.

They had been allowed to leave, alive. Bev wasn't sure any of them truly believed that, expecting to be shot in the back as they made the shameful walk out of Newhaven. It had been made clear, they were not welcome, ever again. If they came near, they would be shot, there would be no warning, no mercy. The tears flowed for a long time.

The return to the camp was a sober and silent affair. They arrived at a scene that was just as heart-breaking. Kingsley's widow lay dead in her tent. She'd slashed her wrist with one of the hunting knives. Her young children sat at her feet; her blood stained their faces.

The following months, as the weather slowly tuned colder, conditions worsened. A cholera outbreak ripped through the camp, killing so many. She had to watch them die, slowly, in pain. In the cold and the dirt.

Bev sat alone in the cold tent, the wind whistling around her. She silently vowed that one day, somehow, she would take what Tom had denied her. The power vacuum left in the camp had been in contention upon their return.

Not only was there Bev and David vying for the spot, some of the other families were also trying to exert their influence, to take control of the camp. Bev had won out, eventually. She had the smarts to keep the camp running and the desire for revenge grew inside of her which shone across as confidence. People slowly started to follow her. She felt David move away from her as the years passed and he struggled to keep his jealousy of her position hidden. She'd have to watch out for him. He'd always be a risk, someone waiting in the wings, to grab this newfound power from her at the first chance he got.

CHAPTER FIFTEEN

The darkness settled over Newhaven, as it did every night. The guard posted atop the gate started his shift, the long night shift. He didn't like that one. It was lonely and usually uneventful. Martin usually took these shifts; he wasn't used to it.

He'd been here for a few hours and was getting restless already. He looked into the persistent darkness, nothing stirred. The air was still and silent. The storm of the previous night had broken, and the long summer days were threatening to return, along with the warm nights they brought with them. He wiped his forehead. Even now, it was warm. He was tired. He wasn't used to this and hadn't slept properly before he came up here. It would be okay, nothing would happen. He settled down into the wooden chair he'd brought up with him. It was an old dining chair, really, but better than nothing.

He started to drift off, with the sounds of the nearby forest rocking him to sleep. It was a quiet night. The others had left hours ago. They should be back tomorrow, then he could go back to his preferred day shift and wouldn't have to deal with these late nights. The crickets chirped angrily nearby as an owl took flight through the trees, its wings beating away the thin branches as it did. He could just about make out the smell of the smoke from the fire burning itself out in the town behind him.

The bang forced his eyes open. It wasn't a sound he could immediately place. It was a familiar sound, but not one he directly recognised. It had been loud and close, like thunder.

The sky was clear, though. He felt pressure on his chest, but he didn't know why. His mind, in that moment, refused to process what had happened. He ran his hand across his shirt, it was wet, something dark glistened from his fingertips. Bringing his hand to his face, in the moonlight he could just make out the blood coating his hand. He hadn't felt anything at all as the shell passed through him.

Weird, he thought, his mind refusing to register the situation with its last act. Then he slumped sideways and slid to the floor with a dull thud. Blood dripped slowly through the boards on the floor, pooling on the ground below.

The attackers, numbering nearly twenty, silently slipped through the long grass, coming to rest before the closed metal door surrounding Newhaven. The sound of the shot from the rifle had been absorbed by the night and no one came running to investigate.

The door creaked silently as they forced it open, as they crept slowly inside.

****

Kate had returned to the others. She'd searched around the area and found no evidence of Martin or the others being there. The building remained silent and dark.

"We need to go back," she hissed quietly. "Newhaven is under attack, and we've taken the best guards and all the weapons out here. It was a trap. It must have been."

"You go," Michael said. "We'll get the others back and meet you there."

"No," Kate shot back. "Maria is in there. My daughter is in there. I've lost my husband; I can't lose my child, too."

"We will get her, Kate, I promise. You need to look after the rest of your people. Trust us to do this; you go back and defend Newhaven."

Kate looked at him. Her emotions threatened to get the better of her. She battled the inner turmoil. She knew he was right; she had a responsibility to Newhaven, but she also had a responsibility to her family. Eventually, she pulled her gaze away.

"Okay," she said quietly. "Please keep her safe. I'll see you soon." Without another word, she turned and sprinted up the track and out of view.

Michael watched her disappear.

Kate didn't stop running until she heard the braying of the horses. She barely slowed as she grabbed the reins and unhooked them from the tree. Then she took off at a canter, making the journey back to Newhaven. She knew Maria would be safe in the hands of Michael. The people from Boneyard were well trained, there was no one she would rather be trusted with the safety of her child.

She hoped they'd be quick. She didn't know how many attackers had arrived at Newhaven. The short message had been harrowing and the not knowing was torturous. She pushed the horse on, faster and faster. She knew it couldn't keep it up. How had they got past them? There was only one road that ran between the building and Newhaven. They would have seen a group of people heading in the opposite direction.

Her mind raced as she traversed the terrain. Something was off about this, but she couldn't put her finger on it. She shook the thought off and kept pushing the horse towards home. Then it hit her. Something Michael had said. The building, it was a rifle range. They shot at clays in the meadow behind it. Behind it. There must have been another exit, a track leading through the meadows and forests, seldom used, that far out. They would lead directly to Newhaven.

It felt like forever before she finally saw the giant walls of Newhaven come into view. She'd had to stop to let the horse recover, it had added valuable time to the journey. She had to hope the people had been able to hold their attackers off. She prayed they were still alive. Newhaven was eerily quiet as she approached. The gates sat open, with no guards on the barricades high above.

She jumped from the horse and broke into a run as she entered the town. There were no bodies littering the ground. She'd imagined a sea of blood running through the streets as her mind brought the worst-case scenarios to her thoughts on the journey.

They'd left Newhaven with nothing. They took most of the weapons and all of the best fighters. It must have been a trap. The buildings appeared deserted. Was it all to draw them out, so someone could take Newhaven?

But then where were they? As she travelled further into the heart of Newhaven, the scene repeated itself. Eerily quiet streets. No blood, no bodies. She slowed, cautiously watching her step. She should have seen something, or at least heard something, by now.

She was standing in front of the farms, the large expanse of fields stretched out before her. The once red barn, now peeling on its outer walls, dominated the landscape. Glancing around her, she headed in its direction.

The horses were still in their stalls, excluding the dozen or so that had gone out with the groups after Benny. Hay sat uneaten on the floor. Someone had been here recently. Whatever had happened, she hadn't missed it by long. With her hands planted on her hips, she looked around her, and then back towards the town. That's when she saw it. The crops were trampled, a thick, dense line through the middle, the indentation of what could have been thousands of people, she'd nearly missed it with only the stars glow to guide her. She followed the track; it ran into the woods that blocked Newhaven from view of the wider world. Once upon a time, a steel fence had run through those woods, keeping that side of the town protected from attack. It had eventually, like everything else, become old and damaged.

It hadn't been replaced. When it was finally reclaimed by the wilderness, they'd let it fall. She regretted that now.

She followed the track to the trees. It disappeared from view as it pushed through the overgrown foliage. She peered through the branches and saw nothing. Something inside of her screamed for her to turn around, to retreat to the safety of home. But what was there, what safety could remain there, if anything had happened to the rest?

What could she do? She was alone. An entire town had disappeared into the dark; how would she fight that, whatever it may have been?

She had to try. It was her duty. Tom would have done something. Bob would have taken after them alone, if he'd had to. In the midst of her panic, she felt a small twinge of sorrow at the thought of everyone she'd lost. She glanced towards the town hall. Tom would still be there; his cold body lay inside. They hadn't buried him yet. She felt guilty at not checking on him as she passed, but soon shook that off. He would have scolded her for wasting time on something as trivial as a dead man.

She had to know. She had to do what she could. She inhaled deeply, then pushed into the trees.

The branches whipped at her; she wondered subconsciously how the entire town could have travelled through here, with no visible signs of damage anywhere. The trees stretched for miles. Their canopy distorted her sense of direction and soon she no longer knew which way she was headed. She saw light, spilling through the thick trunks in front of her; she was nearly at the end. She pushed through, out into a wildflower meadow, rolling in the distance. Nothing stirred for as far as she could see. She turned in a slow half circle, her eyes squinting in the moonlight. It had taken her hours to get back here. They could have a head start on her of miles. She derided herself for not bringing the horse with her. If she hoped to catch up, she'd need to move quickly.

Despite her many years here, she'd never been out this way. She had no idea what lay before her. Others had, of course. Scouting parties and hunting groups had often used this side of the town. Firewood was harvested from here, but never by her personally. She tried to recall if they'd ever mentioned anything out here, but her memory failed her at that moment. Without a better plan, she walked, a steady yet quick pace, headed for the horizon before her.

She stumbled as her foot hit uneven ground. Her ankle screamed in pain as she rolled over it and she sank to the floor, deflated. She was exhausted. How long since she'd last slept? It might have been days now. She couldn't rest yet, she had to keep going. The longer she spent on the cold ground, the further her people would be. Forcing herself back to her feet, she ambled ever on.

As she climbed the crest of the small hill, an unfamiliar landscape revealed itself before her. The cloudless night lit up the ground like a shimmering mirage. She took a moment to catch her breath as she evaluated where she was. She ached, her stomach rumbled, and her throat burned with thirst. The pressure behind her eyes was turning into a full-blown migraine. She couldn't remember when she last drank. She needed sleep. She'd been stupid. She'd left with nothing, not even stopping to collect one of the radios from the town hall. She was out here, alone and with nothing, the rifle on her back the only possession she had.

She collapsed once again to the soft ground, the grass cushioning her fall. She rolled onto her back and closed her eyes. Just half an hour. She just needed half an hour to recharge.

She awoke to the sun high in the sky above her. With a jolt of fear, she sat upright. She'd been out here long enough to know what that meant. It was mid-morning now. She must have slept for hours. She felt better. She was still thirsty, but her head had cleared. The fog of exhaustion had receded. With the sun's light, she could clearly see the meadows around her. An indentation was distinctly visible through the tall grasses. She steadied herself and set off once more. A glint of light caught her eye. She stopped and turned to face it. Wondering if it had all been a trick of her mind, it took her a moment to spot it. In the grass lay a child's teddy bear. It was such a strange sight. The sun must have reflected off the large, black glass eye sewn into its face. It seemed out of place out here. It was old, it would have to be from before the world ended, but not weathered. It had been dropped recently. She tried to place it, but she couldn't be sure if she'd ever seen it before. She picked it up; it was damp with the morning dew. Grimacing, she placed the arm into her mouth and sucked the small amount of liquid out of it. It wasn't much and it barely satisfied her thirst, but it was something.

She thought momentarily about who this could have belonged to. She thought of the children in Newhaven. The idea of them being forced to march through the night, scared and cold, strengthened her resolve, as she rushed further onwards.

Watching the movement of the sun, she knew she was headed southwest. She tried to map the terrain her head. If she was right, they would be headed past the building she'd come from, bypassing the road all together. It must have been how they got past them. She was right, there must be a track through the forest linking the two. This was a trap. She thought of the distance involved. They couldn't intend to march these people all that way, could they?

She couldn't slow down, she couldn't stop. She had to keep going. Even alone, she was the only hope her people had now. She was so hungry. She couldn't remember when she had last eaten, and yet still she moved forwards. She pined for the radio. She must be closer to the rifle range than Newhaven, now. If she could call the others, they might be able to head them off. It was too late for that, thank to her stupidity, she'd just have to continue alone.

With the sun high above her, midday, as she recognised it. She caught the first glimpse of the column, walking in the distance. A long row of people, stretching as far as she could see, over the rolling hills and into the distance. She saw people walking on each side of them, corralling the column. She couldn't see how many from here, but she had to assume they were armed. How else would they have made the entire population of town leave with no apparent fight?

If she could see them, there was a chance they could see her. She'd just have to hope they didn't look behind them. Ignoring the pains in her stomach, she walked on. The column was moving slowly, she was gaining fast. As she drew closer, she could see the people walking to their side were indeed armed. They had masks covering their faces and guns in their hands. Most of the people from Newhaven wouldn't have seen a weapon before, the demographic was young, and they certainly would never have fired one.

She crouched in the grass, hoping it would obscure her from view if anyone looked around. She crept as quietly as she could, ever closer. What was she planning to do? She had no idea. She had nothing with her; she'd left everything back at Newhaven. All she had was the element of surprise, her rifle and a very limited number of shells. What good could that be against an unknown number of armed attackers, holding her people at gunpoint. She once again silently cursed herself for her stupidity. She'd been so set on discovering the truth, she hadn't thought this through. She was so focused on the slow-moving column in front of her, it was far too late when she heard the rustle behind her.

She spun on her heel, hoping she could react fast enough to the threat stalking her. The hand grabbed her arm before she could strike and she stifled a scream, before her eyes widened in recognition.

"Martin!" she hissed; the surprise was clear in her voice.

He smiled at her. "Taking on the lot on your own, I suppose? Tom would have been proud."

She started to reply but was cut short by the emergence of Maria. Her face was bruised, and large black circles surrounded her eyes, but she smiled, that beautiful smile of hers.

"Maria," Kate exclaimed. "I am so pleased to see you. Are you okay?"

"I'm fine. Honestly, it wasn't that bad."

"How-" she started, before Maria cut her off.

"Not now," she pointed to the people, now tantalisingly close. "Let's deal with this mess, first. Then we can catch up."

Further sounds from the nearby grass indicated that more of them had arrived. She saw Michael, crouched low, with the rest of the Boneyard crew following close behind.

"Where's Benny?" Kate asked, looking around when she didn't see him.

"He got pretty badly beaten. He's at Newhaven. Chloe's stayed with him; she thinks he'll be okay."

"How did you find me?"

"Same way I guess you found them. I suspect it was easier in the light. And we had the horses. Don't worry, we left them a little way back when we saw you."

Kate smiled. Now they had a chance. That's all she could ask for.

CHAPTER SIXTEEN

Michael sighed. He watched Kate as she disappeared up the track. He didn't feel comfortable leaving her to head back to Newhaven alone, but someone had to. She'd be okay, she could take care of herself. He could see the pain on her face at leaving Maria, but she had a responsibility to her people. She had to go.

He'd received the call shortly after Tom died. Kate had asked for their help, and they were never going to say no. He'd gathered the best of his community and they immediately set off. There were closer camps they could have called. He was sure they'd also have helped, but none of them were as well trained, or equipped, as Boneyard. Their people also felt, all these years later, some form of reverence for Tom. They always had. It was the actions he and Bob took, thirty-five years ago, that gave birth to their home, at least the home they knew today.

He turned to face the building. Still ominously dark and silent. He raised his hand and gave the international sign for forward. Then, he crept towards the door. The others followed close behind, keeping low and hushed. They reached the large wooden door; Michael reached for the handle and depressed it. It was locked. He scowled to himself, then gestured for the others to head around the side. He pushed at the window; it opened ever so slightly as he pressed against the glass. With as much care as he could muster, he opened it enough to climb carefully through. His boots echoed dully as he stood on the wooden floor inside. He heard the others climbing in behind him.

They crept slowly between the rooms, checking every hiding space as they entered. The building appeared to be completely deserted. With every step they took, Michael felt the anxiety inside him rise. They'd been warned to expect heavy resistance, up to twenty well-armed people. Wherever they were, it wasn't here. Feeling confident they were alone; he took a small flashlight from his pocket and clicked it on.

The light shone against a dusty, derelict wall. Wooden panelling was rotting where it had lain untouched for years. The floor was bare, and few furnishings were present.

They reached the back of the building. A closed door sat disused in front of them. It was the last place they still to search. Michael opened the door and it swung on its hinges with no resistance.

A lifeless figure sprawled on the floor by the window.

"Benny!" Chloe exclaimed, running to his side and throwing herself to her knees. She moaned as she brushed his hair from his face and saw the mess below. He was hardly recognisable, bruising and deep red welts scarred into his skin. His lips were bloodied and swollen, as fresh blood dripped slowly from a graze across his forehead.

He let out a low moan but didn't try to move. Michael let out the breath he hadn't realised he was holding. He was alive. They could deal with the injuries, as unpleasant as it might be for him.

He mumbled something incoherently and Chloe moved her face closer to his.

A moment later, she looked up, her eyes were wide.

"They've got them. They've got Maria, Steve and the others."

"Where did they go?" Michael asked.

Chloe whispered something to Benny and a moment later replied. "He doesn't know. It wasn't long ago. He doesn't think they are far."

"Well, they didn't come out the front." Michael turned to the people behind him. "Come on, with me, there must be another way out of this place. We need to find it." They nodded in agreement and exited the room, leaving Chloe crooning over Benny alone.

The building was dark as they slowly crept along the walls, feeling for a way out. Michael's flashlight illuminated the dull wood immediately in front of him, sparing little illumination for the rest of the room.

"Got something," one of the Boneyard crew whispered. "Over here."

Michael turned to face the sound of the voice. His torchlight barely cut through the swirling shadows. Along the far wall, facing the perimeter of the building was a simple, metal door. It was inset into the brick and didn't look like any of the other doors furnishing the building.

"Must be a fire exit or something," Michael said absently, pushing it with his palm.

It gave and creaked open, revealing the night outside.

A track in the dirt gave credence to the thought that this exit went somewhere. Michael stepped out and looked carefully around. Too dark to see anything and his feeble torch barely up to the job, he frowned as he crept along the track.

Footprints could just be seen in the dust below. The recent rain had softened the ground, it seemed someone had used this recently.

The track led into the trees, thinner at the back of the building and directly to the large steel fence. A small door swung open from a gate inset into the fence, leading out to the forest behind them. It was just about wide enough for two men to pass through. If they hadn't been looking directly at it, they could have missed it.

"Damn," he said softly. "They could be anywhere. It looks like this could bypass the road entirely."

His eyes widened in horror. "It's them. They've gone to

Newhaven."

They returned to the building. Chloe still rested on her knees, with Benny's head nestled in her lap.

"He's awake and he's talking clearer," she whispered. "He doesn't know how long he's been out, but he doesn't think they've been gone long."

"How many of them?" Michael asked with urgency in this voice. "How many of them left?"

Benny groaned as he tried to speak. "Most of them left earlier. Maybe fifteen. The rest stayed, until they caught Maria and the others. They took her," he rasped. "They've taken her. I don't know where."

Michael looked around him. They now had two pressing matters to attend to, excluding getting Benny safely home and he didn't want to be the one who had to make the decision. He'd sent Kate back alone. She was running into a trap, outgunned and outmanned.

"Okay," he sighed eventually. "We'll try and go after the others. We'll need them when we get back to Newhaven. Benny, any idea at all where they went?"

Benny shook his head slowly.

Michael turned to the others. "With me, let's fan out, see if there's anything to give away which way they headed out back."

Within moments, Chloe was left alone in the dark, Benny's head still resting in her lap.

Outside the rear gate, the forest sprawled before them. The moss-covered ground was slippery with the recent downpour, with no sun to dry it. Michael knelt down; he could feel the moisture from the ground, cold on his leg. He shone the flashlight slowly around him, looking for any indentation in the soft earth around him. That many people, there should be a sign.

It didn't take long before he found it. Several sets of footprints, all headed in the same direction. He followed them into the clearing, until they split off in two distinctive directions. A larger group had headed north, which he assumed would bring them out somewhere near Newhaven. A small group of prints led in the opposite direction, circling the building and out to the meadows beyond. That was likely where their camp was located.

He gestured to the others and followed the track south, hoping they hadn't had a chance to get far. He moved as quietly as the terrain would allow, his people following close behind.

A crash through the branches ahead of them forced him to stop, he took cover behind the trunk of a nearby tree. He couldn't see anything, but the crashing footsteps, running, he thought, were getting ever closer. The noise was directly in front of them now. He swallowed the lump in his throat, readied his rifle and clicked on the small flashlight.

Swinging out into the open, his light illuminated a confused-looking face, gazing directly at him.

"Martin!" he exclaimed.

"What... Michael, how...?"

"Later. Where are the others?"

The clamouring sounds of people running answered the question for him.

"They're armed," Martin shouted. "Get to cover."

Maria appeared in the small glow of light next, her face flushed, blood trickled from her lip and a bruise was forming around her eye. The others soon followed, as they dived behind various trunks, seeking cover from whoever was chasing them.

"Ready," Michael called out to the rest of the armed defenders from Boneyard. As one, they stepped into the open, rifles drawn and aimed into the gloom.

The first man, his face obscured by the all-too-familiar mask, came skidding into the lights' glow, he was immediately cut down by the sound of a shot from a rifle in the dark. His momentum carried him as he fell, and he sprawled to an unmoving heap by Michael's feet. He took a moment to kick the gun from his grasp and heard it skid across the wet ground. He noticed someone out of the corner of his eye reach for it, a blur of movement he didn't have time to investigate.

Shouts halted the rest of the incoming attackers in their tracks, outside the reach of the light. A barrage of steady shots pinged off the nearby surfaces, embedding into trees as the ground rutted in front of them.

So, they've decided to go for the direct approach, Michael thought to himself, a rueful smile on his face. They'd have to reload, very soon. The sound of the shots obscured his movement as he flanked around them, moving quietly through the trees. He could make out the dark silhouettes, illuminated by the flash from the rifle muzzle. There were four shooters, that he could make out. He was close now, very close. He could smell the rank odour of unwashed bodies coming from them, he could hear their panicked whispers as they tried to organise themselves.

He could almost reach out and touch the closest one, just as his rifle clicked empty. The man reached for his pocket as the sound of another empty chamber clicked nearby. Michael pulled the machete from his belt and drove it into the man's back, pushing with all the force he could muster, aiming for his heart.

The man let out a weak scream, a gurgle and fell to the ground as the blade pierced through him. Michael hadn't been quick enough, the large blade still stuck out of his back. He reached for it but found too much resistance to cleanly retrieve it. The others had looked around; they had noticed him. He went for his rifle, fully loaded and shot several times in the direction of one of the men. Someone fell, grasping their side as they went down.

They'd all noticed him now and the tell-tale sounds of rounds being chambered told him he wouldn't have long left.

The first shot made him jump; he hadn't been expecting it, it came from further back in the treeline, the other side of them. Someone fell with a grunt, unmoving. The second shot ripped the bark off the tree next to the now reloaded attacker, Michael saw him duck sideways as he was showered with fragments of wood. His movement made him stumble and he put out his hand to break his fall, dropping his weapon as he did so.

Movement beside Michael caused him to look around; the fifth and last person was taking off at a run. They had been close to him; they probably could have killed him if the shot from the other side hadn't come when it did. The stumbling man regained his balance, another shot whizzed just over his head and unarmed, he took off into the darkness, too.

Maria emerged from the shadows, making to go after them. Michael held out a hand to stop her.

"No," he said firmly. "They've gone. We've got you back and we need to get back to Newhaven. Now."

She scowled but lowered her weapon.

Martin appeared from the clearing, looking around at the bodies on the floor.

"Nice job," he said brightly. "Thanks, Michael. Appreciate the assist."

Michael smiled. "Any time. Now, the rest of them, we think they went to Newhaven and there's no one there to defend it. Kate's headed back, but it might already be too late. Benny said the others left hours ago. We need to get back."

"Benny?" Maria asked, her eyes wide. "Is he alive? Just before they took us, I don't know why, but they beat him pretty badly."

"Just barely, but yeah, he's alive."

Relief flooded over her.

Someone coughed nearby. Michael shone his torch over the bodies. One of the men was still alive. The one he'd shot in the side. He sat with his back against the tree, his hand clamped over a wound. Blood seeped down his body, dripping quietly onto the floor. The mask covered his face, but his eyes were wild and full of fire, despite his injuries.

Martin walked to him and grabbed the mask, pulling it free to reveal his face.

He stood in thought for a moment, before realisation flooded him. "David?" He asked.

The man laughed, which quickly turned into a cough and blood dribbled down his chin.

"Hello, Martin," he said through gritted teeth. He'd gone pale, blood loss was claiming him.

Martin knelt in front of him. "Have the rest gone to Newhaven? Why?"

"It's too late," David replied quietly. "They'll be there by now. Your town is dead. It's ours now."

"I don't think you'll be around to see it, I'm afraid David. Looks like you're onto your last."

"That's okay," he replied. "At least I'll die knowing I achieved what I wanted for all these years. At least we've had our revenge. After you people abandoned us, left us to starve." His lips curled into a bloody snarl.

Martin looked at him. The way he remembered their last meeting was much different to the reality David was trying to portray.

He gestured to the two men who stood closely behind him.

"See if we can get him alive back to the building. There's still at least two of them out there and I don't want to be caught short."

The men nodded, then grabbed David under his arms and hoisted him to his feet. They were met with an audible scream as they did so. His feet dragged across the ground as they slowly limped him back up the track and inside the wooden building.

Martin took a moment to retrieve his machete, wiped the blood on the man's shirt and tucked it back into his belt.

"Chloe," Martin called through the open door. "We've got them, all of them."

"That's great," she called back, her voice drifting from the room they'd left her in.

"How's Benny?" he asked.

"He'll be okay. He's beat up, but I think he'll pull through. I'm worried about getting him home. The journey will be difficult for him."

"We've no choice. He can't stay here," Michael added. "We've got some horses; we'll get him on with one of our better riders and get him back that way."

She smiled up at him. "Thank you, but I'll do it myself."

"What happened to yours? We didn't see them on the way in."

She shrugged. "We took them into the trees some way, I suspect they'll still be there."

That was good, at least they should have enough transport for just about everyone to get back. Walking would have put them hours, if not days, behind.

She caught sight of David, being dragged through the hallway outside.

"Wait," she called, as the men did so.

David slowly opened his eyes to the sounds of her voice.

"You," she said, quietly. "I know you."

He tried to smile, but the edge of his mouth only rose slightly before falling back down his face.

"You did this?" She asked.

He nodded, a feeble movement.

His lips moved as he rasped. "I'm glad he's okay. I did like the boy. It was the only concession she'd give me. He wouldn't die. But she made it clear, he'd have to suffer, I thought at least he'd live."

"What?" she asked, confused.

"The boy," he rasped. "He was meant to die, with the rest of them. I had to beg her, I had to beg her to spare him," he manged a blood covered smile, then his head fell limp. The two people carrying him looked at each other, then moved him out of view.

"I don't think we'll be getting anything more out of him after all," Michael said nonchalantly.

"I doubt he'd have said much. Or that it would have been much use if he had. I'm pretty sure we know all we need to." Martin turned to Chloe. "We need to go. Get ready to move Benny. I'll fetch the horse here, but we need to get him out of this place.'"

Michael stopped him with an outstretched hand. "How did you get clear of them?"

"Easy," Martin smiled. "I think we were being led to our execution. It's amazing what you can do when your life is on the line. Most of them went off the other track. There was more of us than them. A few quick shoves, and we were home free. More or less. They really should have tied us up. That was an oversight on their part, I suspect."

Michael shook his head smiling, "amateurs," he said quietly.

Benny moaned quietly as they lifted him onto the horse. He'd almost screamed when they raised him from the wooden floor, Chloe suspected he had several badly bruised ribs, amongst other ailments, at the very least. He slumped over its neck, gasping short, shallow breaths.

"I'll ride with him," Chloe said.

Michael nodded to one of his men. "Make sure you stay with

them. Get them back to Newhaven. We'll need to take off, probably quicker, so hang behind. Come find us when you can."

The man returned his nod and mounted his horse. He moved into position next to Benny and reached for Chloe's arm, helping her straddle over the animal and slide into the saddle.

Martin returned with the rest of the horses. "Two got loose," he said. "We don't have enough, unless a few people fancy doubling up. I think that will be slower."

Michael thought about it for a moment.

"No," he said finally. "I've a better idea." He turned to the rest of his group. "You two," he pointed to a man and a woman, waiting patiently in the doorway to the building. "Head down that track, carefully." He reached into his pack and threw them a radio. "You see anything, let us know. We might already be too late, let's see if we can get eyes on the rest of them."

They nodded back to him and turned to enter the house.

"If you see anything, do not engage. Just keep us apprised of the situation. If we miss them at Newhaven, we need to know where they're going. Stay hidden and watch."

"Got it," the woman replied, smiling before she disappeared from view.

Chloe had already set off; the others were attaching their various supplies to the saddles of their horses and starting to mount them. He did the same, bringing his horse to the front of the group.

"Let's go." He said grimly.

CHAPTER SEVENTEEN

The sun was starting to rise when they finally arrived back at Newhaven. It was deserted. The gates were askew, eerie silence coming from within. The morning mist floated through the long grass, adding to the foreboding feeling rising up in Martin.

The journey had been uneventful; they'd seen nothing and met no one. Exactly what they'd expected.

Martin looked frantically around as they stepped through the threshold to enter Newhaven.

"No bodies," Michael said calmly, coming to stand next to him. "So likely no dead, yet. Keep calm, Martin. We'll find them."

Chloe walked in just behind them, Benny still draped motionless on the horse. He'd slept the entire journey, feeble moans escaping his mouth from time to time. She'd kept up with them without a problem. Benny was hurt, badly. He'd been beaten to within an inch of his life. He'd need time to recover. The journey strapped to the horse wouldn't have helped, but they'd had no other option. They had to get him home.

"I'll get him inside. I know you need to go and look for the others, but I'm sorry, I need to stay with him."

Martin nodded, "I understand. Get him safe and comfortable. We'll be back. Maria," he shouted over his shoulder. "You best stay, too. He'll want to see you when he wakes up and you don't look like you're in much condition yourself to follow us out there."

He expected an argument, a rebuttal as to why she should accompany them anyway, but it never came. Maria looked exhausted.

"We need to head out; we've got to try and catch up with the others, before it's too late." He turned to address the others. "No time for rest, not yet. One more push, then we can all get our heads down. You with me?"

Roars and cheers replied to him.

Several men helped hoist Benny off the horse and carefully walked him into the town hall, his arms draped over their shoulders, as his feet dragged across the ground. Maria slowly walked in behind them.

Martin looked to Michael and the two older men locked eyes for a moment. They both knew just how dangerous this could be. The entire population of the town had disappeared, nearly 2,000 people and there could be only one reason why.

A scream cut through the air, coming from within the town hall, followed by intelligible shouts. They ran towards the open door and burst inside.

Chloe was sheltering Benny in the corner, as the two men advanced on a figure standing in the next hallway, where the shrieking was coming from. They had their rifles raised, pointed towards the sound of the commotion.

"Stop!" Maria shouted suddenly, as all heads turned to look at her. She had a quizzical look on her face. Her head tilted slightly as recognition flooded into her eyes.

"It's you," she said quietly. The figure in the hall stopped screaming.

Martin squinted his eyes. It was an older woman, not someone he recognised. She was wearing simple jeans and a white t-shirt, her grey hair tied tightly to the back of her head. She looked as normal as any of the other inhabitants of Newhaven, but her eyes were wild. Her mouth hung open, revealing few teeth left in her gums.

Martin finally clicked, as Maria had done moments earlier.

"How...?" he started to ask, but Maria cut him off.

"Hi, Caroline," she said softly, speaking like she might to a scared animal. "I'm glad to see you're safe. You're looking better." She smiled, taking care not to show her teeth.

Caroline didn't respond; she just kept her eyes locked on Maria, watching her like a wild animal contemplating fight or flight might.

"Do you know where everyone went, what happened here?" She closed the distance between them and was now crouching low, trying to keep to the same level as the woman.

Caroline cocked her head and looked at Maria through squinted eyes. Recognition flowed through her and her mouth broke into a wide, toothless smile. She rushed forward and wrapped her arms around Maria, holding her tight as the two men moved to grab her.

"No," Maria said, holding her hands to the men to stop them. "It'll be fine. I promise."

"They... came..." Caroline whispered with effort into her ear; her voice still raspy from decades of never uttering a word.

"Who came?" Maria asked.

"They. The men."

With her head resting on Maria's shoulder, she could still barely hear the words coming out of her mouth.

"The men who took Benny?"

The woman nodded her head.

"I hid." She pointed to the store cupboard. "Here."

"Okay, that's okay. I'm just glad your safe. How many of them were there?"

"Many."

"Did anyone die when they came, did they shoot anyone?"

She nodded her head. "One shot," she whispered.

Maria turned her head to look at Martin. "Looks like they've been able to just walk in and take everyone. I guess if they had guns, there wasn't much anyone could do. Anyone who could really fight was out looking for us," she glared ruefully at the people around her.

"Did you see my mum? Did you see Kate?" she asked, turning back to Caroline.

Caroline looked at her blankly for a moment, then nodded and pointed into the distance.

"Down that way? They went that way?" She asked, following the woman's finger.

"The farm. To the forest beyond. That must be where they've gone," Martin said.

"Makes sense," Michael added. "We didn't see anyone on the main road. If they wanted to stay out of sight, that'd be the way to do it. The track out the back of the range, I think it leads directly here."

"But why was the main gate open?"

"Who's to say they didn't open it after they came into Newhaven? Or could they have circled around? Maybe they didn't know about your back gate. Not until they were already inside. It wouldn't be a stretch to think they came through the forest and around to the front. That's what they knew, after all."

"Maybe," Martin replied thoughtfully.

Caroline was whispering unintelligible sentences to Maria, who shook her head to show she had no idea when the men looked at her.

"Are you going to be alright with, er... her," Michael asked, pointing to Caroline.

"They will be," Maria replied. "I'm coming. Mums out there, I need to help find her. Chloe's here with Benny. She'll be fine. Caroline isn't a threat, she's just scared."

No one tried to stop her, as they turned and walked back onto the deserted streets of Newhaven.

Martin looked to the sky, fighting back the tears that threatened to spill. This was on him, all of it. They knew the dangers these people posed. He took everything, all the weaponry they had, all the people they could spare. He left Newhaven with nothing to defend themselves. He thought of Ava, was she okay? She was never one to take anything lying down. He had to hope she hadn't done anything stupid enough to get her killed. One shot. Caroline had said one shot was fired. Who at?

He shook his head to clear the darkness creeping over it. The people who attacked Newhaven, they were heavily armed. Their intentions were still unknown, but he doubted they would be good.

These people had planned this, they'd played them perfectly. Well, nearly perfectly. Where Newhaven spent the years creating a stable and peaceful society, these people had spent them arming themselves, creating a fighting force capable of overpowering anything Newhaven could use to defend against them.

Why hadn't he done more? He was in charge of security, after all. Why hadn't he led expeditions out into the broken world, collecting weapons, ammo, anything he could use to defend these people. He'd wasted their past, running around with bows. How did he not see this coming. It was only a matter of time until someone came along, some group with enough to do something like this.

The decision to develop Newhaven as they had was a group call, of course, but he couldn't help but bear the weight of responsibility on his shoulders alone in this moment. Tom had been against any earlier suggestions of raiding the old army camps. He had deemed the risk too high, they never knew what they might find. If they'd gone into those places, he'd rationally argued, they could bring the virus back with them. Worse still, if they were still populated, they may never have come out alive. He hadn't been prepared to risk it, and Martin had gone along with him, every step of the way.

Even years later, when it became clear the virus wasn't a major concern, they still never made the trips. Something about falling back into their past lives must have haunted them all.

These people had done it, whoever they were. They'd done everything Martin should have. He silently cursed himself. He turned to catch Michael staring at him, watching him from the entrance to the town hall, an unreadable expression across his face.

Martin looked to the ground, he couldn't meet the mans gaze. Boneyard and Newhaven had different outlooks on life, and protection. It appeared in this moment, Boneyard had been right. If he'd followed their advice, how many might still be with them? Would Tom still be alive, the others he'd lost? He felt the dread flowing through him. That feeling was becoming more and more common these days. He had a lot of regrets now he'd entered his later stages of life. They seemed to grow with every passing day.

They found the trail Kate had followed hours earlier easily. Her horse was in the stable, a sign she'd made it back safe, at least. Assuming everyone was on foot, they knew they could catch up soon, as they set out at a canter.

With the morning light illuminating the forest, they saw tracks every step they took. The undergrowth was trampled down. A lot of people had passed through here, and recently. Martin imagined Kate trying to follow this track in the dark and hoped she'd found the right path.

They were making good progress, covering the miles in short time. The horses snorted as they pushed them harder. Before they left, Martin and Michael had taken the packs and refilled them, ensuring each man and woman had food and water, along with a fresh supply of bullets from the store that Michael had brought from Boneyard.

They pushed deeper through the forest, eventually emerging on the other side, overlooking the long meadow sprawling out in front of them. Martin covered his eyes, as the change in light stunned him. It was bright without the dense cover of the trees canopy. He scanned the view in front of him. There was a clear track through the grass, leading over the hills and down into the valley. He pointed, but the others had already seen it. They paused momentarily to take on water, it had been a hard ride, and they knew that they couldn't be far behind now.

At the crest of the hill, they finally saw what they were looking for. A long column of people traversed over the landscape, stretching for a hundred meters, marching in a wide, organised line. They looked like ants in the distance, small black forms trudging slowly over the landscape.

They dismounted the horses, they'd have to leave them here, there was nothing to tether them to. With the grass, it was unlikely they'd go far, they would have to take the risk.

They crouched as low to the ground as they could manage and made their way to the slow-moving mass of people. They were still descending into the valley. The elevation of the ground gave them a good view of the people below them. Maria tapped Martin on the shoulder and pointed to another figure, one not with the main group. Someone was keeping low, like them and gaining on the group quickly. From their vantage, they could see the track being created by this figure, pushing low through the grass.

"Kate," Martin whispered. "It's got to be. Come on, if she's about to move, we need to be ready to help her."

They picked up their speed, keeping themselves concealed. They moved with military speed and precision, their boots hardly making a noise as they trod through the soft earth. Before long, he could see the sunlight shining off Kate's greying hair. He reached out to her, placing his hand silently on her arm as she spun, her eyes wide with fear.

CHAPTER EIGHTEEN

Kate graciously accepted the food and water that Martin handed her. Unlike her, they had thought to stop and stock up. They filled packs with water and fruits. They were also armed and had the radio. The situation suddenly didn't look nearly as bleak.

The column of people marched on in front of them. How far had they come? Kate didn't know. She'd walked, exhausted, for so long. They could be anywhere. A thick row of trees sat off to her left, the open meadow in front. The sea wasn't visible, so they had walked inland. She knew the direction thanks to the sun, but not the distance.

"Martin," She asked. "How far have we come?"

"We don't quite know, but we think it's about twelve miles out of Newhaven now. Maybe a little less. These people have walked a long way for a long time. Honestly, Kate, I'm surprised no one has dropped along the way. It's a young population, but there's still enough of us old ones left who this trip will do no favours to."

"Is everyone from town here?"

"Nearly."

She raised an eyebrow.

"That woman, Caroline. She hid in the storeroom. She's back there now with Benny and Chloe."

"I forgot all about her," Kate mused. "I should have checked. There could be others. I'm sorry. I just left. I didn't think."

"You had to find them; we all get that. Now, we need a plan, or people will die. We can't just go in shooting. That'll never work."

They took a moment to huddle together out of view, trying to figure out how to save all these people without getting them shot.

They split into two groups, each flanking the column, using the long grass as cover. As they drew closer, they could see the fear and desperation on their people's faces. They looked exhausted. Those lagging at the back were being pushed forward by the men with guns. Martin studied them; they didn't look much better. They'd also made the march and it looked to be taking its toll on them, too.

They were just feet behind them now, they could smell the sweat of the marching people wafting back towards them on the breeze. He heard the occasional stifled sob and the muttered words of people talking in low voices. He glanced to his right, where Michael crouched a short distance away, following the same tactic.

The column was being guarded by two men at the back, then one each side, every twenty meters or so. People were walking four or five abreast, whether by design or accidentally and it kept the column at a manageable size for the armed guards.

Martin silently pulled his trusty machete from his belt, gripping it tightly in his hand.

He could hear the man's footsteps as he crunched through the overgrowth. He was close enough to count the hairs on the back of his neck. He sucked in his breath, then in one fatal move, sprang to his feet and stabbed the blade of the machete into the man's back. He gripped the handle with both hands and twisted the blade inside him. The man fell without a word. He saw Michael out of the corner of his eye grab the other guard around the neck, then with a spray of red mist, he expertly slit his throat with a bowie knife. They grabbed at the fallen men's masks and quickly wrapped them around their own faces, moving in step to march with the column, taking their places as the rear guard.

The next guards were just up ahead, walking to the side of the column. This would be trickier, as there was no way of doing this without being seen. They just had to hope the residents of Newhaven would keep their composure. Martin watched as the grass swayed with movement creeping through it. He thought of a lion, stalking its prey. Not that he'd ever seen a lion, but he'd watched enough David Attenborough documentaries in the old days to know how they hunted.

Sweat beaded on his forehead as the grass swayed ever closer to the next guard. Whatever, whoever, was moving through it, was nearly upon him. Maria emerged from the grass. The armed man took a moment to look at her in surprise, before she brought the raised axe down in a narrow arch. With a sickening crunch, it settled into his head, and he dropped where he stood. A quick glance told him that the man on the other side had met a similar, although perhaps not as grisly, fate.

The people in the column immediately around the action recoiled in surprise and horror, their murmurs grew louder as they realised what had happened. Maria held a finger to her lip and walked in step next to them. Those in the rows behind began to look around them, a few looked back at Martin; he tried to avoid eye contact, the less they knew, the better. It was no use; their excitement kicked up into commotion. Several of the guards further up the column turned to look at the source of the noise. Martin fingered his rifle nervously. If they fired, the plan was over. They'd have no choice but to go in guns blazing and then some of their people would die.

They had expected a low success rate with this option, but it was the best they could think of. They knew the risk that people would die was high, but they were not prepared for what came next.

The men in front headed down the column, slowly closing the ground between themselves and the group. They realised something was wrong much sooner than it was hoped they would, and Martin had let off two shots before they had a chance to level their rifles. The noise sent the column into a panicked frenzy, people started running in every direction. The guards at the front, in a fit of confusion and fear, unloaded their rifles into the fleeing crowd. Martin watched in horror as people fell, cut down where they ran. Unarmed people were mercilessly shot in the back.

He felt the rage and anger build inside him. This all happened within seconds of the first shot, the shot he'd fired. He felt responsible for every lifeless body that hit the ground. He trained his sight on one of the people firing and pressed the trigger. He was an excellent shot, even after all these years of not firing a weapon. The man fell, spinning in slow motion in the air as the projectile ripped through him. A mist of red blood remained suspended in the air where he had stood.

As recognition spread between the guards that armed enemies were nearby, their attention moved from the crowd to scanning for the new threat. It didn't take them long to spot Martin and he threw himself to the ground to avoid the barrage of shots aimed in his direction. They'd had the element of surprise and managed to take out at least five of them before they started shooting. Another two had fallen from return fire and the rest were beginning to scatter.

Martin forced himself back to his feet, trying to make sense of the picture painted around him. Screams filled the air. Kate was shouting at people, trying to corral those behind her, but her voice barely penetrated the chaos of noise. Someone was screaming in pain, others in shock. He could see people running in all directions and he had no way to know who was friendly and who was foe.

He saw a figure running towards him, rifle aimed directly at him. He hadn't been ready, he tried to turn and raise his weapon, but deep down, he knew he'd be too late. Age had slowed him, and this would be his final moment. He felt calm wash over him. He'd had a good run and dying for his people wasn't a bad way to go. He prepared to meet his end, but it never came. Out of the grass, a figure sprang, almost catlike, enveloping the encroaching attacker, dragging them to the ground. He ran over to the scene, to be greeted by Ava, straddling the man, a knife plunged deep into his heart. She looked up at him and smiled.

"I knew you'd come," she said calmly.

The shots became more sporadic as people fell or ran. The scene around them was pure disorder. Structure and any hope of a plan had long gone. Ava took the weapon from the fallen man and ran off towards the sounds of gunfire. Martin raised his rifle and looked through the sight. He found a target but hesitated. There were too many people around; he couldn't be sure he wouldn't shoot a bystander in his haste.

He saw several people running into the distance, unsure if they were friend or foe. He felt helpless, there was nothing he could do. The plan had failed. They might have saved most of the town, but he had to assume they'd lost a lot and not stopped the attackers. A lot of them would get away, and then they'd be back.

The gunfire had stopped.

"Stop!" he shouted to the others around him. "They're retreating."

"Then let's go after them," Maria shot back fiercely. The cut of her lip had split open again as wet blood sprayed the air as she shouted.

"How?" he asked. "Can you see who's who? We go after them now and we'll just get more people killed. Let them go."

Maria hissed something under her breath, and he thought better of asking her to repeat it. He looked around to see Michael watching him thoughtfully. He raised his eyebrows at him, and the man simply nodded in reply.

"It was the right call," Michael said, as he and Martin checked another body lay in the blood-soaked grass for signs of life.

It didn't feel like it. They'd counted twenty-four dead so far. There were countless injuries, some that probably wouldn't survive. Others had been lucky and were nursing grazes or superficial wounds. They'd be okay. But getting them back to Newhaven was going to be difficult. Two of the Boneyard crew had been shot down in the ensuing firefight. Martin felt responsible for them all.

He merely shrugged in reply. They had almost finished collecting the bodies. They wouldn't be able to get them back to Newhaven, not yet. They'd moved them all to one location. They needed to identify who they had lost and who might have run off into the trees. They'd need to conduct a search soon to try and locate anyone still missing. They would also need to decide what to do about the camp in the south. It couldn't be far from here, but they had more important things to do now than chase them down. They needed to secure Newhaven and make sure the people there were safe. Michael had called Boneyard and requested additional people and weapons to be sent. Martin was grateful for that; he had a feeling they would need all the volunteers they could get.

"Martin?" Kate shouted. He looked up to see her staring towards the treeline. Three people walked towards them.

"'Friendly?" he asked.

"Looks like it. They're not rushing or trying to hide."

"Maybe someone who ran, coming back now."

"I don't think so, look," she pointed towards them. "Two are armed and it looks like the third isn't coming willingly."

Martin raised his rifle and Kate followed his lead. Michael placed his hand on the barrel and pushed it down.

"They're ours," he said softly.

As they walked closer, he recognised them as the man and woman who had followed the trail behind the building in the woods. The man between them was wearing a mask, he was one of the attackers from the camp.

"Michael," the woman said.

"Hey, Cindy. Good to see you. Been hunting?" he asked, watching the man being frog-marched between them.

She laughed. "Not quite. He ran right into us. We heard the gunfire; we were probably a mile away. We've followed the track, and it led here. This one," she jerked her head towards the masked man, "came running through the forest, basically tripped over us. It wasn't hard to figure out where he'd come from. Oh..." she added as she noticed the growing piles of bodies.

"Yeah," Michael replied carefully. "We had a few casualties, unfortunately. The rest of the town is safe, and the folk back home are sending some more bodies and guns our way."

Cindy didn't reply as her eyes glanced over the two dead men from Boneyard. Her face fell.

"I'm sorry, Cinds. They got caught up in the crossfire. I know you were friends."

She let out her breath. "We knew what we were volunteering for. What do you want us to do with him?" she asked, indicating the man looking nervously around.

"I think it's time for a little dignified chat, don't you?" He smiled. "Kate, Martin, come say hello to our new friend."

The man was walked away from the growing crowd, who were slowly starting to reorganise into a milling group, and taken to a nearby clearing, just inside the treeline. He didn't say a word as they ordered him about. He was sweating and his eyes were darting between them.

Martin tied his wrists with rope from the supplies Boneyard had brought with them, the man's hands had shaken uncontrollably as he did. Once they were out of sight of the others, Martin pushed him to the ground, and he fell to his knees with tears in his eyes. He reached forward and grabbed the mask from the man's face, removing it in one sharp tug. The face revealed below was not what he expected. A young man knelt before them. He couldn't have been any older than Benny. Just a kid, thought Martin. Tears were running freely down his face and his lip quivered.

"Who are you?" Kate asked.

He tried to reply, but the words seemed to get caught in his throat. Martin felt another pang of guilt. The kid in front of them was terrified. They were all victims, in their own way.

"You need to start talking, or things will get much worse for you. Do you understand?" She asked.

He nodded. "I'm just doing what I was told," he managed to stammer out.

"What were you told to do?"

"What we did. Exactly what we did. We were told to come to Newhaven, where there wasn't meant to be any guards left. They said it would be easy. We'd just round up the town and march them home."

"Why?" Kate asked.

"So we'd control Newhaven." He replied simply. "They said that if we had the people, then you wouldn't attack, you wouldn't dare."

"Why do you want Newhaven?"

"The vaccine, of course."

She hesitated. She hadn't expected that answer.

"What vaccine? What are you talking about?"

"For the virus. The vaccine they brought from that island."

She looked at Michael, whose face appeared nearly as confused as she felt.

"There is no vaccine," she said.

"There is! We know there is, and you're hoarding it." There was a touch of anger in his voice now.

"The virus has been gone for years. Probably longer than you've been alive. Why would we have a vaccine?"

"That's not true. We've had people die because of it recently. Whilst you people keep it all to yourself."

Kate shook her head in disbelief.

"So, you tried to kidnap the entire town to force us to hand over a make-believe vaccine for an extinct virus?"

He looked at her quizzically. The colour drained from her face. She knew in that moment he wasn't lying.

"Who was infected?" she asked quietly.

"A few people. They went to the city, looking for supplies. We have to travel far to scavenge now. They came back and within a few days, they were dead. We burned their bodies, of course. But another got sick soon after. Then another. We need the vaccine, before we all die."

"Listen to me. There is no vaccine. There never has been. Whatever they've told you, is just bullshit."

"There has to be," he whispered, looking down to the ground.

"Where were you planning to take all these people? You wouldn't have taken them to your camp if you thought the infection might be there, surely?"

"No," he replied. "We were heading back to the range. The plan was to lock them in there, the grounds, at least, then trade them for the vaccine. It was the only way. Bev already told us you'd turned them away."

"Is that right?" Kate mused. "Did she tell you why they were turned away? They tried to take Newhaven before. Many years ago, now. They killed people. Good people. They failed and were banished for good. We haven't seen them since. We didn't even know she and David was still alive, until we saw them at the rifle range yesterday."

He looked surprised but didn't reply.

"How many people are in your camp?"

"A few hundred. Maybe more now. I don't know."

Her eyebrows once again rose up her face. The camp was much bigger than she remembered it being.

"What about weapons?"

"Plenty. There's an old army encampment in the forest. It had a full arsenal. We've used them for hunting for years now. Bev found them. She found them shortly after you people threw her out, it's how she took control of the camp. She proved she can provide for us."

"How are you people surviving?"

"Barely," he spat back. "We've lost dozens to the sickness now. We've no food, the water is contaminated. We are dying."

She shook her head; this was getting nowhere. She looked at Michael.

"You want to take this one?"

She moved aside as he took her place.

"I'm Michael. I run Boneyard, or that island, as you know it. We do not have a vaccine. We have never had a vaccine. They were testing, many years ago, but it failed. It always failed. There is nothing these people, or us, can do to help you. If what you're saying is true. We are all in a world of trouble."

The man looked at him without replying.

"I promise you, son," he continued. "There's nothing we have that can help your people. Are you sure it was the virus? You said your water is contaminated. Could it be something else?"

The man furrowed his brow. "No, they said it was. It is." He declared confidently.

"You've never seen it. How can you be sure?"

"Bev said it was. It doesn't matter, now. It's sure to have spread here. You'll have no choice soon."

They kept him talking for a while longer. He didn't have any real information they could use. He hadn't been born when the second wave of the virus swept over the world. The deaths he was describing could be anything, especially if they lived in squalid conditions. He was too young to know for sure. He'd never seen the virus.

They were not going to shoot him; he was just a kid. They'd take him back to Newhaven; they had no other choice.

The others had organised the townspeople. The injured were given the horses, either alone or riding in tandem with someone if they were too injured to do it themselves. The doctor was also put on a horse, she'd be needed back at the town as soon as the casualties arrived.

The rest resumed their positions within the column and began the slow trek back to Newhaven.

CHAPTER NINETEEN

Newhaven was a hive of activity. The people had returned and were busy at work to put the town back together. They'd been taken far too easily and vowed it would never happen again. The rifles that had been brought by Michael and those they had recovered from the dead attackers, were added to the arsenal.

The attack had been quick. The armed men and women had shown up in the dead of night. With no weapons to defend themselves, the people of Newhaven had been left with little choice but to surrender and go with them.

One of the guards had been shot, a young man, Paul. He'd been working with Martin for a few months. He was a good kid; Martin had been sad to learn of his death, one more he added to his sense of responsibility.

He shouldn't have taken everyone he did with him. Would they have had any better luck defending Newhaven if Steve had stayed, or Vincent? He felt another pang of guilt. He'd gotten Vincent killed too. Not directly, perhaps, but every death was on his head. He should have gone alone. That's how they would have done it in the old days. He'd have quietly snuck up and found some way to rescue Benny. That's what he should have done. Pauls body had been left where he fell on top of the barricade. They hadn't noticed him when they got back to Newhaven. Ava had recovered it when they returned and it now lay with the others, awaiting burial. The cenotaph would have many new names by the next morning.

He sat in silence for a while longer, letting the people rush around him. He listened to their frenzied movements, thinking about all the people he'd lost.

Ava slid in beside him, gently placing her hand on his shoulder.

"This isn't on you," she said, almost as if she were reading his mind.

He looked at her and smiled.

"I should have left you more. I should have left more weapons, more people. I shouldn't have taken them all. I should have seen that this was a trap." His face fell with every revelation.

"It was me who told everyone to give up. After they shot Paul, I knew we had no chance. But I knew you'd come for us. If it wasn't for you, how many people here would be dead already?" she spread her hands out around her, forming a half-circle to the townspeople. "Never forget what you've done for them, Martin. What you've done for us."

He closed his eyes. She always made him feel better. She was right, but he couldn't shake this feeling growing inside of him. He sighed. They'd need to get on. This wasn't over.

Once Paul had been killed and the people of Newhaven had been forcibly roused from their beds, it was Ava who had stepped forward. With nothing but regret, she surrendered the town to these people. She'd hoped they'd just try and take over, keeping everyone locked in their homes until they could work out a plan to escape, or until the others returned. She'd been bemused when they lined the inhabitants up in the town square and marched them out into the wilderness. It was a few miles before she realised, they were in big trouble.

She had hidden the blade in her belt, covering it from view, as she tried to stay out of the attention of the attackers. She was prepared to die for this place and would do everything she could to ensure their safety. Once the others had caught up, she hadn't needed to, but she took the first opportunity to help after the shooting started. She'd killed two of them, the guard closest to her; she slit his throat when he turned to look at the commotion, and the man aiming for Martin. She'd seen that unfold from some distance away and sprinted to make up the ground, before launching herself into him, ending his life.

A fire was lit in the centre of the town, near the kitchen tent. The people were exhausted and hungry. The first thing they had to do was to get them fed and rested. The attackers hadn't caused too much damage. They hadn't looted the stores or burned the buildings; they just walked in and calmly walked out when they had them under control. Ava truly believed this wasn't about what they had, or at least what they had on display.

The smell of roasting meat soon filled the air. The aroma was tantalisingly delicious, Martin felt himself salivate. It had been so long since any of them had eaten. What were they cooking? It smelled like deer. Someone must have gone hunting on their arrival. He hadn't even considered feeding people. With Tom gone, a lot of the responsibility for Newhaven would fall to him and he knew he wasn't ready for it. Kate would remain the figurehead, of course, but even in his ailing state, Tom had still made the vast majority of decisions on the day-to-day running of the place. Things would change, they'd have to. He wondered if it might be better for the younger generation to take over. He and the others were getting old. They were getting slow. Most of Newhaven was younger and would have more in common with their peers. The town might be safer with them in charge. He thought of Benny and Maria. They could do it, if they had to. There were plenty of suitors and perhaps soon, one of them should be given a chance.

"Come on," Ava said softly, ripping him from his dark thoughts. "Lot's to be done, best to get to it. Michaels waiting for you in the town hall."

He stood, and they walked together to the middle of the town, carefully avoiding the rushing people. Michael was talking to Kate. They appeared to be having a hushed conversation in the corner. Martin moved to join them.

"We need to end this," Kate said. "We need to take the fight to them. We know where their camp is, and we know how many of them there are."

"We also know how many guns they have," Michael interrupted. "You don't have enough. Even with our help, there isn't enough. You'll just get more people killed."

"If we don't, more will die. You heard them. They're desperate and they think we have some magic vaccine. Or more to the point," she looked Michael in the eyes. "They think you do. How long until they come for you?"

"They won't get near Boneyard. It's not somewhere you can sneak up on like this."

"Tom and Bob did," Martin added.

"Thirty-five years ago. Things have changed."

Martin took a deep breath. Kate was hot-headed, she always had been. He agreed with her, but they needed Michael's help to do it, they couldn't alienate him here and lose that valuable support. Michael had always been loyal to Tom. He was friendly with the others and Martin didn't want to risk losing him now. He would have to play it safe.

"I'm in agreement with Kate. They aren't going to stop. Michael, I'm asking you for your help. I'm asking you to stay. I know you've got some additional people on the way. With your guys, we can do this. I promise, it'll be a sensible, thought-out move. We won't do anything rash. We can't do this without you, you know that."

Michael studied him for a moment.

"We'll discuss it," he said eventually. "When the others arrive, we'll have a talk and see what we're prepared to do. Rescuing Benny was one thing, but I can't ask my men to go and fight for you. That's something they'll need to be willing to do on their own."

Martin nodded and smiled. "I cannot ask you for anything more than that, Michael, thank you."

Michael grunted and left the building, leaving Kate and Martin together in the corner.

"We'll do this, with or without them," Kate said, glaring at him.

"I know."

After a moment of silence, which stretched into uncomfortable territory, Martin asked, "what do you want to do about Tom?"

The casket lay on the floor where they had left him.

"We can't leave him here. We need to bury him, soon." Kate said, fighting back the fresh swell of tears.

"We'll do it this afternoon. Once everyone has had a chance to get themselves sorted and rested, we'll take him out to the coast. He liked it there. He can rest overlooking the sea."

She looked up at him and nodded, her eyes twinkling with the tears pooling inside them.

They tried to sleep during the rest of the morning, dozing in the sun. Everyone was back and the last few who had run off into the forest had now been rounded up. Michael was still in Newhaven. He and his men wanted to stay, at least for the ceremony to lay Tom to rest.

The dead from the raid were dealt with first. They were left in the meadow where they had fallen, holes were dug, and the bodies were laid to rest inside. It wasn't plausible to get them all back to Newhaven for the ceremony. The names were read off as they were added to the ever-growing list on the Cenotaph. Tom's name was added last.

A moment of silence engulfed the town. The wind could be heard rustling through the grass, as the birds called in the distance.

Solitary steps followed. Kate, Martin, Michael and Maria emerged from the town hall, carrying the wicker coffin that Tom had been placed into, walking in perfect step. Benny hobbled behind them; his face set in struggle as he fought his wounds to move as silently as he could. Without a word, they headed for the still open main gate. The people of Newhaven followed close behind in absolute silence.

Several of the arrivals from Boneyard stayed behind, manning the barricades and keeping an eye on the young man they'd captured in the forest. They didn't want to leave the town completely deserted, not after all that had happened.

The walk was slow, but with the sun still high in the sky, they arrived at the coastline. The lookout point sat in front of them.

Kate nodded to Maria. She looked around her before pointing to a spot atop a raised hill nearby.

"It's perfect," Kate whispered.

Several men walked forward with shovels in hand and started excavating the ground where she'd pointed.

In the silence, the sounds of their shovels and grunts echoed over the rolling hills.

Soon, the hole was deep enough for the coffin to be lowered inside. Not quite six feet, but enough that they were happy nothing would try to dig him up.

Martin and Michael picked up the coffin, one at each end, and walked it to the hole, laying it on the earth around it, with long, thick straps underneath, before silently stepping back.

Kate cleared her throat. As loud as she could manage, due to the amount of people gathered, she said, almost at a shout, "we lost a good man recently, as you all know. You all knew Tom, on one level, or another. He's responsible for everything we have. He's responsible for everything we've built since we've been here. I loved him, and he loved me. But he loved each and every one of you, too. He spent his life caring for you, keeping you safe. He died trying to do exactly that. It's no secret Tom wasn't the same at the end. He tried to keep it from you all, but there was something going wrong with him. We didn't have the facility to properly diagnose or treat it. It's widely thought it was the start of dementia. Something we need to accept and live with in this world. I think a part of him wanted to go on that rescue mission, knowing the risk, hoping he wouldn't come back. He wouldn't have wanted any of you to see him like that. He was far too brave and proud for that. He'll be happy, knowing he died doing what he loved, for the people he loved..." she paused as the tears flowed down her face.

Blowing her nose, she tried to continue, but her voice broke and came out only as a croak. She dropped her head and looked at the ground. Martin placed his hand on her shoulder and smiled.

"I've got it from here, you're good," he whispered.

He turned to address the crowd, his voice commanding and loud in the silence.

"There's not much left to say. Kate covered most of it. Tom was a good man. Not just the people here, but many people owe their lives to him," he nodded to Michael, who returned the gesture. "Now let's give him the send-off you know he would have liked."

The crowd cheered, chanting his name. Birds took flight from the trees at the sudden sound.

As the crowd kept cheering, Martin, Michael, Kate, Ava, Maria and Steve walked to the coffin, picking up a strap each. They positioned themselves over the hole and gradually lowered it into the ground until they heard the dull thud of it hitting the soft earth below.

Kate picked up a handful of dirt from the mound next to her.

"Rest well," she said quietly, before throwing it into the hole and moving aside. Maria did the same, then the others. The people of Newhaven flocked forward, each of them taking their turn to repeat the action, until the mound was depleted, and the hole was filled.

The waves crashed into the rocks below as the silence stretched ever on.

Without a word, Martin turned his back to the cliffs behind them and started to walk back towards Newhaven. The others followed.

Michael stopped him with an outstretched hand and a frown.

"This is where we part, for now," he said, with a grave expression on his face. "The guys at Newhaven, they've agreed to stay and help you in whatever you decide to do next. We'll leave the weapons and the ammo. You should have enough firepower if you choose to go after them."

"Thanks, Michael. You're a good man," Martin smiled back.

"Be warned, Martin. It's not going to be as easy as you think. If you do this, you'll be adding more names to that statue of yours. Be sure of that."

"If we don't, the list will be longer."

"Perhaps. Please, be careful. I've lost too many of you recently. You're old friends, all of you. When all is said and done. I don't want to lose another. Be safe and look after them." He held out his hand. Martin took it and they exchanged a brief shake before parting to their separate ways without another word.

Kate positioned herself next to him and walked in step. She cast him a sideways glance.

"What was that about?"

"Michaels going. He's going home."

"He said."

"The guys at Newhaven, they're staying. He's left us his weapons and ammo. He's given us everything we need, if we want to go ahead and do this."

"I think we need to, don't you?"

He paused mid-step and she had to take a half step back to stay in line with him. He gazed off into the distance, not looking at anything in particular. She watched his face closely, as the muscles in his jaw twitched. He had something to say, but didn't want to let it out. She knew him well enough to pick up on his ticks after all these years.

"It's okay. Go ahead. What's on your mind?"

"It's just that... Michael was quite cautious. He really doesn't think we should go after the camp. He thinks we should leave them be. I get that, I really do. But I fear we'll just give them time to lick their wounds and come after us again."

"Even with the extra guns, could we hold them off?"

"Maybe," he sighed. "But give them time, they might find a way in, some plan or trick, which will just let them roll over us. We've been in such an age of peace for so long, I don't know whether we remember how to fight anymore. A lot of the people here," he gestured to those walking around them. "They've never been in a fight in their life. There's a chance we could get them killed, whatever we do. Do you think we have the skills to successfully attack this camp? Do we have the people, the training? We've got the guns, sure, but do we have enough people to use them?"

Kate pursed her lips, he had more to say, and she'd stay silent until he felt ready to let it out.

"And...," he said slowly. "I'm concerned. I'm worried about what those people were saying. The virus being back. Do you think it's true?"

"I don't know. I hope not."

"If it is, they're the least of our issues. If it's true, the virus will wipe them out, soon enough. Attacking could mean we bring it back here. We could inadvertently bring around another wave of horror here. Honestly, Kate, I don't know what to do. Each way I look at it, it seems bleak."

She nodded in thought. "I know what you mean. But here's the thing, I don't think it's back. I think something killed people in their camp, but I don't think it's the virus. I think it's just something they couldn't diagnose, and they've panicked. The problem with panic is that it spreads. It makes people irrational. It makes people dangerous. If they believe it, they are sure to come for us."

"We always thought it might be back. You remember what the folk from the government told Tom and Bob, over at Boneyard? We always wondered if it might be true. Why not now?"

"I just think we'd have seen it, or heard about it, before now. "

"It's not like we've got the internet or news channels anymore. We'd never know until it's staring us in the face."

"We still see travellers now and again. Someone would have heard something. Someone would have said something."

"What about Bev?"

"Nah, she's just vengeful. I wouldn't be surprised if she spread the virus story to gear everyone up to attack. She knows better than that. I don't know what disturbed narrative she's managed to thread through her head over the last however many years, but it doesn't paint us in a good light, that's for sure."

A sense of understanding settled between them. The short and concise conversation had been all they needed.

"So," Martin said. "We're doing it?"

"Yeah, we're doing it."

They turned and followed the flock of people back to Newhaven, fading into the crowd.

CHAPTER TWENTY

The night had descended into party. Officially, a wake, but even in this new world, that meant the same thing. The beer and wine flowed, brewed right here in Newhaven, of course. The night fell as people danced in the light of the fire. Reminiscing about those they had lost, they shared stories of days gone by. Percussion instruments, mostly homemade, could be heard reverberating around the barrier, which protected the town from the wilderness.

The entire town had turned out, young and old, for this celebration. After the events they'd been through, they needed a way to blow off some steam. This was for each and every one of them, as much as those they had lost. Only a select few stood guard, watching the darkness, keeping the revellers safe. Unusually, they sported rifles, the first time anyone on those walls had done so in well over a decade. They cast glances to the people enjoying the festivities below them, but kept their attention focused solely on the still grounds outside Newhaven.

Someone shrieked in inebriated glee below them, and they clutched their weapons wearily.

Maria slid into the bench next to Benny. He was nursing a beer, wincing every time he moved his lips to drink. He'd moved away from the bulk of people around the fire, not feeling like being around them. He hurt; he had taken a beating and was still healing. The day had taken yet more of an emotional toll on him. He just wanted peace and quiet.

He smiled at her, then winced in pain. "Sorry, how are you

doing?"

"I'm good," she replied.

"Seriously," he pushed. "You've been through a lot, and you've lost your dad. I am sorry about that, Maria, I really am."

"Seriously, I'm okay. I promise."

"It's okay not to be," he said, softly. "With all of this, no one would blame you for not being."

She looked around at the people dancing in the distance, the yells of alcohol fuelled joy cutting through the night air.

"I know this is a wake for everyone who died, including my dad. But listen, this is what he'd have wanted. I didn't know about the dementia thing. They kept that from me. That must have cut him up inside. He'd have loved this, knowing we were all having a good time. Toasting his memory!" she raised her glass into the air.

Benny did the same, as his ribs cried out in pain at the sudden movement. The glasses were not traditional pint glasses, of course. They had been blown in Newhaven. They were not a uniformed size, nor clear. The opaque finish hid the liquid sloshing inside, although they provided the same result as a clear, factory-finished glass of old.

The town had plenty of craftsmen, now. People had learned how to do the basics from scratch. Glass blowing, blacksmiths, brewery. These were all tasks that had required a skilled hand in the years after modern technology had left them. The world had reverted hundreds of years and people, for the most part, were much happier that way. Money was no longer a thing. People worked because they wanted to. They wanted to better themselves and their community.

Benny and Maria knew no different. This had been the way all their lives, like most of the younger inhabitants of Newhaven.

"He'd have loved this," Maria repeated absently. "A party. The way to go. None of this sadness and people moping. Just get drunk and enjoy the night."

"Yeah, I'm sure he would," Benny replied with a smile. "I'm sorry, Maria. I really am. I'm sorry for what happened to him. It's no way to go."

She looked at him fondly. "Isn't it?" she asked. "He wouldn't have known much about it, I don't suppose. It's that, or a slow slide into illness. I think it's a pretty decent way to go."

"Huh," Benny replied. "I'm not sure I'd agree with that." He'd heard the stories of Tom's death; it didn't sound that decent to him.

"He never told me either, you know," she continued. "I had no idea he was ill. I mean, I could see something changing, but assumed it's just because he was getting old. I didn't know his mind was actually going. He hid that well."

"I suppose he was always going to. I've never known your dad to show any weakness. I guess why would he start now."

"That's right," she slurred. "Why not." She frowned at him, pouting her bottom lip comically. "This is sad. Let's not be sad. Let's celebrate his life, not mourn his loss!" She raised the glass once more and swirled it around her head, dripping the contents on the floor around her.

"You might want to calm down. Much more of that and you won't end up remembering much of this night," Benny laughed.

She giggled. "I've been wanting to ask you, Benny. What did dad do? Why do those people hate him so much?"

"Honestly, I'm not sure. From what I've gathered, he didn't really do too much. They were here, a long time ago. I think I sort of remember that one man, David. I'm not really sure, we would only have been little. It sounds like they attacked Newhaven, tried to take it over and lost. Tom and the others threw them out, banished them, effectively. Then conditions in their camp got worse and worse, to the point where a lot of them died. Some disease or another. Some of the guards who held me think that broke Bev. Made her a little bit crazy."

Maria laughed. "A little bit?" she squeaked through the

laughter. "That's obvious."

"Yeah. Maybe. I understand that she and your dad were okay. You know, they got on, at least. It was someone else, whoever ran the camp at the time who kicked it all off. I think Bev understood at first. But as more died, she began to resent Newhaven and Tom, in particular. Eventually, it just all built up inside her. What is it, nearly twenty years of thought? I think she's got a bit obsessed. Not even the others seem to fully understand it. They're just doing what she tells them. Some of them were around when it all happened. I heard them talking. Even they don't know where she's truly got this narrative from."

"That's silly," Maria said with a frown. "They'll all get themselves killed, over nothing."

"Yeah, well, that's people, I suppose." He sighed.

"They should all just have a drink, get merry, like me. Then we'd all be friends. But they might want to take it easy, or they'll all get drunk."

She giggled again, then smiled at him, that big, toothy grin of hers that he loved so much. He gazed into her eyes, his stomach was in knots; he could feel the metaphorical butterflies, fed by the poor imitation of alcohol, bursting free. She gazed back at him, her eyes widened, the colour drained from her face, as she leaned over the bench to throw up on the floor.

He laughed as he reached for her hair, pulling it away from her face.

"Maybe it's too late for that."

She giggled, quickly cut off by a hiccup. He downed the rest of his glass. No use being the only sober one in town. The music droned on in the background, the whoops and hollers of people floating on the breeze. Benny and Maria sat there in silence. She hiccupped from time to time, and he smiled to himself, stroking her hair as she rested her head on his chest.

His glass was empty, but he had no desire to move to refill it. He had everything he wanted right here. He heard

Maria's breathing slow, before quiet snores emanated from her. Something smashed in the distance, followed by a scream, then laughter. The town had truly put the horror of the past twenty-four hours behind them and were determined to make the most of this night.

He looked around, Maria resting her head against his chest. He loved his town. He loved these people. Any thoughts of leaving were extinguished right there and then.

He'd had the desire to leave for some time now, but in this moment, he knew this was exactly where he needed to be. Exactly where he wanted to be. These were his people, and he loved them like they loved him. He'd never leave here. He needed these people, and they needed him. He could see that now. They'd rescued him from Bev and the others, he owed them his life.

"Come on," he said softly, raising Maria to her feet. "Let's get you to your bed."

She grunted as he led her slowly across the grass towards her home.

The music had stopped, and the large fire was now burning itself out. It was the early hours of the morning, by best estimates. Martin watched the darkness from the vantage of the barrier. Not a big drinker, he'd volunteered to take the watch, while his men and women joined the party.

He was tired, but there would be no relief tonight. They were mourning, not just for Tom, but for many of their own. Paul, Vincent. They'd both been killed in the last few days. By these people. The people in the camp down south. He'd long since decided that Kate was right. They needed to go. He'd let the others sleep their night off. Then they would set off. They'd find the camp and end those responsible for the bloodshed.

If they didn't, they'd be back. Of that, he was sure. He yawned into his sleeve. There'd be a long time until he could rest, and it was lonely out here alone. He sat, contemplating the events of the last few days. He tried to piece it together in his head, but the pieces wouldn't fall into place. Where had Bev and this camp, even come from? He hadn't cast them so much as a thought for so many years. He'd never have looked for this threat from them. So much time had passed, how did they keep a grudge for so long?

A lot had been learnt these last few days. They hadn't seen Bev since the day she was forced to leave. He tried to piece the years together. They'd returned back to their camp and things had got bad. He understood Bev had managed to claim power, but he didn't understand how. She was a nice girl, but he'd never honestly seen her as the leader. He would have thought David would have taken that mantle. The boy they'd caught in the forest had told them about the early days, the best he knew, at least. Bev had found the weapons, the ammo. She'd proven her worth by providing for the town. She'd changed over the years. The hardship had made her into a new person. A worse person, but a stronger person. People followed strong people. That was something he'd learned the hard way, back when he was still enlisted, before the end finally caught up with them.

He watched the sky. It was a clear night; the stars were visible. Their beauty with the omission of light pollution was one of the things he enjoyed most about the end of the world. Sure, almost all humanity had died out, but it wasn't all bad. He chuckled at his poor joke, then abruptly paused as the voice rang out behind him.

"Something funny up here?" He turned to look at the speaker of the familiar voice. Ava stood there, coffee steaming from a mug in her hands.

"Hey," he said, his voice barely audible over the beating of his heart. "Gave me a scare there."

She smiled. "Didn't want to disturb you, but I thought you might want this." She handed him the cup, which he gladly accepted.

He sipped the warm liquid. They called it coffee, but it wasn't really recognisable to the drink he'd had in his younger days. There had been some unsuccessful attempts made over the years to grow coffee and what they'd ended up with had been a concoction of something he'd never been able to identify. He was sure it was actually a mixture of tea leaves and various roots or bark to flavour. He'd never really understood how it was made; he just drank the stuff. Still, it was better than nothing.

"What's running through that mind of yours?" she asked, dragging him from his wonderings.

"Just thinking about how we deal with this camp. Michael thinks we should leave them be. Kate thinks we should go in guns blazing. I think, if push came to shove, I'd side with Kate. And I think if we're going to do it, we need to do it soon. I just can't shake this virus talk. If it's real, we're in a world of trouble if we head that way."

Ava shrugged, barely noticeable in the dark. "If we don't go, we're still in a world of trouble. If it is, then it'll get us, one way or another. Might as well deal with the camp. Only one thing to worry about then."

She was right, of course. The first and second wave hadn't even been slowed by segregation. It always found a way through, and once it infected someone, it spread like wildfire. They sat in silence for a while longer. Martin finally broke it.

"Are you with us? If we go, will you be with us?"

"Yeah," she replied. "I was here when they came; I saw how easily they just took us. Something needs to be done. I'm with you."

They sat in silence and let the noises of the night wash over them.

"Go on," she said, after a while. "I'll cover. I got some shuteye before coming out here. Go get a few hours. It might be a big day tomorrow."

He smiled. "Nah, I'm good. I'm exactly where I want to be."

She looked at him with her head askew. "What's in it for you, Martin? What's this all about?"

"Keeping everyone safe. Like we always have."

"No, it's more than that. Something's going on with you. You've always protected these people. I think you're out for vengeance. I think you're out for Bev."

He didn't reply.

"I wouldn't blame you. It feels like she's behind all of this. I know David's dead. She seems to have taken the mantle. I remember that day, clearly. You did nothing wrong, none of us did. She's created this story. I think you want to put an end to it. Do you blame her for Tom's death?"

He mused on her words. "I suppose I do. If they hadn't taken Benny, we never would have gone after him and maybe Tom would still be with us."

"Hmmm," she replied. "Maybe."

They sat in silence for some time, listening to the cracking of the dwindling fire in the square behind them. He let his mind wonder again. It went back to happier times. He was younger and Newhaven was still in its infancy. They were the days he missed the most. He'd been busy, sweaty and dirty at the end of every day, but he knew he was making a difference. He was helping to build a future. The future that he could see now. He was sure in that moment they'd made the right decision. There was no way he could let this all fall apart. Not after so many had put so much into it.

"You know what, I think I will take you up on that offer. I could do with closing my eyes for a little while."

She smiled and Matin walked down the sloped plank leading

from the top of the barrier. The coffee sat cold where he had left it.

CHAPTER TWENTY-ONE

Kate looked around the small group, assembled in the early morning light. Some of them looked worse for wear. Perhaps the alcohol last night hadn't been a great idea after all. She felt her head. She's also overdone it slightly, she supposed. She could feel the beads of sweat settling on her forehead, even in the low heat of the morning sun.

Around her stood eleven others. Martin and Ava, two of the younger guards from Newhaven and the seven people who had stayed from Boneyard. She'd only spoken to a few of them and hadn't yet picked up their names. She made a mental note to ensure she knew them before they reached the camp. It was the least she could do, considering the risk they were taking for her and Newhaven.

Maria had wanted to come with them, of course, but Kate had rejected her offer. She was in no state to do this and Kate couldn't bear to see her in harm's way again. Not after all she'd already been through.

"Alright, guys," she said. "Thank you all for volunteering for this. We could have taken more, there was no shortage of people willing to undertake this with us, but I think we've got the best of the best and everyone we need. The plan is simple. We need to remove the ability of that place to ever do to us what they did again. They don't know we're coming and that's how I want to keep it for as long as possible. We'll try stealth for as long as we can." She saw Ava absently tap the machete strapped on her hip out of the corner of her eye.

"We're on the horses for as far as we can, then, like usual, we walk the rest of the way. I had a good talk with our guest last night, the boy we brought back from the attack. He's lost a lot of his bravado and spilled fairly easily where they are. The rifle range building isn't far. He says it's a few miles further down the road. We can travel either way, down the road, or through the forest. It makes no real difference at this point. I'm voting for the forest. In case they try another sneak attack, we've more chance of coming across them there. We've left enough people and weapons, here to defend this time if they do, but we have to be prepared. Everyone happy with that?"

One by one, the group of people around her nodded back. Stoic looks etched across their faces.

"Happy days," she said quietly. "Let's go."

They travelled light, each person carrying just a small pack, containing a small amount of food, left over from the festivities the night before and a bottle of water. They had rifles slung across their shoulders and machetes or long knives tucked into their belts. Martin had a bow slung over his other shoulder and a quiver of arrows strapped to his saddle.

They mounted the horses and set off, disappearing into the thick undergrowth and out of sight.

They trudged along in silence, the hoofbeats rustling on the fallen leaves. Beams of sunlight cut through the canopy, creating a mosaic of light through the trees as they pushed their way through onto the overgrown path leading deeper into the forest and headed south.

The silence was palpable as they slowly traversed the ground towards their target. Ever vigilant, they expected an attack from behind each tree, but it never came. The trees remained quiet. Before too long, the track widened, and the rutted ground indicated it was used much more frequently than the rest they had travelled on.

Hoof prints littered the ground, resting in the dry dust. They stopped still and listened. Nothing reached their ears other than the sounds of the birds in the trees and the crickets' chirping around their feet.

Kate held up a hand to the others, her fist balled in the air. Slowly, she unravelled her fingers and pointed down the track.

Martin watched her closely, taking in how old she looked in that moment. He was sure he didn't look much better, but it was telling. All of those who had survived the first wave of the virus, then the second, were an aging generation. Most of the population, probably of the planet now, as diminished as it may be, wouldn't remember that.

They wouldn't remember the terror, the horror, the death the outbreak brought with it. Soon, it would be just them left. He hoped they'd make a better go of it, second time around. He was sure some of the old-world benefits would return. These kids were smart, pretty soon, they'd figure out how to get the electricity back, how to get computers working again. Hell, maybe they'd even have the internet back, one day. He frowned. He almost hoped not. The last thirty-five years had been some of the best of his life, free from the confines, the shackles of what modern life had been for them before everything changed.

He shook his head to clear it. They had a job to do, and he needed to stay focused.

The track narrowed and soon they came to a split, one track leading to the range they had been held captive, the other descending deeper into the forest. The took the path south and rode on.

"Here," Kate whispered, bringing her horse to a halt a short while later. "We walk from here on in."

The others nodded as they dismounted and tied up the animals.

Soon, they were creeping through the trees. They didn't know exactly where the camp was, only that it must be close. They listened for any noise, sight, or sign of any form to tell them they were nearby.

Someone whistled. Martin looked around; it was one of the men from Boneyard. Sam, he'd introduced himself as. He was pointing down the track, towards something in the distance the others couldn't see. They made their way to his position and crouched next to him, looking towards the compound he pointed at.

It was a shanty town, at best. A mishmash of tents, canvas structures that looked like tarpaulin hung over nothing more than tree branches, dotted with a few small, wooden structures. The ground was muddy and wet, even after the recent dry weather. The camp was a few hundred feet in front of them. From this distance, they could just make out several men sitting around a smouldering fire. They looked to be armed, but not alert. Their rifles were propped against the same log they sat on. Their heads were dropped, and they each appeared to be lost in their own thoughts.

"Not what I expected," whispered Martin to no one in particular.

"How have we never found this before?" Kate asked.

"We've had no reason to," Martin replied. "We don't tend to go this far out, not this way. There's nothing down here."

"It's a bit odd," Kate replied. She turned her attention back to the men. "I suppose they could just have had a tough day. They might not have much left?"

"It's not like it's the middle of the night. There should be more of them. There should be people all around here. You remember how many people the kid told us lived here? Where are they all?"

Kate thought for a moment. He was right; something felt off about the situation before them. She remembered something the prisoner had said, didn't they move from their original camp? Was this just the remnants of their prior home?

"Let's move up. Carefully," she whispered back.

Martin nodded and edged further forward, with the others following closely behind. They crept closer and the men did not look up. He heard Ava pull her machete next to him, the blade scraping off her belt and the soft sound of boots crunching off the fallen foliage below them.

He held up his hand, indicating they should halt. They were close to emerging from the cover of the treeline. He scanned the scene around him. The camp looked deserted and for a moment he worried they might have gone to attack Newhaven again and they'd missed their approach. He soon calmed, remembering that they'd left weapons and more guards his time. Any attack on Newhaven now would not go well for potential invaders.

The men by the fire were close enough now that he could clearly see their faces as they slouched around. They were not asleep, yet not quite awake. Resting in the heat from the embers. They were dirty, unkempt. He wondered if they had access to showers or simple sanitation here. He knew several of them had died; they were blaming the virus, but looking around him, he wondered how they could be sure. The place was a cesspit. Disease must be rife and rampant.

Had they really lived like this for all these years? Had they resided in this squalor for most of their adult lives? He had a sudden flashback to Bev, young and fresh-faced when she first arrived at Newhaven. It made him sad to think of her aging in a place like this, in these conditions. She hadn't been a bad sort. It was the others who started the problems. She just got caught up in it. He couldn't dwell on that now. She was clearly in charge here and out for revenge. A lot had changed since that first meeting, for both of them.

The men sat around the fire, there was three of them, he could clearly see now, facing in their direction. If they looked up, they'd be staring directly at them. He looked down the scope of his rifle. It would be so easy to take them out, but that would alert the entire camp to their presence. Despite its abandoned feel, he couldn't be sure there wasn't more of them around. He played with the string on the bow. He'd never be able to end the three of them quick enough. He mulled over the best action to take. Their options were pretty limited, from the angle they'd be entering the camp. They couldn't sneak up on these men, and any silent attack would be too slow, one of them would raise the alarm. The rifles would certainly raise it.

He was still running through various situations in his head when Ava tapped his shoulder, jerking her head to the side to move him out of the way. He looked at her quizzically but did as she asked. She silently handed her pack and rifle to him. She reached to the ground and collected a handful of dirt, smearing it across her face. She ruffled her hair until it fell in messy clumps around her face. She smiled, placed the machete behind her back, then walked into the clearing.

"Help me," she sobbed, somewhat theatrically, playing the role of dazed and panic-driven damsel wonderfully.

The men glanced at each other, clearly surprised by her sudden appearance. They didn't make for their weapons; they stood and walked towards her; arms outstretched as if to catch her if she fell. As soon as they were within range, in one majestic motion, she withdrew the machete from behind her back and swung it deep into the neck of the closest man. They all halted, mesmerised by the arc of blood spraying from the wound. Her machete penetrated about a third of the flesh on his neck, before coming to a halt against bone.

Without thinking, Martin raised his bow and let fly the arrow perched within it. The shot was perfect, resting with a sickening thud in the chest of one of the other men. Ava tugged the machete free, before turning to face the last and hacking it down hard into his left shoulder. He screamed. The sound cut through the clearing, before it was abruptly cut off by the thud of another arrow settling into the man's neck. Martin had pierced through his windpipe, and he fell to the ground, blood pooling around him in the dust and dirt.

The other crept forwards, rifles aimed all around them, waiting to see if anyone would respond to the scream. After several long moments of silence and no hordes of angry people streaming at them across the camp, they relaxed slightly.

Searching the camp around them, it appeared deserted. The tents and canvas structures were empty. A few rusty pots sat discarded within some, but the smell of damp, must and mould seemed to indicate that this was not the home of the group they were after. After several more moments searching the debris, they collected themselves back by the fire, the bodies of the dead still bleeding around them.

"What the fuck is going on?" Martin asked. "There's no one here. There hasn't been anyone here for some time."

Kate shrugged. "Maybe they moved on. This place is a shithole. It stands to reason. They can't be far, though, surely? That boy, he did say they'd had to abandon their original camp. I think this was it."

"Why were they here?" Martin asked, kicking one of the bodies with his boot.

"Not sure. Lookout, maybe? Or perhaps they were nothing to do with the camp. Maybe they were just passing through."

"No," Ava added. "The way those men acted when they saw me. If they were just passing through, they'd never have believed that. They're nearby. I'm sure of it. I'd bet these guys were lookouts. They probably should have been in positions somewhere, but were taking a break, didn't expect to see anyone."

"Could be," Kate said. "That does make a lot of sense. This place doesn't look fit to live in. If they're close, then I guess it's a fair bet that someone would need to pass through here."

She knelt down and began to search the pockets of the dead men.

"Here you go," she said after a moment of rustling, revealing a bright orange flare gun. "I'd bet this was to warn the camp if they saw anything. They must not have any other way to communicate.

They formed a tight circle, staring at the flare gun in Kate's hand. Such a strange relic, that bright, toylike plastic in the shape of a gun. It's not what any of them had expected to see.

"Well. That's one way to do it," Ava said after a brief pause. "Whatever works for them."

"It gives me an idea," Martin said. "I didn't say a good one, but an idea, none the less." The others looked at him, the same thought slowly forming in their minds.

They took a moment to form their plan. It was simple, basic, but plausible. They were going to hide and let off the flare. They'd wait for the people of this camp to come to them. The abandoned camp was perfect for a guerrilla fight. They could spread out, take up position across the clearing and take down anyone who entered the kill zone.

They took some time to set simple traps. They hid the bodies of the three men they had killed and tried to kick away the drying blood into the dead leaves, scattering the ground. They'd had to use what they could find, as they brought nothing with them. They removed the rope from the hanging tarpaulin, lashing it tightly around the base of the trees, creating a simple trip line at the main exit and entry points into the clearing.

They would use the trees for cover, wait until those from the camp arrived, presumably from the track leading off the other end of the clearing, that's what they hoped, at least.

Once they had laid their preparations as best they could, Kate took the orange pistol and fired it into the air. The gun released a stream of sparks and smoke, as the projectile flew high into the bright sky, then exploded with a distant boom; a cloud of smoke erupted high above their heads and settled onto the air.

They retreated into the shadows and waited. They didn't

know how long it might take. It could be moments; it could be hours. It would depend entirely on how far this place was. The flare had caused a quick relocation of the nearby wildlife, the birds had taken to the sky, squawking angrily as they flew, leaving an eerie silence in the normally vibrant forest around them.

Kate could hear her heart beating in her chest as she tried to control her breathing. After what felt like a lifetime, footsteps could be heard crashing through the forest, coming from the track off the clearing, just as they had predicted.

Several men and women, all heavily armed, appeared in the light before them, looking cautiously around. They glanced at the fire, the embers still glowing between the rocks and said something quietly between themselves that Kate could not hear.

"Get ready," Martin whispered into her ear.

More people arrived from the opposite side. There were over a dozen of them. They looked just like the three men they had earlier killed; dirt stained their skin, and they dressed in a similar way, old, simple clothes pulled across their emancipated bodies. Their eyes were full of anger, though, burning with the same hatred she'd seen when she caught up with them after their first attack on Newhaven.

Another noise took her attention, someone had fallen over the trip wire at this end of the clearing, she panicked, she hadn't seen anyone come this way. They were about to be discovered and they hadn't fired a shot. They were outnumbered and out gunned. She spun to look at the rope, two figures were tangled on the floor, trying to regain their balance. Shouts could be heard from the group now just meters away, rifles were cocked, the familiar clicks cut through the din. They were pointed at the figures on the floor. Kate's mouth dropped open in horror. It was Benny and Maria.

CHAPTER TWENTY-TWO

Kate watched in horror as the men and women converged on the fallen forms of Benny and Maria. They were shouting incoherently, weapons pointed towards the ground. Maria acted first, dropping her rifle and raising her arms out in front of her as she tried to scoot to sit upright. Benny was struggling. Kate could see he was still hurt and in no fit state to have made the trek. They must have left soon after the main group.

He stopped struggling and followed Maria's lead, the armed people from the camp seemed to relax slightly as they searched the trees nearby and found nothing. One of them was examining the rope that had tripped the pair. Soon, they'd put two and two together and figure out it hadn't been Benny and Maria who had laid the trap. They had to act; they needed to do something, and they needed to do it soon.

Several weapons were still pointed towards the pair, an all-out attack now would likely lead to their deaths, something Kate could not risk, or even comprehend. She looked towards the others, she could just make them out, knowing where they had hidden. She saw the fear on their faces echoing her own. The plan was in ruins. She frantically glanced around, looking for any way out of this. She had two options, best she could see it. Let them take Benny and Maria and hope they didn't just kill them. Or she could do something really stupid and pray the others would pick up on her train of thought. She decided on the latter option. After the events with this group recently, she couldn't risk that they would keep the pair alive. She hoisted the rifle onto her back and stepped out from behind the large tree trunk she was crouched behind as quietly as she could manage, standing with her arms in the air.

"Hey!" she shouted. Several people turned to look in her direction, shock spreading on their faces. She kept her eyes trained on Benny and saw the recognition wash over his face as he noticed her. That look turned to dread as he realised what she was doing. The weapons that had been trained on them were now being lifted to aim for her. At least four rifle barrels were now aimed towards her; she watched them shake as the holders struggled to keep their hands still. The second she was happy none of those barrels were still pointing at Benny or Maria, she dived to her left, narrowly being missed by the first shot that headed her way.

She heard the return fire from the people of Newhaven almost instantly. A man was screaming; a quick glance showed he'd been hit in the thigh. He'd dropped his rifle and was clutching at his leg with both hands, rocking back and forth where he sat. The scream ceased as Maria dived forward, plunging a knife into his chest.

Others had retreated to the trees and tents on the far side of the dilapidated camp, shooting haphazardly from behind whatever cover they had been able to obtain. They shouted incoherently between them, trying to muster some form of organisation, albeit unsuccessfully. They didn't take the time to aim down their sights, rather just fired at seemingly random targets they could not see.

Kate was struck by how unprofessional this group appeared. She'd expected a well-armed, well-trained, militia. So far, this had not been it. She aimed down her sight, focusing on a man in the crosshairs and pulled the trigger. The man fell and slumped onto his side, dead. She turned her attention a few meters to her left, a woman was crouched behind one of the tarpaulin tents, her silhouette visible through the thin fabric. She aimed for the centre of it and depressed the trigger again, the shadow dropped and did not move again.

She saw the others methodically shooting, too. The people from the camp were falling at such a rate that she was now struggling to find targets. Two of the men from Boneyard emerged from their hiding place, walking in tandem, letting off shots at sporadic intervals as more of the people fell.

A man ran out from behind a tree, a war cry coming from his mouth as he lunged towards them. He wasn't even aiming, his rifle held horizontally in his arms, almost as if he intended to use it as a club. He made just two more steps, before a bullet stopped him in his tracks and he skidded to the ground, coming to a halt on his side, the rifle still clutched in his hands. Kate shook her head, *what a waste*, she thought of all the people that had been butchered these last few days. With the population of the planet as low as it was, they needed to work together, not start up yet another territorial war that had already fractured what little was left of civilisation.

They'd pushed them back to the track from which they had appeared a short time earlier. She saw Ava out of the corner of her eye, hacking at a man with her machete, his screams cut mercifully short as her blade sliced through his flesh. Those left turned their backs on the group and ran. Further shots dragged two of them to the ground as they tried to make their escape, as a further two disappeared from view, down the muddy trail.

"Check them," Martin called, as people walked between the fallen, checking for signs of life. They reported back within moments; they were all dead. Twelve of them in total, plus the two had escaped. Fourteen people had responded to the flare. The two who had escaped would be a problem, they'd be sure to tell the others. The element of surprise was over.

Kate ran to Maria. She was stood next to Benny, who had

pushed himself against a tree, resting his back against it as he sat on the floor. Her eyes scanned the scene around them.

"What are you doing here?" she hissed.

"We wanted to help. We thought you could do with the backup."

"You silly girl," she cried, as she drew her into a hug, pulling her close to her as she winced. "What would I have done if they'd killed you?"

She shrugged in reply. Her face was still swollen and bruised. Benny looked worse than ever sat in the dirt by their feet. How they had made it all this way, she would never know.

"Had to do something," she mumbled. "You were gone by the time we woke up. Could have at least said goodbye."

"You'd have wanted to come, if I did."

"I wanted to come, anyway. Got to feel for Benny, though. He's not doing so well."

"Does Chloe know he's here?"

Maria wouldn't meet her gaze.

Knowing they could soon have the entire camp to contend with, they needed to move, and quickly. The arrival of the group from the camp had made it obvious which way they needed to head. They stood at the edge of the clearing, looking down the path, which snaked around the trees and soon could no longer be seen.

"Down there?" Kate asked.

"No," Martin replied. "If they come that way, we'll run right into them." He pointed to the trees. "Through there."

She nodded and followed him into the dense foliage, the others keeping close behind. They crept carefully through the overgrowth, listening for the telltale signs of approaching boots. Keeping close enough to the track, they advanced towards what they assumed would be the big battle. The first real battle any of them would have experienced in a very, very long time.

As they drew further into the forest, the first sounds hit them. Softly, at first, whispers on the wind. Growing ever louder, they could now hear the strained voices, shouts and commands being exchanged. People were close, and by the sounds of it, they were preparing for war.

"Damn," Martin whispered. "There goes any hope of a quiet attack."

He crept to the edge of the tree line as his eyes widened at the sight in front of him. The abandoned camp they had passed through was nothing in comparison. This camp kept the same basic structure, that same mishmash of tents, tarpaulin and wooden structures, but the scale was much larger. The camp, from the outside at least, was huge. It sprawled as far as he could see. There was no barrier; nothing to keep the outside world at bay, the tents pushed up to the trees provided the only form of perimeter.

People ran this way and that, most of them armed. There didn't seem to be any discernible order to their actions, despite the larger man standing in the middle of the camp, shouting orders at groups of runners.

He turned back to the others and wordlessly mouthed for them to press further into the trees, flanking around the camp, a head-on attack here wouldn't go well for them.

They pressed into the branches, coming to a halt against the edge of a large, long tent, pushed right up to the tree line. Martin held his ear against the thin fabric, no sound greeted him from inside. He carefully removed his machete and sliced a long line down the exterior, before pushing the loose fabric aside with his hand to reveal the empty interior. The heat was stifling, the sun having been on the canvas all morning, beads of sweat began to form on his forehead as soon as he stepped foot inside. The zipper on the far end of the tent was firmly closed. A small pile of blankets lay messily in one corner and a rickety table was pushed up against the other. The smell was intoxicating, the musty, mouldy smell of damp and dust assaulted his nostrils. He stifled a cough, spluttering as quietly as he could into his sleeve. He pulled the bottle of water from his pack and took a quick gulp. The others, seeing him drink, took the opportunity to do the same.

Maria was standing by the zipper at the other end of the tent. She had her face pressed against it. Frowning, she whispered, "I can't see what's on the other side. We could leave here, right into the middle of them. What's the plan?"

"Wait till dark?" Kate suggested.

Martin shook his head. "What if they go after Newhaven again and we're caught here hiding in this tent?" he pointed to the blankets. "Looks like someone is living here; we need to be long gone before they get home. I think they might notice the giant slash in their home." He glanced around him. "Here," he said finally, pointing to the far wall of the tent. The machete still clutched in his hand, he cut a further rough slash down the far end of the tent. The sunlight streamed in, dust dancing in the light. He pushed his head through the gap. "It's clear," he whispered, before stepping through, back into the outside.

One by one, the others followed him through, hugging to the outside of the tent as best they could in an attempt to keep themselves concealed. The noises of movement were still loud all around them, but this part of the camp seemed to be empty. Martin slowly crept to the corner of the tent and peered his head around, looking in the direction of the majority of the commotion.

"This'll work," he said quietly, pointing the glinting blade of his machete to the next row of tents. A small, dusty alley between them was shaded and empty. No one was looking this way, the attention of the people in the camp appeared to be on the main entrance, converging on that small dusty track. Martin waited for his opportunity, then ran the distance between their current hiding place and the alley across. The others followed, pushing themselves into the cover of the tents once they had crossed the path between them.

Martin led forward, the noise was growing ever quieter and distant. He inched around the corner of the next tent, and came face to face with a man walking the other direction. The shock of the situation caused them both to freeze as they silently stared at each other. The man was not armed; he was older than even Martin, his wrinkled face not showing fear, but confusion. The recognition slowly dawned over him, as he opened his mouth to shout.

Martin rabbit-punched him in the jaw and he collapsed to the floor before any sound other than a slight whimper could leave his mouth.

"That was close," Ava whispered, coming to a halt at his shoulder.

"Yeah," he hissed back. "Need to take more care. This place is a maze." He rounded the corner where the man had appeared, taking more care as he slowly placed each foot in front of the other. They were deep into the camp, now. The sounds of shouting were distant. The place was huge. Larger even than it had looked when they glanced down the perimeter.

The camp must have been large enough to house thousands of people, but many of the tents appeared uninhabited, their canvas sides rotting and the poles rusting away where they sat. It was sparsely populated here. Only once or twice did they have to hide around the corner of a tent while a person rushed past. They'd traversed where Martin approximated was the middle of the camp. The floor was a slurry of mud and rubbish. Despite the shining sun, the tree canopy overhead kept the ground cool and prevented it from fully drying with the quantity and weight of footprints that appeared to have trampled over it each day.

"This should do," Martin whispered. "We'll work our way

back up and try to take them out from behind."

"Can we?" Kate asked. "There's a lot more of them than we thought. There's fourteen of us. They're all armed. I'm starting to doubt this plan."

"Too late to go back now," he said. "We'll have to do what we can." He turned to Benny. "Lad, you're not going to like this, but you need to leave. You're in no fit state to fight, and if we fall, someone needs to be able to let Newhaven know." He reached for his pack and produced a radio. "Sneak back out, the way we've come in and call them. Let them know what's happening and to prepare for an attack if we don't come back."

"No way," Benny stuttered, his voice still raspy. "I'm staying."

"No," Kate hissed firmly. "You're not. He's right and you know it. Maria, go with him. Get out of here. It's the only way we can make sure Newhaven doesn't get taken by surprise."

"You can call them right now. There's no need for us to go to do that," Benny complained.

"Not if they have anything to communicate with," Martin replied. "We don't know if they can listen in. We can't risk it. Please, just go." He and Benny locked eyes for a moment, before the younger man finally looked away, his gaze falling to the floor.

"Fine," he said quietly.

Martin turned to look at Maria, black bags around her eyes. She nodded, although she made no expression with her face. Without another word, the two of them turned and crept back the way they'd come.

"We shouldn't have let them come this far," Kate whispered to Martin.

"No," he agreed. "I didn't think there would be this many of them here."

"You think this will work?"

"Nah."

"It's been a good run."

He smiled at her. A sad smile, given away by his eyes.

At the end of the tent they were hidden behind, the track opened up into a wider road. It looked well-trodden, although it was still deserted at the moment. He got the impression it was one of the main walkways through this place. From here, he could see up the tree lines they'd first entered this place from. People were still running up and down the path, weapons in their hands. He tried to count them, but there were just too many, moving too much.

"I'd say there's at least forty of them, all armed," he sighed.

Kate looked behind her. "Where's the rest?" She asked.

"The rest what?"

"The rest of the people. Why is this place so empty?"

He frowned as he thought about what she'd asked.

"I don't know. We've killed quite a few of them, recently. Maybe this is all they have left. Let's deal with one problem at a time. Attack from behind, we might be able to get a good half of them before they even know we're here. They're running around like headless chickens. You never know. Our training might get the better of them."

"Just these people, for this entire camp?"

"Maybe you're right but worrying about that isn't going to help us now. Let's just deal with what's in front of us."

She didn't look convinced, but she smiled back at him regardless. The others had been silent throughout almost the entire journey. She turned to face them.

"This isn't looking good. If anyone wants to leave, I understand. You're free to go, go back to Newhaven and prepare the defences. They'll be nothing held against you."

She looked at each of them, meeting their eyes one at a time. No one moved. One of the men from Boneyard, she still hadn't learned his name, put out his balled fist, then extended his thumb upwards, giving her a broad smile.

"Alright then," she said. "Let's do this."

CHAPTER TWENTY-THREE

Benny winced as he crouched in one of the many dusty alleys. He and Maria had returned the way they had come and met no one on the return trip. They stepped over the unconscious man, still flat out on the floor where Martin had punched him down.

Benny glanced at his face as he passed, he was older; his hair was thinning and his face gaunt. His clothes were old, frayed and had many small holes. His face was streaked with dried dirt, where his mouth lay agape and his rotten, blackened teeth were visible.

He shook his head in disgust and continued to creep through the camp. They arrived at the last tent, the one they had cut their way through when they first entered from the treeline. He could see from here that the action had been slightly pointless, as there was no barrier or fence. They could have just walked around it. He shrugged to himself; it didn't really matter.

He glanced down the length of the canvas and stopped dead as his blood ran cold – a man stood just meters away, his back to them, a rifle strapped over his shoulder, looking carefully down the row of tents.

Benny pushed back into the shadows, extending his arm to stop Maria in her tracks. She raised an eyebrow at him, and he pointed to the man before bringing his finger to his lips. She nodded in acknowledgment and pressed into the tent next to him. The man milled around for a short while longer. He didn't seem to be looking for anything in particular, but just stood in the way. Benny ran the options through his head; could they kill this man to get him out of their way? He didn't see how. A shot would certainly alert others, and the machete in his belt wouldn't be much good, due to the distance to the man; he wouldn't get anywhere near him without being seen.

Maria tapped him on the shoulder. He turned to look at her. She held a rock in her hands. Not a large one, roughly the size of her palm. She launched it over the tent, putting as much force into the throw as she could; they heard the small thud as it hit something a few rows over. Benny glanced at the man, who still had his back to them, looking towards the sound of the noise.

He silently gestured to Maria as they crept across the clearing, hiding themselves out of view around the tent, before the man turned around to face where they had stood, apparently not overly interested in the source of the noise. Benny felt his heart beating rapidly in his chest as they moved from the tent and entered the thick undergrowth of the forest stretching out before them. With every clumsy step he took, he heard leaves and twigs cracking under his boots. Every rustle of leaves reverberated through the silence, sounding to Benny like it was magnified to a deafening volume. He was sure they'd be heard in their escape and expected the throngs of men to come crashing through the trees at any moment.

Trying to move as slowly as he could muster, he headed in the opposite direction to where they entered. Knowing the people of the camp were congregating around that area, they'd decided to try and loop around, using the thicker forest as cover, until they could rejoin the main track further up where they hoped they wouldn't be spotted.

The trees thinned and Benny came to a halt, studying the ground around him.

"What's up?" Maria asked, quietly.

"Look," he said, pointing to the barren ground. "This has seen some heavy movement; it's bare." He followed the trampled earth with his eyes, which led to the far end of the camp, away from where they had planned to head.

"Should we check it out?" Maria asked.

"Yeah, I think we need to," he replied.

They headed cautiously along the track and trampled ground. It flanked the camp, leading around to the far end. They came to the edge of the treeline and halted, the scene in front of them causing them to falter.

The trees ended abruptly, the valley below falling away as far as the eye could see. It was full of people, hundreds of them. They were toiling in what looked to be crude fields. They looked a bit like the fields Bob had lovingly cultivated back in Newhaven, but rushed and attempted by an uneducated hand. Some form of crop was clearly growing, but there was none of the straight, tended rows they were used to. The clumps of growth were uneven and saturated by weeds.

The ground looked exhausted, nothing more than clumps of dried mud and rock, with little growth for the area being tended. Benny had worked with Bob for a few years, and although he wouldn't consider himself an agricultural expert in any way, even he could see that this setup was terrible.

The men and women working in the field looked downtrodden. There was none of the smiling, laughing, or joking that he's become accustomed to on Bob's fields, where the chore had been lively and fun. People trudged here, heads down, with homemade implements in their hands.

Looking around the area, he noticed several people standing on the periphery of the ploughed area, he didn't want to call it a field, as it clearly was not that well defined, holding weapons. Were they guards?

The thought ran through his mind that all of these people,

perhaps everyone in the camp, could be prisoners.

As if sensing his thought, Maria asked, "what do you think is going on here?"

"I'm not sure this place is as voluntary as we thought. I think there's a group of them, those with the weapons and everyone else is just here to work. It'd explain the squalid conditions back there."

"So, what do we do?"

"First thing, we need to call home. We need to let them know what's happening. Then we'll decide what to do about this."

Maria nodded and reached for the radio in her pack. She clicked it on and held the button down.

"Newhaven," she whispered. "Please come in."

After a moment of static, a tinny voice replied.

"Maria? Is that you?"

"Steve!" she exclaimed. "I expected Chloe. Glad to hear from you."

"Chloe left earlier. I tried to stop her, but she was having none of it. She's gone out looking for you pair. You didn't tell her where you were going. Where are you?" his voice cracked through the radio.

"I know, we'll apologise to her later. We're at the camp. The others have gone inside, there's a lot of them. If it all goes wrong, they want you to be ready. They wanted you to know what we're up against.

A pause followed.

"How many?"

"At least forty, all armed, maybe more. They're here now, but if Martin, mum and the others don't get this right, they could be headed for you."

"Understood."

"Listen, there's more."

She repeated what they could see to Martin.

After another moment's pause, he replied. "I don't think you should go into this, Maria. Not just you and Benny. It's not safe."

"We've got to do something; we can't just leave them like this. There's only four or five guards here, we'll be okay."

"Listen, I'm not saying I disagree with you. I'm just not sure it's the right time."

"Will there be a better one? With this camp guarding against Martin and the others, I don't think we'll see any reinforcements sent here. If we leave it, then we may never get them free."

He didn't reply for a long moment. "Listen, Maria, as I said, I'm not saying I don't agree with you, but your mum will kill me if anything happens to you, and I didn't at least try."

"I understand. I'll make sure she knows you tried."

"Wait, Chloe is probably headed your way. She went out a few hours ago. It's not a stretch to guess where you guys headed. She's got a radio. I'll have to let her know."

"That's fine, try and get her to come home. You might need her there more than we do here."

He laughed.

"That will go well, I'm sure. Best of luck, kid."

"You too, old man."

She clicked the radio off and looked at Benny. "You ready for this?"

"Yeah," he smiled, which quickly turned to a grimace as his face ached.

They crept quietly down the hill, heading to the valley below. Keeping as low as they could manage, machetes drawn. The guards were not paying much attention. It appeared that this was routine, and they guessed that nothing much tended to happen out here, usually.

They reached the first man, standing at the periphery of the ploughed area, his rifle leaning against a tree stump, smoking a cigarette and staring out into the distance.

Benny briefly wondered where he had obtained a cigarette from. They couldn't have been manufactured in over thirty-five years. He wondered if they had managed to grow tobacco, and if so, how much of a waste that must have been.

The smoke wafted over them, the sickly-sweet aroma sticking in their throats. Maria raised her machete, its sharp blade glinting in the sun. With a single, fast movement, she plunged the blade through the back of the man's neck. There was a sickening squelch as the blade dug through flesh, as dark red blood ran down the back of his neck, soaking his stained shirt red. He fell to his knees, gurgling, before rolling over sideways, dead. The cigarette still smoked on the floor where it had rolled from his grasp. Maria grimaced as she pulled the blade free from the man's neck. A small spray of blood erupted from the slash it left, which quickly subsided to a trickle, running down his neck and pooling on the floor.

Benny gave her an impressed smile as she wiped the blood from the blade on the back of the man's shirt. She pointed further up. The next man was just visible in the distance. He was looking away, paying as little attention as the first. They edged forward, Benny taking the lead this time. He approached the man from behind and just like Maria had done, he raised his blade to the man's neck and thrust forwards. He missed. The machete bit into the man's neck, before bouncing sideways, meeting nothing but air. The man grabbed at the wound, as he let out a low moan. He spun; one hand still clasped to the cut. His eyes widened as he saw Benny and Maria behind him. He reached for his rifle as his mouth opened to shout.

Maria lunged forward and forced her own machete into his stomach; he instinctively reached for the blade piercing him, the start of a shout turning into a gurgle. Benny drew his arm back and slashed at the man's throat. The sickening thud as the blade bit into him over and over cut through the air. Arcs of red blood splashed over the air, coating Benny's face and shirt. He didn't stop, he kept slashing at the man until he fell. Gasping, he looked at the scene before him in terror. The man's neck was nearly entirely severed, only a small sliver of sinew kept his head connected to his body.

He looked at Maria, his breathing laboured, her eyes were wide as she stared at him.

"It's okay," she whispered. "It'll be okay."

He tried to smile, but his face wouldn't follow the command. He felt the tears welling up in his eyes and looked away.

"Let's go," she whispered. He was happy for the distraction; he didn't think he'd ever get the sight of this man out of his head again.

There were only three of them left now. They were probably just about far enough away, that a rifle shot might be mistaken for the sound of commotion within the camp, if it came to it. This side of the ploughed area was now clear of armed guards. Two stood across the other side, out of sight from their current position and one more stood watch from the top of the fields, where he should be able to see everything occurring below him. He was obviously as oblivious as the other two, as he hadn't noticed their demise. It was only a matter of time, however. Soon, he'd glance this way, and when he couldn't see the guards, he'd investigate. They had to move on, quickly.

They increased their pace as they kept out of sight, using the patchy crops and overgrown grass as cover. They could hear the men and women around them, using these insufficient tools, trying to drag them through the dirt. The valley levelled out onto flat ground on either side, if they left the cover of the crops, they'd be spotted for sure.

"Who are you?" The voice made them jump. It was flat and

lifeless, and it was coming from behind them.

They spun, in shock and fear, to see a woman against the backdrop of the sun, high in the sky. She wore a stained and dirty dress, patched in various places. Her hair was tied in a simple ponytail at the back of her head, which barely hid the tangled mess that portrayed a woman who hadn't washed it in a very long time. The people of Newhaven, including Benny and Maria, took these things for granted. Their showers were plentiful and always available. Warm water was ordinary, hygiene in Newhaven, for the world they lived in, was a very high standard. They'd come to realise, that was not the norm.

"I'm, erm…" Benny stuttered, not sure what to say. If this woman shouted, would they have to kill her? She was thin, thinner than would have seemed healthy. Her face was gaunt, and her eyes sunk into her skull.

Maria took over. "We're from Newhaven. It's okay, we're here to help you. We're here to set you free, so you can have a better life."

It was a gamble. If these people weren't actually being held against their will, there would be nothing to stop this woman from yelling, from giving away their presence. There was little they would be able to do about it in time. She was a few feet from them; they'd never cover the distance quickly enough to stifle a shout. She had a homemade plough in her hand. It was nothing more than a slightly straight branch, with a sharp, heavy-looking lump of metal strapped to one end, crudely sharpened to a narrow point. If she swung it, Benny was sure it could cause some damage.

"Oh," she said quietly. "That's good." Her tone remained flat.

Benny and Maria looked at each other, then turned their attention back to her.

"We need you to remain quiet, okay?" Maria said.

"Okay," the woman replied, then she turned and trudged back into the crops without another word.

Benny let out the breath he had not been aware he was holding. He looked back towards the man at the top of the field. His eyes grew wide as he saw the rifle pointing directly at him.

He grabbed Maria's shoulder and pushed her sideways towards the ground. She complained as she fell and he dived down next to her, just as the flash from the barrel came into his vision. The sound of the round whizzed over his head. The man was shouting something he couldn't make out, as his ribs screamed in pain, the others would be here soon. He grabbed for his rifle, stashing the machete back into his belt. The element of surprise was over, they'd be going in loud now. He tried to find the man, but another shot sent him crashing back to the relative safety of the ground. He heard running footsteps but couldn't locate where they were. He panicked, tried to grasp for his rifle but fumbled. His ribs screamed at him, still not healed from the earlier beating and made worse by the long trek they'd undertaken.

He'd landed on Maria when he dived to the ground and she still squirmed under him, not able to raise her own weapon. The man was over them now, pointing his rifle towards them, a sick smile spread across his dirt-streaked face. Others were running, too. He could hear them, but they were not yet in sight. He closed his eyes, they'd failed. He was tired. He hurt. He was done. At least they'd managed to raise the alarm in Newhaven. At least they would be prepared. A sad smile spread across his face; he would hold onto that, hoping that they may have saved the town, or at least given them a fighting chance. It was all he had left, as he lay in the dirt, waiting for the shot that would end his life.

Instead, he heard a thud, followed by a low grunt and the sound of a body falling to the floor. He opened his eyes, the woman who had spoken to them earlier stood over him, the homemade implement still grasped in both of her hands, small droplets of blood falling from the metallic edge.

She looked at him with no expression on her face, her eyes

still lifeless. Then she flew sideways as a spout of blood erupted from her chest, the sound of the shot following shortly after. She landed on the ground near them, her eyes still open, staring at them, dead on the floor.

Benny's mind raced. He's seen her fall before he heard the shot, the armed guards must not be close, but they were getting closer. They'd have only moments to prepare, hoping the foliage around them would provide some cover. He got his hands around the rifle and levelled it in front of him, scooting sideways to free Maria from under him. She did the same. He heard her deep breaths, as they sat up, rifle barrel pointing in front of her. Then they heard the screams. Not the screams of fear they were accustomed to, but screams of pure hatred, screams of repressed anger. He raised his head just above the nearby stalks, giving him a view across the crops. He saw the last two armed men, but they were no longer looking his way. The people who had been tending to the crops were converging on him, tools raised above their heads, shouting and shrieking, creating inhuman sounds as they rounded on their oppressors. A few shots were heard coming from their rifles, as several people fell out of sight, falling into the grass as bullets ripped through them. The crowd did not slow and soon they set upon the men. Tools rose and fell, as they hacked into the guards, the screams cut short, but the sickening thuds didn't stop for some time.

Benny let his body sink back to the floor. He could hear his own shallow, shaky breathing as people moved to surround them.

CHAPTER TWENTY-FOUR

Martin watched Benny and Maria creep back up the dusty alley and disappear behind the row of tents.

He turned his attention back to the men and women far in front of them. He'd just have to believe Benny and Maria had the skills and sense to get out of here safely, and alive. He had full faith they would, they were capable kids.

The movement up ahead was calming down. He wasn't sure if they'd finally found their positions, or if they were starting to believe the group wasn't coming. From the abandoned camp to here, they must have expected an attack long before now. Not knowing the group had snuck in and were now watching from behind them, Martin wondered if they were starting to give up on the idea of a frontal attack. He also wondered if soon they would go out looking for them. That might even up the chances. If some of this group left the camp, they'd have less here to contend with, and would deal with the others on their return, or even hunt them in the forest, if they had to. As the commotion up ahead began to quieten, a new noise could be heard, coming from further back in the camp. Vicious, hacking coughs. He could hear them. He knew that sound, it was a sound he hadn't heard in a long, long time. It was the coughing that might be associated with a cold or infection, it was the cough that was all too common back during the second wave, the outbreak that ended humanity.

He looked at Ava, her eyes wide, she had heard it to. The young members of the group looked around them, they didn't recognise the fear this sound brought to the others.

"No," Ava whispered, her voice full of fear. "It can't be."

"We'll need to be sure. We've got to check it out," Martin replied. He turned to the others. "Stay here. I'll be back shortly." He turned to leave and felt Kate fall into step next to him. He glanced at her; she was looking into his eyes.

"I'm with you," she said. "We need to know."

He nodded and the pair of them slowly made their way towards the sound of the coughing.

A large green tent stood in front of them. It looked a lot like the old military tents they had seen many times set up in various town centres. The entrance was a folded back strip of green canvas, held in place by a thick, browning rope. The interior was dark and musty. He could hear the coughing, multiple people, at least. He did not dare to step foot into this place, but had to see, he had to know.

Before he could act, Kate stepped in front of him and put her head through the opening, looking into the dark. As her eyes adjusted to the low light, she saw rows of metallic cots, thin, stained mattresses lying atop of them. There were maybe twenty of them, lined up in rows in the tent. At least half were occupied. The people lay in them fidgeted uncontrollably, thrashing back and forth as they coughed. Blood stained the walls and floor.

"My god," she whispered.

A person in the bed closest to her turned on their side to face her. The face was gaunt, the eyes sunken, grey skin stretched over their cheekbones. Their face, she couldn't tell if it was male or female, was bloated, blood ran in small drips down their chin. Their eyes flashed in recognition and the figure slowly raised an arm towards her, trying to speak, but letting out only a low moan. The voice quickly turned into a violent coughing fit as they recoiled into a small ball on the thin mattress.

Kate stepped back, hoping for the safety of fresh air. She looked towards Martin and shook her head. Without another word, they backed away from the tent and the low moans and coughs of the people left to die inside.

"It's back," she whispered. "We've seen that enough to know. It's back. God, it's back."

The others patiently awaited their return. Ava glanced between the people in front of them and the track Martin and Kate had taken towards that awful sound. She soon saw their silhouettes returning, growing closer with every step. They hadn't been long; she couldn't decide if this was good or bad. She waited as they arrived, waiting for them to report what they had seen.

Kate glanced at her and shook her head. Nothing more needed to be said, not now.

"Let's just deal with the immediate threat," she whispered.

They moved their focus back to the people they had come to deal with in the first place. There would be no chance of a sneak attack here, there were too many of them. They'd need to go loud, take out as many as possible and hope the element of surprise would be enough. Martin secretly doubted it would, but they had to try. All the people around him had volunteered for this and all were prepared to give their lives to keep Newhaven safe. He cast an eye over the seven members of Boneyard. He respected these people more than they would ever know. They were here fighting with him, for a home that wasn't theirs. He knew they held Tom and Bob in high reverence and was thankful for that. It was likely the cause of their loyalty, and he was sure they wouldn't be able to do this without them. He was sure they wouldn't be able to do this without their weapons.

The people of this camp had obtained their large arsenal of

weaponry from a looted army base many years ago. Martin now felt that Newhaven should have done the same. If he returned after this, he'd be sure to try. They couldn't be caught out like this again.

They had been watching the people of the camp for some time and yet he hadn't seen Bev anywhere. There had been a distinct lack of any real command. There also didn't seem to be any obvious place she would be. He'd expected there to be some form of command tent, something a bit plusher than the desolate tents that this place comprised of. He wondered if there might be more to it, although he couldn't worry about that now.

It had been long enough. They'd be crouched here for too long, they needed to make a move and they needed to make it now. He checked his rifle, and the others followed his lead. He heard the clicks of chambers being inspected.

He stepped into the open. No one noticed him as he raised his weapon. He looked through the sight and located a man's back. Square in the crosshairs, he pulled the trigger and watched as the man was plunged forward by the force, dropping face-first into the dirt. Everyone froze; it seemed like time itself had stopped for a moment. Martins barrel smoked as eyes began to turn his way. Without another thought, he shifted his aim and fired again, another man fell before they could react.

Chaos erupted, people dived to every side, scrambling for cover as they fumbled for their own weapons. He heard shots from behind and around him, the others now had targets in their sights, too.

A bullet ripped through the canvas of the tent on his left and he dropped lower to the ground. The group from Boneyards had flanked through the rows of tents and were now shooting at the armed people in this camp from both sides, opening up three fronts that they had to try and defend.

More people dropped, and for the shortest moment, Martin had the fleeting feeling that they could win. They must have killed a third of the defenders now, or wounded them to the point where they could no longer fight. It had been quick, and blood filled. The ground was streaked a bright red, rivers of flowing blood washing towards him. He shook his head to clear it, knowing that couldn't be true. But that's what he saw. He saw the flowing rivers of red, gushing down the path, engulfing the tents in its wake. He rubbed his eyes and when he opened them again, the scene before him had reverted to normal. There was blood, clearly visible, pooling on the floor, but the rushing river had never been real.

He contemplated for a moment what he had seen. Was he hallucinating? Here and now, that would be the worst timing he could manage. Someone must have sensed his hesitation, or seen him pause in his shock, as he felt the impact of the bullet ripping through his chest. He fell hard to the floor. He could hear Ava somewhere behind him calling his name. He didn't feel scared, he felt at peace. He wasn't in pain, but he knew enough about gunshots to understand that was just adrenaline and shock. If he was lucky, they'd keep him pain-free until he died. He forced himself to look down. The red stain was expanding from his midriff. He knew he was dead. It was just a matter of when. The blood was seeping out quickly. It wouldn't be long. It wouldn't be long at all.

"MARTIN!" Ava screamed as he flew backwards, settling onto his back in the dirt. A cloud of dust erupted around him from the impact of his body. She ran to him, dropping to her knees, cradling his head. His face had turned grey, his lips a shade of blue. His breathing quivered as his eyes lay unfocused.

"Oh, God, Martin," she sobbed.

He reached up a shaky hand and brushed his fingers against her chin. A smile spread over his face as his eyes glazed over. His breathing slowed, then stopped. Ava sobbed as his eyes continued to stare at her.

She felt her sorrow turn to hatred. She aimed her gun up and fired at nothing in particular. She fired until the chamber clicked empty. Tears flowed down her face as she discarded her weapon and unhooked Martin's from his dead shoulders. A shot sent in return ricocheted off the ground by her foot, then another buried itself deep in Martins leg. The hatred boiled over as she rose to her feet. She ran, diving to the side to keep in the cover of the row of tents lining the track. She didn't stop, she ran closer until she could clearly see the faces of the people shooting at her, the people who had killed Martin.

She reloaded her weapon and took careful aim, using her years of training, she killed three of them before they could fire back in reply. She saw from the corner of her eye the people from Boneyard were close; she watched as one of them fell silent after being found by a wayward shot from up ahead. His friends turned to look as he fell and two more of them were cut down in quick succession, their blood sprayed onto the moulding canvas behind them.

The pause in return fire galvanised the people of the camp as they regrouped and started firing towards Ava and the others. Ava threw herself sideways, taking cover behind the row of tents. Their flimsy structures ripped apart as bullets passed through them and she forced her head to the floor.

She heard boots running to her left; they were flanking them. This was it; they were going to lose this fight. Martin had already died. She would be next. The only solace she could take from this was that they'd taken out a large number of the camp defenders. Any attack on Newhaven would be greatly reduced. She smiled to herself, they had given them a chance, that's all they could ask for.

"Enough!" A familiar voice called out from somewhere over the rows of tents.

The footsteps ceased and silence descended over the camp, broken only by the light moaning of the wounded.

"Throw your weapons and come out into the open. Let me see you," the voice shouted, echoing off the nearby trees.

Ava lay on the ground, not trusting the words. She heard the sound of a gun being tossed nearby. A shadow rose to its feet, visible through the tent.

"Hello, Kate," the voice said.

"Bev," Kate replied.

Ava glanced up the track and could see Kate, unarmed, with her arms raised. Bev was standing in front of her, a pistol in her hands. Three men flanked her, rifles pointed at Kate's chest.

"Now the rest," Bev shouted.

Ava heard the sounds of the others copying Kate's lead and threw her own rifle into the clearing. Standing, she looked around. Three of the people from Boneyard remained, Kate, herself and one of the younger guards from Newhaven. That's all that was alive. Half of them had been killed in the assault.

Bev glared at Ava and tilted her head slightly in recognition.

"Nice to see you all," she said, a big smile spreading over her face. There was no kindness in the smile; it was pure malice.

"Where's Martin?"

"Dead," Ava spat, pointing to his body further down the trail.

"Shame," Bev said. "Always liked him. Not to worry. Unfortunately, he'd have had to die here, anyway. You all will."

"Why are you doing this?" Kate asked. "We were fair to you and your people. What happened isn't on us."

"I know," she replied simply. "You live like kings, while we die in squalor. That can't continue. These are my people, now, and I promised to look after them."

"Great job you've done so far," Kate replied, looking at the dead around her. Bev snarled in reply.

"Where have you been hiding?" Kate asked.

"Around," Bev replied, nonchalantly. "It's a big camp, with lots to do. People to see, you know how it goes."

"Those people," Kate pointed to the tent deep in the camp.

"What's wrong with them?"

"The virus," she shrugged. "We told you. It's back. We've lost a dozen now, maybe more. Soon, it will take us all. The rumour is that Boneyard created a vaccine. I know it's a slim chance, but we had to try, and we'll continue to do so. What else can we do?"

"You could have talked to us. You could have asked."

"You would have said no."

"No, we wouldn't. You don't seem to understand, Bev. We wouldn't have just let you die, if we could help it. We're not like that."

She laughed. "You've done it before."

Kate shook her head. "It wasn't like that. You must know that."

Bev opened her mouth to reply but was silenced by a noise coming from behind her. The forest was alive with shouts and whoops. She jerked her head at two of the guards, who scurried out of sight into the forest with rifles drawn.

The silence inside the camp was palpable, as the shouts grew closer. A shot was heard in the distance and several of the guards turned to stare at the treeline.

One of the guards, returning at pace, sweat beading on his face, ran to Bev and whispered something in her ear. Her eyes widened, then she began shouting to the others around her. She turned back to face Kate, before shouting to the guard nearby.

"Kill them, all of them." Then she turned and walked away.

The guard raised his rifle, pointing it directly at Kate. She closed her eyes, awaiting the bullet that would send her to meet Tom. The shot was deafening. She didn't flinch; she didn't feel anything. She was still stood. Slowly, she opened her eyes to see the guard on the floor before her, dead with a bullet wound in his head. Confusion spread over her face as she looked around.

Chloe ran from the treeline, firing as she moved. Several more people fell before they knew what was happening. Kate, momentarily dazed, just stood there, watching the scene in front of her. People ran everywhere, now. Someone was emerging from the trees on the other side. People she didn't recognise. They were dressed in ill-fitting clothes, hanging loosely over their thin bodies. Some had rifles in their hands, but most ran with what appeared to be homemade farming tools raised above their heads.

They were screaming, inhuman sounds left their mouths and pure hatred burned from their eyes. They mobbed the guards, hacking at them as they ran over them.

Kate reached for her discarded weapon, shooting at the armed guards, who were now focused on the throng of incoming people. She saw Benny and Maria appear from the trees, shooting as they came into view. Her heart fluttered at seeing them. The guards were down to just a handful, now. They were trying to run, only to be cut down when they ran too close to the mob, or by bullets piercing their backs.

The others had also retrieved their weapons and were helping to cut down the few fleeing guards. The tide had turned, and this could only end one way.

Bev was backed into a corner. She was firing at the incoming people, but they surrounded her, shouting and jeering. Her face looked terrified, and then her rifle clicked empty.

Kate watched, unmoving, as the crowd drew tight around her. She screamed, trying to use the rifle as a club, swinging it madly about her. Someone managed to get a hand on it and pulled it from her grasp. The crowd drew closer still and she fell to her knees, covering her head with her hands. She shrieked, letting out a continuous scream of frustration and pure terror.

Kate's view was blocked, as the blood-curdling scream pierced the air. She saw a plough raised high into the ground, then forced back down with a sickening crunch, as the scream cut out prematurely. More tools were raised high above their heads, as more nauseating thuds followed. She looked away. This was mob justice, perhaps deserved in this case. She couldn't watch. The crowd were taking their revenge out on her. She was dead, Kate knew it, yet still they did not stop.

Maria approached and reached for her, her arms extended and pulled her into a close embrace.

CHAPTER TWENTY-FIVE

Kate stood, watching the devastation around her. Every tent had new holes, caused by wayward bullets, blood stained the floor and bodies lay, some mutilated, everywhere they looked.

The people who had arrived through the trees, the labour, were picking through the remnants of their camp. They lived here with the guards but were never equals.

Back in the early days, under Kingsley, the camp had been a bitter and difficult place to live, but they had all been equal. Once he'd died, Bev made her grab for power. With a vacuum to fill and little opposition, she'd managed it. She was a young and bright girl, back then. She had ideas on how to improve things and a positive outlook on life and the future. When the cholera struck in her first winter, she lost so many. It changed her. She became hard and distant. Anyone who was considered not to be of use to her was put to work in the fields, the kitchens, or general cleaning. Anyone who refused was denied food. Bev had told them that if they wanted to eat the camp's stores, they had to contribute to the upkeep. Most people eventually accepted the new regime. It was better than starving to death or taking their chances alone in the wilderness.

Her methods became more brutal as time went on. The change in her was visible as more of her people died, usually from avoidable illness. She often spoke of Newhaven, and of Tom in particular, reminding her people that they had nothing, while Newhaven had it all. When she eventually snapped and became consumed with the idea of revenge, it couldn't be pinned down to a single day, more a combination of the hard years and continued losses.

Eventually, the pretence of voluntary labour was all but gone. Armed guards were posted to watch them. They'd beat anyone deemed not working hard enough, or fast enough. Life was hard, but Bev reminded them it was harder outside of the relative safety of the camp. They had no barrier, people could feasibly have simply walked into the forest, if they had wanted to. As the camp grew, they moved to the current location. The first camp, the one across the track which the group had first encountered, wasn't big enough. There was no place to grow food and the years of poor sanitation, and no lavatories had made it all but unliveable. They'd taken everything they could carry. Everything else, they'd looted from the nearby army base. They'd been marched out there, it was a full day's hike and loaded down with supplies, dried foods, tents, scraps of canvas. That had all been used to build where they were now.

The attacks had been caused by the first infection returning back to the camp several weeks ago. Although their life was dire over the earlier decades, the infection brought home their fragility here. Bev had made the decision to attack Newhaven, even though it was clear she didn't truly believe they had a vaccine or cure for what was coming. Only she would know her true motives. Kate supposed it could simply have been revenge, an attempt to right what she saw as the wrongs that had been done to them, before it was too late. Or perhaps she believed that if they could take Newhaven and hide behind its walls, she could somehow keep the virus at bay, and herself safe.

Weapons and ammunition were taken by the guards when they discovered them, the labourers were never trusted to transport those. The weapons were held in a tent in the centre of the camp where Bev stayed. Armed guards protected them day and night. There was no way for these people to get access to them. Not until now.

The attack by Benny and Maria on the guards at the fields, plus the attack on the camp, had provided them with the ember to spark their fire of rebellion. They bore no ill feelings to the people of Newhaven, and once Bev and her crew were dead, they had embraced them with open arms.

The hatred the camp seemed to show towards the people of Newhaven was instigated by Bev, as they had expected. Her true motives were still unknown, but the suspicion was that she'd harboured a growing hatred of Tom and the rest after the sickness ripped through the camp and killed many of her friends. Once she watched Kingsley's children die that first winter, she never truly recovered. Although deep down she knew it wasn't their fault, she needed someone to blame. Someone to galvanise her people against.

Kate offered the survivors refuge at Newhaven, of course, but the offer was refused. This was their home and now, with Bev and the others gone, they could work to build the home they wanted.

An old woman stepped forward to be the spokesperson for the group, without ever introducing herself. She explained all this and told them that for years, the camp had been split into two castes: those who worked and those who fought. The armed guards were fed the better food, slept in the better tents and enjoyed a life of much higher standard than the workers.

They toiled in the fields for twelve hours a day, ate whatever leftovers were available and slept often in the cold, with little in the way of blankets or beds available in the camp. Their life had been hard, and too often short. The sick in the tent further down the camp were all labourers. The first to show signs of infection had been part of a foraging party, sent to the city, days walk away. They'd returned, and soon after fallen sick. Since then, the sickness had spread. They couldn't be sure if it truly was the virus, sanitation and nutrition was so poor amongst them, it could have been anything. Kate still worried about this assessment; she'd seen so many infected in her time, these people looked so familiar in their symptoms. It sent shivers down her spine to think about it.

The old woman promised to take care of their dead. They couldn't return with them, so they would be buried here in the camp. Ava knelt over Martin's body, weeping as she whispered to him.

They left the camp as a group, smaller than the one that had arrived, but in good spirits, knowing the threat had been removed. The journey home was less stressful for all of them. They collected the horses and set off at a relaxed pace, Benny and Maria took up position at the rear of the group, Kate and Ava led up the front, with the rest in the middle. They didn't expect any trouble, although it was always beneficial to be prepared. The sun was on its descent by the time they arrived at the gates to Newhaven. Steve watched them arrive, as they drew closer, they could see the smile spread across his face. Despite the late hour, the surviving people from Boneyard took their leave, headed out of town and towards the coast, on their own way home. Kate thanked them profusely as they parted and sent her condolences for their dead.

"Kate, Ava," Steve shouted down as they approached. "It's great to see you guys." He paused and looked at the group. "Where's Martin?" he asked, the concern clear in his voice.

"I'm sorry, Steve, Martin didn't make it." She looked to the ground, not wanting to meet his eye.

"Oh," he replied simply, his voice an octave lower than it had been.

They entered the gates into Newhaven to a sight they hadn't seen in a long time. A line of guards greeted them, all armed with the rifles left by Boneyard. The barricade, long untouched, had been reinforced as far as they could see. The town had been busy. People came running up to them from all directions, happy smiles on their faces. The smiles faded as they realised how few had returned. Kate ignored the questions asked of her and walked to the cenotaph. She ran her fingers over the names carved into the side.

"There will be more names to add to this in the morning," she whispered.

A mug of beer was pushed in Benny's face, which he accepted gratefully. Maria took a look at the cup being offered to her and turned it down; her face had gone slightly green; she was still feeling the effects of the prior night.

Questions were fired their way from all directions, people talked over each other, everyone wanting to know what had happened and if they were now safe. Eventually, Kate had to put a stop to it. The story of the infected back at the camp had spread through Newhaven like wildfire. Most people here had never seen the virus, or what it did to people. They wanted answers, they wanted to know what was coming.

These were answers Kate simply did not have. She knew no better than the rest of them what was around the corner. She was old and tired. She'd had enough of it all.

"That's enough," she shouted, with enough conviction to cause the crowd to silence.

"We'll go through everything tomorrow. We're exhausted and I think we would all appreciate a good night's sleep. All I'll say now is we're safe, the threat is over. Now, I'm going to bed."

The crowd cheered and moved to let her through.

Kate collapsed into her bed, the noise outside was quieter here. She felt her heavy eyelids drop as she curled up in her bed, fully clothed. She wasn't sure her head had even hit the pillow before she was out.

The crowning of the birds woke her early the following morning. How long had she slept for? She sat upright, rubbing her eyes. Her muscles ached, her bed was soaked in sweat and her face felt like she was recovering from the worst hangover of her life. But that couldn't be right; she hadn't drunk anything. She felt her forehead; she was burning up. Her blood ran cold as the tickle in her throat erupted into a coughing fit. She spluttered into her hand, that familiar, raspy cough. She looked at the small droplets of blood on her hand and wiped the trickle from her chin.

She sighed; she'd expected something like this. At least she'd soon be back with Tom.

She knew the end was coming for her, she just hoped it wouldn't take anyone else with it. She sat in silence, reflecting on her life, the events that had brought her here. She smiled, as the memories came flooding back. The day she met Tom. The first meeting with Bob. When they finally settled in Newhaven, when they knew they'd finally be safe. The day her son, Benny, had been born. She felt the pang of guilt thinking about him. She couldn't say goodbye, just in case he caught it. She'd always assumed she was immune; she had thought they all must be. She figured that's how they had all lasted this long. Maybe she was, to the earlier strains. Maybe it really had just taken all this time to mutate, to a point where any immunity was useless against it. Maybe this would be it, no matter what she did next.

She had to hope she was wrong. They couldn't have survived this long, to be cut down in this way. She wouldn't be able to bear the thought. Only she and Martin had entered the tent, and Martin was now dead. That just left her as the threat to Newhaven now. She knew what she had to do.

In the light and quiet of the early morning, she left her home for the final time. She looked around the town as she walked towards the barrier. Careful not to touch anything, she smiled at the memories this place had provided for her. She'd be leaving it to a capable generation. She thought of Benny and Maria; they would do great running this place. One guard sat alone on the barrier. It was Steve. She didn't know if he'd even been to bed from the prior night. He was a good substitute for Martin. He stood as he saw her approach.

"Going out?" he asked as he walked down the ramp to the ground.

She said nothing but held up her blood-stained sleeve, keeping her distance from him.

"Kate…" he said softly.

"Yeah," she smiled sadly. "It's time to go."

"You don't need to. We could see what we can do. You don't know for sure what it is."

"I know," she said. "I can feel it, Steve. It's my time. I'm okay with it."

He looked down. He knew she was right. Silently, he unlocked the gate and pushed it open, standing back to let her pass.

She passed him before halting and turning back. "Steve?"

"Yes, Kate?"

"Tell Benny I said goodbye. And that I love him. I know he'll understand, but this will be hard for him for a while. Tell them all. I love them. I really do."

Steve nodded as he wiped a tear from his eye.

"You got it, boss," he whispered.

She turned and headed off towards the coast, towards the resting place of Tom, with the sound of the birds as her only companion, Newhaven slowly fading into the distance behind her.

The End.

Printed in Great Britain
by Amazon